THE END OF SUMMER

CHARLOTTE PHILBY worked for the *Independent* for eight years as a columnist, editor and reporter, and was shortlisted for the Cudlipp Prize for her investigative journalism at the 2013 Press Awards. A former contributing editor and feature writer at *Marie Claire*, she has written for publications including the *New Statesman, Sunday Times, Guardian, Telegraph, Elle, Tatler, Inside Time,* and has been a guest on shows ranging from NPR's *Note to Self* podcast to BBC Radio 4 *Front Row*. This is her fifth novel.

Also by Charlotte Philby

Part of the Family
A Double Life
The Second Woman
Edith and Kim

THE END OF SUMMER

CHARLOTTE PHILBY

THE BOROUGH PRESS

The Borough Press
An imprint of HarperCollins*Publishers* Ltd
1 London Bridge Street
London SE1 9GF

www.harpercollins.co.uk

HarperCollins*Publishers*
Macken House,
39/40 Mayor Street Upper,
Dublin 1
D01 C9W8

First published by HarperCollins*Publishers* 2024
1

A catalogue record for this book is available from the British Library

Hardback ISBN: 978-0-00-846642-8
Trade Paperback ISBN: 978-0-00-846643-5

This novel is entirely a work of fiction.
The names, characters and incidents portrayed in it are
the work of the author's imagination. Any resemblance to
actual persons, living or dead, events or localities is
entirely coincidental.

Typeset in Adobe Garamond Pro
by Palimpsest Book Production Ltd, Falkirk, Stirlingshire

Printed and bound in the UK using
100% Renewable Electricity by CPI Group (UK) Ltd

For my mum, Jo, and my much-missed grandmother, Joan –
never horrid, but rarely, knowingly, very good indeed . . .

There was a little girl,
Who had a little curl,
Right in the middle of her forehead.
When she was good,
She was very good indeed,
But when she was bad she was horrid.

Henry Wadsworth Longfellow

PROLOGUE

Tuesday 17 September 2024

It is the beginning of one of those end-of-summer days that the Hérault does so well, when it finally comes, the air so still it is as if time itself has stopped in respect for this moment. Everything about the scene is so perfect that Judy could almost have written it: the clear morning heat so dry and dazzling that it causes her to pause awhile over the patch of garden she is tending.

Behind her, the old abbey stands back from the road, a pale sandstone building set against a blue sky.

Standing in its shadow, her weight tilts forward on to the handle of her pitchfork as something inside her shifts. Her eyes linger over a spray of late pink and white blooms that will soon be gone, their petals stretching out wide as if already in surrender.

Lifting a hand to her forehead, she adjusts the straw hat she and Rory found at the market in Bédarieux not long after their first ever visit together, a foolish smile forming on her lips at the memory of those lazy Saturday morning excursions to the nearest town.

As if peering back into another world, she pictures them as they were, without a care.

It was never about the money, though she accepts this might be hard to believe. They were happy – of course they were. What wasn't there to be delighted about? They were young and they were free. Yet, even then, as they made their way through the market, two lovers idling between stalls selling lavender bags and jars of duck *confit*, she had found herself occasionally glancing over her shoulder, out of habit, the slightest breeze causing her to shiver as they walked hand in hand through the crowd.

Standing here now under the bright early-morning sun, a single strand of straw coming away between her fingers, which she uses to work away the soil from under her nails, Judy blinks away the threat of a tear, focusing on the view beyond the garden, an impression of the Pyrenees just visible on the horizon.

She is not yet sixty – still a couple of years away from it – but she knows how quickly things can change. It's like that old coin trick her mother taught her on the long train journeys to school, when she was a child. One moment the coin was there; the next it was gone. The secret, of course, is for the watcher to be looking in the wrong direction when the magic happens.

But life is full of distractions.

These are the thoughts passing through Judy's mind in those perfect few moments before what follows. And then the phone rings inside the house, the shrillness of its cry reverberating against the cool hallway, shattering whatever it is that is holding her there; signalling the house of cards' final, inevitable collapse.

She pauses, instinctively. There's no rush, she thinks, kicking the clump of dry dirt from the nose of her tennis shoes as she makes her way past the chicken coop, towards the back door. She has waited for this moment for almost forty years; it's no more than she deserves. Besides, she is no slave to technology, not like the local boys – the poor will-less creatures who gather in the *tabac* with their moped helmets tucked under their arms, their intense young faces fixed to their screens.

Judy Harrington is no slave to anyone, nor anything. Not at her age, not ever.

Inside, the old rotary phone continues to rattle on its cradle.

'Coming, coming,' she calls out, playing along – for whose benefit?

She feels it coming, barrelling towards her along the cool open hallway that is already full of ghosts. Rory: her darling Rory, still in his forties, waltzing past the coat rack with their daughter in his arms. Francesca giggling, her thick dark fringe bobbing above the rim of the pink star-framed sunglasses and Minnie Mouse T-shirt she wouldn't take off that summer, her bare feet trailing the floor. Judy's granddaughter, Lily, just two summers ago, aged seventeen – her hair pulled into the same Princess Leia buns Francesca had worn when she was the same age.

The life Judy had never thought in her wildest fantasies that she could have.

And then she blinks, and it is gone.

Silence falling between each piercing ring, Judy settles back against the wall. Slipping off her sandals, she lets the cool marble floor soothe the soles of her feet as she focuses on the spiral staircase that leads up to the bedroom where she and Rory once lay entwined in soft cotton sheets, their bodies curved into one another's. Finally, she picks up the receiver.

'Hello?' The familiar rumble of London traffic on the other end of the line makes her yearn, briefly, for the city. For another life.

'Mum?'

At the sound of her daughter's voice Judy's throat swells, her body intuitively understanding what comes next.

Her gaze wanders to the window, settling on a cluster of white flowers that have long since gone over. The sight of them evokes a memory – herself and Rory planting asphodels on one of those first lazy weekends away from London after their daughter was born. Judy recoiling as her new husband enlightened her on the Asphodel Meadows in stories of the Underworld of ancient Greece: *A place where ordinary souls are sent to live.* Laughing, she had pleaded, *Ordinary? Christ, anything but that.*

'Mum, is it true?'

It is one of the hardest things imaginable, hearing one's only child in clear distress and being incapable of doing a thing to help. At least nothing more than she has already done.

'There are journalists on our doorstep. Tell me it's not true.'

Before Judy can reply, she spots it – the police car curving around the road at the end of the garden – and despite herself she is met with the strangest sense of relief.

'Darling, I can't talk now. I'll have to call you back. I'm so sorry.'

'Mum—'

Replacing the phone on its cradle, Judy slips back into her shoes and turns towards the main hall, hearing the thud of boots as the *gendarme* climbs the steps.

Closing her eyes, Judy inhales as she adjusts her cardigan and opens the door. '*Bonjour, Patrice.*'

In the hall, the phone rings again but they both ignore it. The officer nods, unsure where to put himself. There is no other way to do this, they both understand.

'*J'arrive,*' Judy says, smiling reassuringly. She will not make this more difficult for either of them than it has to be. Patrice deserves this much, at the very least.

Anyone passing from the road will be able to see what is unfolding here on the steps of the old abbey. But the officer has not come in all guns blazing; he will have volunteered to his colleagues to come alone – a single man, willing to take the fall should anything go wrong.

But what could go wrong? Judy is old now. She is no threat. *It's OK – I know Judy,* Patrice will have said, vouching for her. *She's lived in the house up there for years.*

He hasn't used his siren. She is grateful for this. Whatever follows, the name 'Judy Harrington' is known and still largely respected in the village, and she appreciates the courtesy that she is being shown; she will not do her old friend the disservice of making this more complicated than it needs to be. My God, she will miss this place. But she has had a decent run; the story had to come out at some point.

My truth. Christ, she hates that expression. Sometimes she feels as if she doesn't understand the world any more – people wanting to tell their stories to anyone who will listen; people demanding trigger warnings on books and television programmes. Life doesn't come with a warning – things just happen, and it's up to us how we respond.

'*Je vais juste mettre les poules à l'abri, et fermer l'autre porte, si vous le permettez, Patrice,*' Judy says, nodding towards the chickens that must be locked up in their coop, and the back door which must be closed, before she accompanies the policeman to the station.

Moving slowly, she makes her way back through the hallway and down a set of internal stairs towards the garden as the officer follows, her mind drifting back to one of the first times she and Patrice had met, more than three decades earlier. A newly appointed policeman then, Patrice had been driving along the road that follows the edge of the village when he'd spotted five-year-old Francesca wandering close to the river, apparently having made her way out of the back door. Judy and Rory had just arrived from London for the summer, as usual, and they had each been too distracted to notice their only child slipping out of the back gate, taking the path at the end of the lane that led to the house and tiptoeing along the ledge that took her to the footbridge, where Patrice had found the girl throwing sticks into the current. Judy had been airing sheets on the front veranda overlooking the driveway, and had blinked in disbelief when she'd spotted the car pull up and the policeman lead Francesca, her dark fringe shadowing her face, from the back seat. Taking the dusty stone steps two at a time, Judy had felt time speed up and slow down again as she ran down to meet them on the sun-drenched street, scooping her child up in her arms, covering Francesca's face in kisses while Patrice explained where she had been found. The realisation of how easily she could slip away had sent a shiver though her body that had caused the blonde hairs on Judy's forearms to spike.

Over thirty years later, the vision of them all retreats in her mind, and is replaced by an almost numb acceptance of what must follow.

Opening the back door into the garden, she makes gentle clucking noises as she moves forward along the path, shooing the birds towards the makeshift hut she constructed not long after she relocated here permanently.

Breathing in, she takes a moment. This is it.

'I've always loved this view. On a good day, you can see all the way to the Pyrenees,' she calls over to Patrice for want of anything else to say, stepping inside the shed and reaching under a small shelf to the left of the door, where the key is kept.

Pulling out the rifle, she tucks the butt under her arm. Holding the barrel steady with her left hand, with the right she places a finger on the trigger, and turns to Patrice.

'I'm so sorry.'

'Fran, what did she say?' Hugo's voice cuts through the silence.

For a moment I am so stunned I can't speak. The phone in my hand seems to be suspended between two worlds as I hold it out in front of me, looking up at my husband in disbelief.

'She hung up.'

'Try again.'

'I did, Hugo – she's not bloody answering.'

In the silence that follows, my mind adjusts to the scuffle of reporters vying for space on the pavement outside the picturesque Kensington townhouse that still officially belongs to my parents, one of them dead, the other—

A pain in my temple cuts through my thoughts.

Not now, I tell myself. For now I need to stay calm; to try to work through what is happening. But before I can stop it, an image forms: my father's body splayed out on the black and white chequered hallway; unfamiliar voices rising up around me.

Shaking my head, pushing back against the rising tide of memory, I clear the mental image of the officers trailing their muddy footsteps through our family home.

And still the journalists are just there, waiting outside the door, sharks circling in excitement at the first taste of blood. The second taste, actually. Not that it's in any way satiated their thirst.

From here in the study, I can see the photographers in the front garden training their lenses, sniper-like, on the final flourishes of the wisteria that hang above the first-floor veranda, zooming in as they roll left towards a steep flight of steps leading to the recessed doorway.

When Hugo reaches out a hand to reassure me, I flinch.

'Fran, what did Judy say?'

'I told you – she hung up on me. *Fuck!*' Slamming my hand against the three-pedestal desk that had been my father's, I notice the green leather top slightly curling at one of the edges. My mother hung up and now I am left here, dealing with this. Whatever the hell this is.

'But she didn't deny it?'

'Deny what? I didn't get—'

I touch my phone so that the screen comes back to life, and my eyes linger briefly on the image that greets me. It was taken the night before my daughter, Lily – now legally an adult; how is that even possible? – flew out to southeast Asia on the trip of a lifetime. Lily, whose phone is simply an extension of her fingers, had directed the group shot outside the Churchill Arms on Kensington Church Street.

'It's a self-portrait. Please don't say selfie,' she had corrected Hugo as she adjusted the lens so that the three of us each appeared to be carrying one of the pub's overflowing hanging baskets on our heads.

'*Self-portrait?* Pretentious much, Lils?' Hugo had laughed in response, holding open the door, the familiar roar of the bar greeting us as Lily and I stepped inside.

I had been so touched when my daughter had suggested it – a Thai meal, just the three of us in the back room of our favourite pub, ahead of all those she would have without us. But, when the night came, the walls of the conservatory lined with butterflies of all shapes and sizes, framed in glass boxes, I'd found myself ambushed by a flood of emotion I hadn't been prepared for. As we sat there in our usual spot, tears of love and pride and selfish regret had glistened in my eyes, the wine we drank going straight to my head. By the time we left I'd felt giddy with nausea, though I'd managed to hide it behind a too-wide smile. There had been no reason to feel like this; the anxiety expanding in my chest was completely out of sync with the celebration we were having, the excitement I should have been feeling for what lay ahead. And yet the sensation was visceral, part of me breaking away: the child I had given birth to when I was almost exactly the same age as her – and spent the following years sheltering with all the paddings of love and money and privilege – drifting away from me, towards a world that I could no longer control or protect her against.

Pushing the thought aside, now, I sit straight.

'I'm booking a flight to France,' I tell Hugo, opening Google on my phone with shaking fingers and scanning routes to Montpellier and Toulouse; then, when that fails, to the next nearest airport. 'Dammit. There's nothing until tomorrow.'

'Have you tried Carcassonne as well?'

When I look up, I find myself almost incredulous at seeing him still standing there. 'There's nothing until tomorrow – I just said.'

The hardness in my voice isn't aimed at him, not really. Our eyes meet and I feel a sting of guilt. When I look away, my attention glides towards the rows of books that line one wall – my father's tomes on old- and new-world wines alongside volumes on the English legal system; my mother's favourite novels, the special edition of *Lady Audley's Secret* in pride of place.

My family's past and present closing in on us like pincers.

'This is a nightmare,' I think aloud.

'I'm sure it's a mistake. Everything will be fine.'

I almost laugh at that. 'Oh, come on, Hugo, don't be so fucking dim.' It's relentless, his inability to recognise the possibility of any eventuality other than the one he wants – even when the truth of it is staring him in the face. Though it's also what makes him such a good lawyer; far better than me. We are different beasts: Hugo born to wave the flag of righteousness in front of a captive audience; me – a family law solicitor – to quietly get the job done.

I'm not being fair. I'm making Hugo sound weak and passive and self-aggrandising when he is no such thing. He's not perfect – who is? – but he is essentially good. Which is why he sometimes fails to see what's staring him in the face. This might sound like a trait that is at odds with being one of the country's most successful barristers, but the truth is to the contrary. Hugo's job is to build a narrative and manufacture everything else, however seemingly contradictory, so that it fits around that. He is so good at it that I imagine when he wants to he can even fool himself that what he's saying is true.

It is, presumably, why we have lasted as long as we have.

'There's a seat first thing tomorrow morning,' I say.

'I'll come with you.'

'No.'

'In the meantime, we'll get the best representation for Judy, I'll make some calls. Everything will—'

'They're saying she did it, Hugo. They're saying my mother *killed* my father—'

From outside there is a bang on the lion-headed brass knocker that leads down on to the street, and I cry out without moving, 'Will you *fuck off!*'

10

'Try to stay calm.'

'They're on our doorstep! They aren't allowed—'

'I'll tell them to leave.'

'No,' I snap, before continuing more calmly, forcing my mind to slow. 'That's what they want. I just need to think.'

My attention catches on the doll's house in the corner of the room, which my father commissioned for my tenth birthday from the specialist shop in Covent Garden. The same shop where, when I was a child, Judy and I would go to choose new additions from shelves of miniatures, picking out tiny bunches of grapes and intricate decorations no bigger than a baby's fingernail.

Today, the doll's house remains a perfect replica of our family home as it was in the mid-nineties, with tiny potted poplars standing either side of the recessed front door. Inside, the rooms are painted and papered in the same in-vogue colours and textures my mother had picked out from the catalogues at Peter Jones.

I had made myself look away when the police officer pulled open the front of the doll's house in the days that followed that awful, unforgettable event, as if expecting to see the aftermath playing out within its walls: blood splashed along the black and white floor tiles in the hallway where my father had fallen. But when I looked it was of course untainted, and the sight of the spot just as it had been before had been enough to make me run and throw up.

When Lily was young, I had briefly considered updating the model house in keeping with the changes that had been made over the years – but, when it came to it, I found it impossible to alter a thing. I could no more move a chair in the doll's house than I could pull my own teeth.

And so it remains, untouched, a mausoleum commemorating life as it was – the same stamp-sized Picasso line-drawing on the stairs; the miniature vase in the hall, still intact.

Standing, I feel lightheaded as Hugo's fingers brush against my arm. Barely acknowledging him, I walk out of the study and into the tiled hallway. Through the stained glass front door to my left, I spot the shadows of the reporters, calling out my name. Their silhouettes in the doorway remind me of a time, years before, and I shudder, pushing the memory away.

Is your mother in there, Francesca? Is Judy home?

Turning away from the voices, I move towards the stairs that run through the centre of the house. Forcing myself to breathe, I glance between the gallery of framed portraits of myself, Lily, Hugo and my parents in various configurations over the years. And there, glaring in its emptiness, the blank space where another picture once hung.

'Fran, where are you going?'

Hugo follows me into the hallway but I don't turn around. 'I'm going to get changed.'

'Why?'

'I need to go to the police station.' My voice is monotone. 'I need to know what she's done.'

There is a faint knock on the bedroom door before Hugo enters, pausing as our eyes meet.

Pulling the turtleneck sweater over my shirt, I sit at the edge of the bed, allowing the reality of what is happening to settle over us.

'Sorry. I shouldn't be taking this out on you,' I say without moving, hoping my voice conveys the contrition I feel. This is not his fault.

Straightening my back, I rub my eyes with my left hand,

the phone still clutched in the other, the tab for the flight scanner I used to search for flights from London to the south of France still open on the web page. Only when I pull my left hand away from my face and see the black streaks on my fingers do I remember the mascara I applied in the bathroom after my morning run less than an hour earlier, clearing the mist from the mirror and watching my own reflection emerge through the haze of steam.

'You don't need to apologise,' Hugo says as he steps inside the master bedroom that once belonged to my parents. 'I'll come with you to the police station.'

Watching him there beside the walnut dresser that has stood on this spot for as long as I can remember, I wish I could say yes.

'Hugo, please – this is something I need to do alone,' I reply.

'Why?'

Letting myself tip into his arms, I take the cleansing pad and run it over each of my eyes in turn. My voice cracks. 'I don't know what's happening. Why won't she answer the phone?'

'Fran, whatever it is, we can—'

'Please don't.' I can't bear his blind optimism. In the silence that follows, I stand. 'I'll call you once I know more.'

PART ONE

Judy

New York City, late June 1985

Aunt Susan's apartment stood on the top floor of the kind of brownstone Judy knew from the movies. The view over this corner of south Brooklyn was the same to which she had awoken every morning for the past twenty-one months, the street sloping down towards the river.

This city.

God, she would miss it, of course she would. She was only human, after all. But she was also barely nineteen, the world was her oyster. New York was only ever going to be a stepping stone, just as London was before it.

As far as Judy could tell, anyone who truly believed that if you were bored of London then you were bored of life simply lacked imagination. The same went for NYC.

The morning sun shone bright with promise as she finished writing the note, which she placed on the table at the centre of her aunt's kitchen table, along with her keys.

Thank you – it's been fun! J x

Her aunt had left early that morning for her job at NYU, and in her absence Judy smoked one of her cigarettes as she sat by the window, tapping her right foot absent-mindedly to the beat of the hip-hop that drifted in from the street below.

Running her fingers over the heavy curtains that had once hung in the living room of her mother's and Aunt Susan's childhood home in the Western Highlands of Scotland – a world away from Brooklyn – Judy let the material fall from her grasp and exhaled a line of smoke, smiling to herself as she let her mind draw circles around the day ahead.

It had been the same scene every Tuesday morning since she had arrived: the same old Buick parking on the street outside her building, the owner – a heavily built white guy in double denim – getting out of the car and heading to the brownstone opposite, slipping around the side towards the basement door and disappearing for twenty minutes before coming out again, getting back in the car and driving away.

'What's he doing in there?' Judy had finally asked one day, calling out to her aunt who was pulling on her Mary Janes, running late for work. 'Who leaves their key in the ignition in Brooklyn?'

'Dealing drugs, probably,' Susan had replied, her tone her signature blend of aloof and condemning as she cast her gaze briefly over the run-down façade of the building opposite, a couple of kids playing with a yo-yo on the street in front of the steps. 'And you shouldn't be spying on people. You'll get yourself in trouble.'

'Makes sense, I guess,' Judy had agreed under her breath, chewing intently on her bubble gum as she watched the man get out, so cocksure that he didn't even lock the door before sauntering over to the house opposite without bothering to glance around.

On this particular summer's morning it was 8.57 – a little earlier than usual – when the Buick and its owner swung around the corner, Genesis blasting from the stereo.

Taking this as her cue, Judy carefully picked up her bag,

glancing at the note and the set of keys on the table before heading out to the first-floor hallway. She made a kissing sound at the neighbour's cat, scratching its neck as she made her way along the hall before taking a flight of stairs to the front door, her right hand running down the banister. Without looking back, she smiled to herself as she took a step outside and was welcomed by one of the first days of proper summer, taking this as some kind of sign as she inhaled the smell of blossom and pretzels that wafted in from the deli on the corner.

From the open window of the Buick, Genesis still blared out, and Judy watched the driver as he crossed the street, without a care in the world.

Closing the front door of Aunt Susan's brownstone behind her for the final time, she held her chin high as she walked purposefully down the steps, her bag slung over her back, stopping to light a cigarette from the packet she had lifted on her way out, taking two pulls of the filter while she waited for the guy opposite to enter the house.

Imagine being so predictable.

Shaking her head, Judy counted out three beats, and then tossed the half-smoked cigarette to the kerb. The embers fizzed in the gutter as she moved around to the driver's side of the car and pulled it open, climbing in, securing her bag in the front passenger footwell and taking a final glance in the wing mirror before releasing the handbrake.

There was a hint of anticlimax as she pulled away, entirely unnoticed by the old man shuffling a pack of cards on the stoop a few doors down, or by the kids kicking an old tennis ball to one another on the corner as she passed.

A galloping sensation seized her chest every time a siren passed, as she made her way through the city, the Buick pushing forward at an unusually brisk pace thanks to traffic lights that seemed, fatefully, to be on her side. She needn't worry about a police chase, she had been sure of that much. Drug dealers didn't call the cops when their cars were stolen.

Surely, though, someone would stop her. After all, drug dealers might not call the police but they weren't averse to meting out justice in their own special ways.

Except they didn't. Not as she moved through Queens, her eyes flicking every few seconds to the wing mirror. Not as she traversed the Whitestone Bridge out of the city, her heart soaring as New York receded to a toy-town in the distance.

Once she was on the motorway proper, Judy wound down the window and whooped at the top of her lungs.

She had got away with it, just as she always knew she would. But now was no time to get cocky. Reaching into the side of the bag in front of the passenger seat, she pulled out the map and studied her destination: Wellfleet, Massachusetts.

Now it was time to keep her eye on the prize.

Two weeks earlier, a bright, blue New York sky had been shining as Judy made her way through Prospect Park and into the library on Grand Army Plaza, the pen she had borrowed from one of the bars near Times Square tucked into the top pocket of her shirt, along with her fake ID.

She had given herself the day off from her usual weekday routine after she'd found one of the rich-kid-tourist rucksacks in the bar at the base of the Rockefeller Center stuffed with $500 in freshly printed bank notes.

Five hundred dollars cash. What kind of person kept that amount on them in New York City, much less failed to keep it properly minded while they hit on every girl who passed? The kind who wouldn't miss it too much in the scheme of things.

Five hundred dollars. It was enough to make a girl lose all perspective. But not for long.

Still high from her unexpected windfall – she had never made more than a couple of hundred dollars in twenty-four hours before, and that was on a good day – she had planned to spend the morning browsing through the selection of magazines and maps at one of the reading rooms under the enormous Art Deco windows through which she sometimes felt she could reach up and touch the sky. Later, she might head back to one of the bars she hadn't hit up for a while, if she felt like it.

OK, so it wasn't exactly the life she had imagined for herself the day she'd upped and left London for New York. But the routine was good, and the money, too. If Judy had ever worried that her proxy guardian wouldn't buy it, she needn't have. Aunt Susan was too busy with her own small life to ever question her niece's claims of having found a job at a coffee shop on the other side of town from both her home and her own job at the university.

And why would she question it?

Working the bars had been fun at first; a natural progression from her days working the snooker halls of north London in the holidays when she was home from boarding school. Except this time her mouth did some of the work along with her fingers. It was an art, of sorts: doing her make-up and hair so that she looked twenty-five, making up false names with a back story to match each new character. Becoming more elaborate with every rendition, Judy found herself almost challenging the men she met to call her out, though none ever did. They were simply too keen to believe that the beautiful young woman at the bar had chosen them to buy her an Old-Fashioned; to sit and tell her their jokes and their stories, while she matched the old bastards drink for drink.

And so it continued, for months on end.

When she ran out of inspiration for characters, Judy went to the old newspaper and magazine section of the library and ran through the obituaries, pulling out names and spending hours working up character traits and fleshing out back stories for the women she briefly became. She was Michelle from Ohio, working as a dancer at the studios downtown; Lorraine from Quebec studying to be a teacher. She was an archaeologist having some me-time between digs. And – her personal favourite – Ursula, a vet passing through the United States on her way back to the spider monkey sanctuary on the Yucatán Peninsula where she worked as a volunteer.

This final incarnation Judy had picked out of a copy of *National Geographic*, illustrated with photographs of blue rivers and bright pink flamingos and the swarms of yellow butterflies that flocked through Quintana Roo at certain times of year.

Isla Mujeres. She let the name settle on her lips. She liked the way it sounded: the Island of Women.

One day, Judy told herself, she would visit that place for real.

Lately, though, she was starting to get itchy feet, her attention drawn more by the characters themselves than the job at hand. Despite her best efforts to keep it interesting, after almost two years of variations on the same routine, she had grown bored. She also worried she was pushing her luck. There were only so many bars suited to her kind of work in New York City, and, once she'd hit one up, she had to give it a rest for a while. The game she was playing was a gamble. You never knew, when you slipped your hand into the pocket of a stranger's coat, or bag, what you might find. It was like Kenny Rogers sang in that song her mother used to play on the old gramophone between rotations of Joan Baez and the Rolling Stones: the key to success was knowing when to fold.

What Judy needed was something solid. A long-term plan. The hustle had been good as a starting off point – and she had just made her first major win. She had $500 in her back pocket, didn't she?

The question now was how to use it.

These were the thoughts passing through her mind that early summer's day, a fortnight before her escape. There had still been a chill in the air as she'd turned the page of the *New York Times*, dated four months previously, and spotted the obituary of one Montgomery Basil Harrington.

Later, Judy would ask herself what had drawn her to that particular story, besides the ludicrous name. The truth was, she would never know for sure. Judy was impulsive, which was both a gift and a curse. Maybe the selection was largely random: a case of right place, right time. She needed a plan, and here one was.

Harrington Senior leaves behind a son, Rory Harrington. Harrington, who lost his young wife, Caroline, to cancer a year ago, will take over his father's role as chairman of the International Wine Society.

The article had been accompanied by a photograph of an attractive young couple, the caption reading: Rory and Caroline Harrington at the annual International Wine Society ball in July, held every year in Wellfleet, Massachusetts.

Rory Harrington. She said the name aloud.

Somewhere behind, a car horn beeped, and Judy smiled to herself as she pulled right towards the motorway exit, picturing the route she had committed to memory; a straight line running 285 miles north from Aunt Susan's apartment in

South Brooklyn to Wellfleet, Massachusetts. The venue for this year's annual International Wine Society gala, in two weeks' time.

The beginning of a new life: a life she had chosen.

It was not yet lunchtime when she pulled into the car park at the bar opposite the motel, somewhere near Warwick, Rhode Island.

She was already hungry – running on adrenaline did that to a girl. Worse still, she had run out of cigarettes.

Parking in the most shielded position she could find, Judy took a moment to reapply her lipstick, admiring the stretch jeans she had found in a store on Madison Avenue. Pulling down the visor in front of her, she watched the empty parking lot through the rectangular mirror.

It was startling, sometimes, when she spotted herself like this, her reflection on some surface or other catching her off guard: for a moment she would see herself not as Judy but as the spit of her mother, just as Aunt Susan clearly had done, judging from her expression the moment her niece had arrived at the flat, the blonde curls that were entirely Esther partially pulled back from her face.

Judy couldn't help but laugh when she thought of Aunt Susan looking her up and down with more than a hint of disapproval, her eyes hovering over the cycling shorts and cropped T-shirt, her final conclusion – a muttered *chip off the old block* – delivered with a sigh. But Judy understood her resentment. Esther had always been the beautiful one, the talented one, the one people wanted to be around. That much was obvious from the single photograph of her mother and aunt together, as much as from the passing comments. The photo had been taken a few years before Judy was conceived, just a few months before her mother's accident. Esther and Aunt Susan, chalk and cheese.

In it, Susan's shoulders were slightly hunched forward, clearly as uncomfortable in her own skin as she was in her proximity to her sister, as she prepared to travel to the other side of the world to make a life for herself away from Esther's shadow.

Esther, then still a talented ballerina, would soon be heading off to London.

And here, years later, was Judy, to remind Susan of everything she had been trying to escape.

Judy did nothing to correct her aunt's view of her little sister. She was too loyal to her mother for that. But let's just say it had been a long time since Susan had seen her.

Pulling down her sunglasses, Judy picked out a book from her bag – a dog-eared paperback she carried for sentimental reasons, serving as much as a prop as a distraction – while she waited for the right guy to arrive. When he did, a while later, Judy knew instantly. Not him, of course, but his type. She could smell men like him a mile away: too-tight jeans, cheap shirt. Old enough to know better, arrogant enough to play along.

Marking the page of the novel with a worn piece of newspaper that served as a bookmark, she set it down on the front seat as she watched the man lock the car door behind him and flick away the butt of his cigarette before heading into the bar.

He was already two beers deep by the time Judy walked inside a little while later, leaning against the counter and glancing around, smiling shyly in the man's direction when their eyes met.

Up close, his nose was red with drink. A thin moustache ran along his upper lip.

Carefully, Judy slipped the rucksack from her shoulder onto the floor. It contained everything she had bothered to bring with her from New York: purse, book, screwdriver, passport, cash, a change of clothes padding out the yellow vase she kept for sentimental reasons, and the pair of car registration plates she had removed from an abandoned vehicle by the basketball courts at edge of the Hudson River, in the days before she left. She had also taken the newspaper cutting about Rory Harrington, heir to Montgomery Basil Harrington's fortune. Everything else, she could get once she arrived. It was better to travel light, in every respect.

'I'll have one of those,' Judy said to the girl behind the bar, indicating towards the man's beer. 'And a whisky.'

'Hey, Molly, I'll get hers. And the same for me.'

Judy worked hard not to show the disgust she felt as the man looked her up and down, grinning as he addressed the waitress.

'Really? Oh that's so kind.' Judy smiled.

'Hard day?'

'Something like that.'

'Where's your accent from?'

'Australia.'

'Is that right?'

'Why, do I sound funny to you?'

'You sound funny but you look good.'

Giggling, Judy bit her lip. 'Thanks for the drink.'

They moved from the bar to a booth after three rounds, at her suggestion. His coat was slumped on the bench between them and she could smell the alcohol on his breath as she leant in, her hand running briefly over his thigh.

'So I said, "Oh I'm sorry, I thought it was a snake!"'

The man wheezed with laughter, slapping his leg. 'No shit.' He was so drunk by now that she had stopped pretending to match him drink for drink, after genuinely knocking back two of the shots and spitting the third on to the floor while he searched for his cigarettes. 'What did you say your name was?'

'Adelaide.'

'Adelaide. You're one crazy kid.'

'I'm drunk is what I am, and I blame *you*.' She leaned in again. 'Now, how about you line up a couple more of these while I go to the Ladies' and sort my face out?'

'Your face looks fine to me.'

'Don't go anywhere.'

Judy heard him call something after her as she walked unevenly across the floor of the bar towards the saloon-style doors, turning so that he saw her hold on to the wall for stability, giggling visibly before moving into a room which stank of piss.

Walking straight now, she moved purposefully across the bathroom, her face furrowed in concentration, spurred on by the feeling of the car keys pressing against her leg in the pocket of her jeans.

Pushing open the door of the first cubicle, she peered in and saw that the window above the toilet was sealed shut.

Shit.

Retreating, she moved to the second door and pushed it open. This time, with a smile, she saw that the window was propped open.

Bingo.

The window frame was little wider than Judy and was located at chest level once she stood on the toilet lid, wary that the whole thing might come away from the wall at any moment.

The drop into the back of the car park was around seven feet high, cushioned by a dusty gravel landing. Taking it head-first was not an option so she worked as fast as she could, using the space between the two walls of the cubicles – which thankfully left a few inches between wall and ceiling – to pull herself up enough to get her feet on the sill and lever herself through the gap.

With a deep breath, she let herself drop, a sharp pain running through her foot as she landed at an angle on the tarmac. Fuck.

Breathing in, she stood and glanced over her shoulder, aware that she had already been gone several minutes. Despite her companion's inebriation, he might soon come looking for his piece of skirt.

It was amazing, the pain a person could put up with when they needed to, Judy reasoned, setting her jaw in an expression of determination as she moved as stealthily as she could manage through the car park.

Staying out of the line of sight of the bar's only side window, she used the keys she had swiped from the pocket of the old drunk's coat to open his car and drive off, leaving the Buick abandoned in the space opposite.

Francesca

It is cool in the tiled hallway, the London sky outside dark and brooding, any promise of an Indian summer already forgotten.

Inhaling deeply, I silence the scream building up inside. I am not yet ready to face whatever it is that awaits me, though I know I have no choice. Taking another, steadier breath, I pull on the mid-length black Acne jacket Hugo bought for my thirty-eighth birthday, earlier in the summer, joking at the time that it made me look like a surprisingly stylish pallbearer. Or, I had countered, an even bigger surprise: a stylish solicitor.

He made a face like he didn't get it. Even then he couldn't mock the career we both must have known, on some level, was a poor imitation of his own.

When I was feeling particularly ungenerous, I wondered if it quietly suited Hugo that his wife had never transferred to the bar – that he was always the more serious lawyer, advocating for justice while I solicited for clients at a small firm in Camden Town. But that was my issue at play, not his. Jealousy simply wasn't his style. Hugo never wanted anything but the best for me, and for Lily. Even knowing what he knew.

In the darkness of the hallway, I slip on the black Italian loafers with the gold buckles I left there the previous evening, standing straight and picking up my handbag from the antique console table before opening the front door.

The sudden assault of the reporters catches me off guard, even though I have been expecting it. Walking purposefully down the slightly too steep steps, just as I have seen Hugo instruct his clients to do outside court – keeping my eyes blinkered ahead, chin held high – I feel my feet suddenly unsure on the path I have trodden countless times before.

One of the journalists has left open the gate to the street. Feeling the gaze of camera lenses following me as I pass, I step through into an outside world that is both an escape and a threat. A neighbour's cleaner looks up momentarily from where she is polishing the brassware on the doorstep before immediately returning her attention to her task.

I turn left, my fingers shaking as I take the keys from my bag.

'Is it true?' A veteran tabloid reporter, whose face I recognise from appearances on the Sky News morning review slot, follows me to the driver's side. 'Don't you want to give your mother's version of the story? Otherwise the papers are going to have a field day.'

Without a word, I open the car door and slam it behind me, taking a moment to gather myself behind the safety of the tinted glass. Closing my eyes, I allow a picture of Judy to form as she was the last time I saw her. And then I stop my mind there, gripping the steering wheel and counting to three before taking the key in my hand and placing it in the ignition, with a single thought.

Mum, what have you done?

Judy

Joining Route 195 at Providence, Judy took the signs towards
Cape Cod until she spotted one of the second-hand car dealerships she had looked up at the library and marked out on
the maps she had photocopied before leaving the city.

Smiling to herself, she pulled in, noticing the man in his
office run a hand over his hair at the sight of her approach.

'Hi, there,' Judy said with her best American twang.

'How can I help?'

The dealer wore thick-lensed specs, his thinning hair parted
to the side and slick with grease, collared T-shirt buttoned
low to reveal his chest hair. If he had been auditioning for
the part of untrustworthy second-hand car salesman, you
would tell him to tone it down a little.

'I need a car,' she said.

'Well, then, you're in the right place. I'll show you what I got.'

He eyed the young woman as they circled the forecourt,
his gait wide-set as Judy stopped in front of the Ford Mustang
II and turned to him with a triumphant smile.

'Part-exchange, you say?' he repeated a few minutes later,
looking between his Mustang and the station wagon she was
offering up, along with $350 by way of payment. Sure, it

was a better car than this deal should have afforded her – even if the Mustang was fourteen years old with a series of dubious marks along several panels, which a more discerning customer might have presumed were indications of a serious crash. But she was feeling lucky, and it wasn't like this guy was inundated with business.

It was a 1972 model, the dealer explained as he ran through his spiel, which she listened to with a half-hearted interest. Judy didn't care about the details. She knew enough already: she liked it, and she needed it. Before the guy from the bar – or the police, for that matter – caught up with her. Though she hoped the false plates she had attached to the front and back of the old drunk's station wagon while parked in an opening in the woods would see her good for a while.

'You want to wait inside, out of the heat, while I do the paperwork?' he asked, finally.

Judy shook her head, adjusting her sunglasses. 'I'll be here.'

The smile fell from her face as he walked away, her eyes following the dealer inside, casing the joint for signs of one of those closed-circuit cameras some businesses had started to use; though, honestly, it was unlikely that Billy Sumners Autos was the kind of establishment where external records of its business transactions were encouraged.

Through the window, the papers he was holding rustled under the fan whirring on the laminate desk as he glanced up at Judy and then down again, his eyebrows narrowing. She felt herself tense as he returned, moving slowly in the afternoon heat. She waited for him to ask for ID or proof of ownership; to quiz her on the licence plates.

Instead he simply nodded.

'You're good to go,' he added before handing her the keys. 'You take care now.'

'Oh,' she replied, 'I always do.'

The following morning there was a warm summer breeze, a curl blowing across her face as the Mustang cruised along the highway.

She drove for a couple of hours, leaving the motel before the sun rose – having half-expected to find the car gone, or to be awoken by the sound of police hammering at her door as she slept.

Suppressing a yawn, she felt in the internal panel of the car door for the cigarettes she had bought from one of the gas stations.

What she actually needed was food. Food and hot coffee. The way she calculated it, she had enough cash for either lunch or dinner, but not both – not if she wanted to survive the month. And it was not yet even 10 a.m.

Turning up the radio to full, she sang along to Donna Summer, pressing her foot more firmly on the gas as she took Route 6 north, crossing over 6A onto the stretch once known as the Old King's Highway. Water ran along one side of the road, accompanied by signs warning of great white sharks, and a series of old white clapboard houses lined the other.

The sign for Wellfleet stood at the edge of the track cutting through acres of vineyard.

Had the wind been moving in a slightly different direction at that very moment, she might not have given a second thought to the heavily pregnant woman kneeling at the edge of the road, attempting to attach a large handwritten sign to a wooden post. In the split second it took for Judy to register the figure with the hammer and tack in one hand, a sudden gust caught the laminated sheet of paper the woman was holding in the other and threw it up in the air, dropping it again face-down on the windscreen of her car.

Applying the brakes and pulling carefully over to the side of the road, she looked up and saw the words staring back at her through the glass on the passenger side, clearly legible: HELP NEEDED.

Judy McVee didn't believe in fate, but she did believe in making her own luck. She also believed in just enough planning, and keeping just enough space open for improvisation.

She felt a sense of anticipation as she turned off the engine, stepping out of the car and removing the sign from where it had wedged itself in the windscreen wipers. Scanning the small print – *Well Springs Vineyard, open Monday to Saturday, 8 a.m. until 4 p.m.* – she walked over to the woman, who was a few years older than herself, dressed in denim dungarees. She was still kneeling on the ground, a nail held between her teeth. In one hand she held a hammer; the other hand was now empty.

'You looking for this?' Judy asked, holding out the sign.

'Good catch.' The woman laughed. 'Sorry about that. I was sure I had it secure but that sudden breeze got me. It's like that along here – unpredictable.'

'Here, let me help.' Judy held out a hand for her to heave herself up. 'How far along are you?'

'Thirty-seven weeks.'

'Wow, congratulations.' Judy pushed away the hair from her face and smiled, returning her attention to the words on the paper. 'Well, maybe this is a sign, because I really need a job. I mean, it is literally a sign.'

The woman looked back at her, amused, holding out her hand. 'OK. Well then, let's start with the basics. I'm Marnie. What's your name?'

'Judy,' she said. 'I'm Judy Porter.'

There was a straightforwardness to Marnie that Judy appreciated straight away. The older woman brushed the dirt off her knees as she explained that the role would be nothing fancy, mainly taking coats, seating customers and serving drinks at the newly opened bar and food shack at the edge of the vineyard. Making wine was one thing, she explained, offering her prospective employee the back story of her plan for an expansion of the business her family had run on this strip of coastline for more than a century, one hand supporting her lower back as she leant on the bonnet of Judy's car. What they had at Well Springs – acres of family-run vineyard with a seafront property attached – was a potential goldmine, what with tourism taking off as it was on the Cape.

It wouldn't be easy to get off the ground, Marnie was quick to add, but she had drawn up business plans to allow for an on-site kitchen and bar that would harness the attention, and the wallets, of those visitors who, as it was, drove out here to sample grapes and buy a bottle or two at the vineyard, wholesale, before heading back into town for food.

'Why supply our wine to restaurants for them to make a mark-up on the profit, when we could take the profit ourselves?' Marnie mused, with a shrug.

Why indeed?

The job would only be short-term – seasonal – but if Judy wanted it . . . who knew where it might lead?

'I only plan to be here for the summer anyway.' Judy smiled back at her. 'Unless something happens to keep me here. So, as far as I'm concerned, it's perfect.'

Judy

Cape Cod, July 1985

The party was already in full swing by the time she arrived. From the edge of the driveway, Judy noted the swell of violins and the clinking of champagne glasses, practised laughter emanating from somewhere just out of sight.

Watching the doorman's eyes light up as she approached the iron gates that guarded the property, she took a cigarette, slowly, from the silver tin in her clutch, making a show of searching for a book of matches and then stopping, berating herself with a demonstrative shake of the head.

A single blonde curl fell from the middle of her hairline, across her cheek.

'That's me.' Glancing down at the clipboard, she pointed to one of the few names that hadn't already been struck through. 'You don't have a light, do you?'

Removing the cigarette from between her lips, Judy noticed the filter was stained Cherry Tomato, the shade of Max Factor tucked inside her handbag. My *purse*, she reminded herself, cheerfully – she was in America, after all.

Her expression was tinted with the vague amusement of a girl who was used to being admired, despite her own silliness.

'Welcome, Ms Sullivan,' the doorman said, patting his pocket and coming up empty.

'Don't worry, I'll get one inside.' She shrugged and smiled, scanning past him towards the expanse of perfectly cut lawn on either side of a gravel drive.

The last of the evening light cut lines across the estate, the gravel crunching under heels that were half a size too big.

Keeping her expression neutral, Judy accepted a flute of champagne from one of the uniformed young women who weaved discreetly through guests gathered on the grass. Pulling her black mohair shawl up around her shoulders and looking around, she saw instantly that she was wearing the wrong thing. Ordinarily she might not have minded, except the material was also a little warm for this time of year – a little scratchy, too, now that she thought about it. Making a mental note to find something more suitable to replace it, she reached the house – one of those large white soulless things people around here did so well, its rooms lit up through vast glowing windows.

She was halfway through the doorway when she spotted him by the stairs, flinching at the sudden recognition. She hadn't exactly known what to expect, but, looking back, she could swear something shifted in that first sighting, the wheels beneath her spinning out of control.

Downing her glass in one, Judy watched the scene unfold from over the edge of the impossibly thin crystal rim. Although he was apparently immersed in conversation with an older couple who were laughing performatively in response to whatever it was he was saying, she spotted a note of agitation or boredom in the slight tapping of his fingers against the expensive seam of his suit trousers.

Oh, he was good at this. Judy could tell that much as he half-turned towards a waitress and reached for a flute of champagne.

But the slightest of flickers in his eye betrayed the fact that he would probably rather be floating face-down in the illuminated pool on the other side of faux-French doors than embroiled in this particular debate on the merits of Ronald Reagan versus his vice president George Bush.

You can't kid a kidder.

Taking a breath, Judy moved a few slow steps forward before turning and letting her leg brush up against his. They turned towards one another at precisely the same moment, with a sudden frisson as their eyes met for the first time.

He was a little taller than her; taller than she had pictured, with brown hair that she imagined would turn grey rather than recede. A silver fox in the making. With or without the wile? That was yet to tell.

There was a slight smile on his mouth, more sheepish than self-assured. As he considered her, she hoped she was imagining the blush she felt in her cheeks. She hadn't expected the depth of the blue in his eyes; for a moment she could almost feel herself falling. It was the same sensation that would shove her out of sleep as a child, causing her to sit bolt upright, struggling for air in the middle of the night as the other girls in the dormitory remained fast asleep in their bunks.

'I'm so sorry,' Judy said, her voice breathy. 'I didn't see you there—'

'It's my fault.' He cleared his throat. 'I'm Rory Harrington – I don't believe we've met?'

He spoke with the same sense of rehearsal that she did, but his was less specific: a public courtesy honed over years of private school and the kind of subliminal etiquette training that came with growing up among the very rich. Manners to gloss over a million fault lines. Yet there was something about this man that seemed genuine too. Judy worked on instinct, and her gut told her that he was what Aunt Susan might tersely have referred to as 'a good egg'.

The thought wrongfooted her. It was harder to know how to proceed when she no longer understood what she was working with.

Steering a path through the jumble of thoughts, Judy cleared her throat and laughed with an expression she imagined was demure but inviting. It was a dangerous line to tread – he surely wasn't the kind of man who wanted anything too easy – and she felt herself tilt one way and then the other, seasick under his steady gaze.

'I don't think we have, either – not before you tried to bulldoze me to get to the champagne. I'm Judy.'

'Just Judy?'

'Just Judy – exactly, how did you guess? But you can call me Just, if you like. All my friends do.'

He laughed and they fell silent for a while, before he spoke again. 'Well, Just Judy, your glass appears to be empty. Please, let me get you a drink to apologise for the stampede.'

'You're very generous with other people's champagne,' she replied, matching the playfulness of his tone, following through groups of discreetly manicured couples in summer dress towards the waitress's outstretched silver tray.

As he guided her through the crowd, she felt several sets of eyes on her back where the dress dipped slightly at the base of her shoulders – a dancer's back, her mother liked to say. Instinctively, Judy's fingers felt for the tiny horseshoe pendant resting just under her throat, hanging from a thin gold chain.

'Is that an English accent?' Rory asked as they rounded in on the waitress.

'You're a detective as well? In that case I probably shouldn't be talking to you.' She leant in, conspiratorially. 'I'm on the run, you see.'

'Is that right?' He took a glass from a large silver tray and handed it to her, his cool blue eyes assessing her face. 'You don't look like a fugitive. Who's looking for you?'

Judy couldn't be sure if she had outwardly faltered. 'No one, as far as I can tell.' She sighed. 'Sad, isn't it?

'I hate to be the one to tell you this, but right now I can see at least three sets of eyes watching you.' He took a considered sip of his drink. 'I'm not sure you'll get away with anything for long. Who are you here with?'

'I'm alone, actually.' Giving him a moment to take her in unchecked, Judy glanced over his shoulder, one way and then the other. 'I was invited by a woman I met at the vineyard where I work, but I haven't seen her since I arrived. I'm beginning to think she was just being polite. Or maybe I got the wrong house. Who do you know here?'

Looking back at him, Judy held his gaze, watching his pupils expand, and smiling in response.

'Everyone – for my sins.'

She let her attention once again circle the hallway, which filtered off on either side towards further rooms with high ceilings. The surfaces were covered in lifeless bouquets of flowers, giving the impression of a funeral parlour.

'So, what brings you to New England?' Rory spoke quickly, as if worried the conversation might dry out.

'After my father died, I decided I'd spent long enough sponging off his money, so I made up my mind to make some of my own.' Judy paused. 'Why are you looking at me like that?'

'It's strange to think of you working at one of those places. You just—'

'A beautiful young woman can't have an interest in fine wine?'

'I never said I found you beautiful.'

'Well, that's a relief.' Judy pushed the hair away from her face. 'I have an aunt in New York City. I wanted to leave London and travel, do my own thing. My mother wanted me to be a dancer, like her—'

Judy could almost hear the screaming of brakes as she slammed to a halt. The trick was to offer up just enough truth – not too much. But in this situation, she was still feeling for the line.

'Besides, I'm too old now.'

He laughed. 'Too old – really?'

'I'm nineteen, practically middle-aged in the dance world.' Judy rolled her eyes. 'And yes, too young to be drinking in America – but I'm English, and we can do what we like from the age of eighteen. Apart from eat swans.'

Rory smiled, puzzled. 'So what is for you then, Just Judy?'

'I haven't decided yet.' Her words lingered in the space between them as she lifted the glass to her lips, holding his gaze. 'It's such a beautiful part of the world. You live here?' Her attention flitted around the room, settling briefly on the older woman Rory had been talking to earlier, the one with the Bette Midler perm. She was wearing a silk scarf that Judy recognised from a mannequin in the window of one of the shops in town; she had stood in front of it for a while, a few days earlier, hypnotised by the lustrous greens and reds, its abstract patterns arranged in such a way that they looked different with every glance.

'I only stay here in the summer. No one in their right mind lives on the Cape year-round.' Rory took a swig from the glass he had been nursing and wrinkled his nose almost imperceptibly. 'I have a house along the bay; it's been in the family for years.'

Taking a sip from her own flute, Judy winced slightly.

'You don't like the champagne?'

'It's OK.' She waited and then leant in. 'If I'm honest, I don't understand why anyone living in one of the finest wine-producing regions in the world would bother to ship in champagne for a party. It's—'

'Vulgar?' he offered without lowering his voice, and she bit her lip in mock horror.

'Rory Harrington, what a thing to say. Can you keep a secret?' Leaning in, she brushed her lips against his cheek. 'I'd actually prefer a beer.'

He smiled as she pulled back and grinned at him over the rim of her glass. 'You know, I can't tell when you're being serious or not.'

'I'm never serious. It's one of the few rules I have,' Judy replied. 'So, do you stay there alone, in the house?'

'Most of the time. Since—' He stopped and cleared his throat, nodding in reluctant recognition at someone approaching. Turning in the direction of his gaze, Judy spotted the woman with the silk scarf, except she had now removed it. Her shoulders were bare, exposing the full monstrosity of her dress.

Recognising her moment, Judy smiled at Rory and raised her glass. 'Well, excuse me, I must find the loo. Sorry, the *bathroom* . . . It's been a pleasure meeting you.'

'Oh.' He looked genuinely taken aback and she felt a pang of guilt, tinged with triumph. 'And you, Judy. Perhaps I'll see you another time, if they don't find you first?'

She laughed at that, holding her wrists together in front of her, mimicking being pulled away in handcuffs. 'Perhaps.'

Judy

Cape Cod, July 1985

Judy was running along the path that followed the shore, her thoughts overlaid by the wailings of Madonna, when she heard her name being called somewhere in the distance.

It was just past 4.30 p.m., a light sea breeze and rolling clouds offsetting the early afternoon sun. Adjusting her head-phones, she reluctantly slowed her pace as she tilted her head in the direction of the sound.

'Just Judy . . . I thought it was you.'

Catching her breath, she bent forward slightly as she watched the man making his way down the bank towards her. From this angle his features were bleached out by the sun, but she could see that he was dressed in tennis whites, with a racquet thrown casually over his shoulder.

Moving her feet up and down on the spot, the Velcro on her Reebok pumps making a slight swishing sound as she attempted to keep her muscles from seizing up, she smiled when he finally came into clear view.

'Oh, it's you,' Judy said, adjusting her visor to shield her eyes from the glare. 'I thought you were the Feds, finally caught up with me. Rory, isn't it? I didn't recognise you without the suit.'

'I could say the same thing . . . though I dare say you pull off the Boris Becker look better than I do. What are you listening to?'

He was indicating towards the Walkman still whirring in her bumbag. Pressing pause, she replied, 'Madonna.'

'Any good?'

She laughed, waiting for him to confirm that he was joking, and then her eyes widened. 'OK, whoa . . .'

'What can I say? The last time I bought a record was 1933.'

'Right. And let me guess, it was Wagner because you were feeling particularly jaunty that day?'

Shaking his head with a smile, he looked her up and down in her white running shorts and matching vest top, which were both damp with sweat. If he noticed the slight nick in the material where she had pulled out the tag, he gave no sign of it.

'So where are you heading?'

'That way,' she said, pointing vaguely in the direction of the track that lined the beach in front of them. She increased the pace of her toe-stretching to indicate she was ready to continue her run. 'Nice to bump into you again.'

Taking a swig from a plastic water bottle, she pressed Play and pulled the headphones back over her ears. When he reached out and touched her arm, the sudden contact caused her skin to goosepimple.

'Hey, you play tennis?'

Pulling one of the headphones away from her ear again, she shrugged. 'Only very competitively.'

'Oh, right – so, you think you could beat me?'

'I couldn't possibly speculate, but you should know I don't hold back,' she said, with a genuine smile. 'Also, I have no idea how to operate a defibrillator, so . . .'

'Excuse me, I'm only thirty-four years old. How about a match, if I promise not to die on you?'

'Sorry, I have plans,' Judy said, apologetically. 'Perhaps another time, if you don't mind being destroyed by a girl.'

'Tomorrow? I have a court at my house.'

Tuesdays were her day off. Considering the question for a moment, she studied his face. 'You're quite persistent, aren't you? Where's the house?'

Turning, he indicated towards the road above where they stood. 'It must be fate, because you just ran straight past it.'

Judy

Cape Cod, July 1985

She arrived a few minutes after two, dressed in a white sports vest and matching Pringle shorts, both freshly procured from the store in town. The clouds that had littered the sky the day before had dispersed, making way for a clear blue canopy overhead.

'I wasn't sure you'd come,' Rory said when he greeted her at the door, dressed in a variation of the outfit he'd been wearing when he had accosted her the previous day on her run.

'You've already warmed up – that's cheating,' she said, noting the slight sheen of sweat running over his back as they moved through the vaulted hallway into the house.

In the centre of the hall, a cluster of orchids had been precisely arranged in a large glass bowl. It was hard to imagine him choosing such decoration – in fact it was hard to imagine anyone living here at all.

Through the windows of the sitting room to the right, the view over the bay was just visible. If it weren't for the sand dunes and the reeds, it might have been the view from one of the top-floor classrooms at Judy's old boarding school, perched on the Sussex Downs, overlooking the English Channel.

'You got me,' Rory answered, turning and considering his visitor's lightly tanned face. Judy's cheeks were pinker than usual, her hair especially unruly from time spent swimming in the sea. 'Where have you been?'

'I came straight from the beach. It's hot today. I'm sorry, I didn't bring a racquet.'

'We have spares. You could have gone in the pool,' he replied. 'Or perhaps you have one . . . You didn't mention where you're staying?'

'No pool; it's an apartment above a shop – possibly the worst in all of Wellfleet. But you live and learn.'

'The best places do get booked up this time of year.' He led the way through a wide, bright kitchen with a glass vista looking out over the water.

'It's OK, I don't plan to stay there long.'

It was impossible for Judy not to gasp as they entered the garden, the lawn rolling towards tennis courts and the ocean beyond. 'What a view! This is absolutely stunning.'

'It's pretty special. I'll miss this place.'

With a jolt, she turned to face him. 'Where are you going?' Did she imagine him flinch?

'I don't know yet. I'm selling it.'

'Why?'

The question felt too intimate and Judy sensed him pull away the moment she asked.

'Sorry, you don't have to answer that,' she continued, hurriedly. 'I'm just – it's so lovely, it's hard to imagine wanting to leave.'

He exhaled. 'That's OK. Just some bad memories. It's time to move on. Anyway, I've been very lucky, generally – and, from what you say, it sounds like I might need some of that luck for our match.'

'Oh,' she grinned as the mood between them realigned, 'you're going to need all the luck you can get.'

* * *

'Well, I can't say you didn't warn me.' Rory was attempting to steady his breath as they made their way across from the tennis court back towards the terrace. The lawn, which had been mown in an unnaturally neat series of lines, was surrounded by manicured gardens that reminded her of Queen Mary's Rose Gardens, where she would sometimes sit and read as a girl, when she wasn't at school.

Indicating for his guest to take a seat at the rattan sofa covered with floral upholstered cushions, Rory filled the glasses on the table where a member of staff had placed a pitcher of fresh lemonade and another of iced water. Judy laughed apologetically, taking the drink and pushing a strand of hair away from her face.

'My mother was semi-professional.'

'Semi-professional – I'm not sure I know what that means. Is that like a not-very-good professional player?'

Finishing the lemon water in several extended gulps, Judy made a thoughtful face. 'I think it means you play tennis for part of the day and drink Campari for the other part? It's not the worst job. There's a court in Regent's Park, which is close to where I grew up. She and I would play together every morning when I wasn't at boarding school, come rain or shine – and in London it was almost always rain. Hence why I now look like I've just had a shower, fully dressed, after an hour of playing in this heat . . .'

Absent-mindedly, Judy ran a finger over the beads of sweat clustered on her shoulders, which were pink with sun.

'You brought a change of clothes?'

'No. But I did bring my swimming things, so I'll head to the beach again on the way home—'

'Well, then, that settles it – we'll have a dip in the pool. And you can borrow something to change into afterwards.'

Judy made a face. 'No offence, but I'm not sure I'll fit into a pair of your chinos.'

'My wife . . . she was a similar size to you.' Rory cleared his throat, smiling at the maid who arrived just then to refresh the jug. 'Thank you, Arlene.'

'Oh.' Waiting a moment until they were alone again, she continued. 'I'm so sorry, I didn't realise—'

'You have nothing to apologise for. She died, two years ago – you weren't to know.'

When Judy pictured Caroline's face, staring out of the pages of the newspaper, there was an accusation in the corners of his dead wife's mouth.

A breeze ran over the grass. Blinking, Judy spoke again, her voice gentler. 'That's awful. I'm really very sorry—'

'As I say, you have nothing to be sorry for.' Rory swigged, his voice more insistent as he looked, disapprovingly, at his empty glass. 'I could do with something stronger. How about you?'

'She must have been young,' Judy continued, emboldened.

'She was a couple of years younger than me. She was thirty when it happened. Her clothes are all still in the wardrobe; I couldn't bring myself to throw them out. Sorry, I don't know why I offered, you probably think it very weird—'

'I don't think it's weird at all.'

There was a moment's silence, the two of them considering each other afresh, and then Rory nodded, slapping his thighs with his palms, his previous good humour returning. 'OK. Well, good! I'll get us some drinks. Arlene can take you upstairs to find a set of fresh clothes. You can change into your bathing costume and I'll meet you back at the pool.'

* * *

49

'You can just pick something out, I'm not fussy about what I wear . . . Arlene, wasn't it?'

Leaving her tennis shoes at the back door as instructed, Judy followed the maid inside, allowing her eyes to roam the confines of the house more freely in Rory's absence.

Arlene didn't answer as they headed upstairs, where polished wood gave way to carpet on the first floor. The landing up here, like most of Rory's house, was painted white, a single photograph hanging on the wall: Rory and his late wife, both around the age that Judy was now, dressed in black tie, the woman's eyes seeming to follow her as she continued into the master bedroom.

Letting her toes knead the chenille, which was soft and plush underfoot, Judy stood in the doorway, taking a moment to assess her surroundings: the floral quilt on the meticulously made bed; the wooden dresser with the oval mirror and uphol-stered stool positioned to its right. The far end of the room was an expanse of windows framed in thick corresponding floral drapes gathered on either side with matching ropes.

The overall effect was almost set-like: the space as perfect and undisturbed as an empty stage before the actors descend to perform the most tedious play in history. God, if Judy had this much money, she would have fun with it. Hell, she would go to Portobello Road market every day and buy all the flam-boyant furs and jewellery that money could buy. Just because she could. Just because she was alive and one day she would be dead, and what better reason was there to do anything?

She shivered, suddenly, from the intensity of the air-conditioning.

'Follow me, please,' Arlene said, leading through a door into his-and-hers walk-in closets, perfectly symmetrical shelves and open wardrobes lining either side. Ahead of them, a mirror ran from floor to ceiling, and Arlene – shorter and more heavily built than Judy – met her eye, briefly, in the reflection before looking away.

The scent of lavender emanated from a hand-stitched silk sachet as she opened one of the drawers, which made a satisfying rolling sound as the woman pulled it out and selected a plain magnolia-coloured T-shirt from the top of a carefully ironed stack of clothes and hung it over her arm.

Picturing her own clothing situation at the apartment above the shop on Main Street – the single bag brought with her from New York, now with the additional few extra items she had acquired since arriving on the Cape – Judy watched on as the maid closed the drawer again with a meaningful click and then opened the wardrobe, picking out a pair of shapeless drawstring trousers.

'What a stylish choice,' Judy said brightly, unable to wholly hide her sarcasm as she took the items from Arlene's outstretched hands and placed them on the floor next to the striped linen bag containing her damp beach towel and the red Sears bikini she had worn for her morning swim. The sea salt had long since dried, forming a coating of crystal frosting over her skin, and she studied herself unselfconsciously in the mirror, peeling the tennis vest and sports bra up and over her head in one deft movement before pulling at the waistband of her shorts and white cotton knickers and shaking them to the floor.

Flustered, the maid turned away. 'I'll wait outside.'

'Suit yourself,' Judy replied, sweetly, watching the door close with a pointed tug as Arlene moved into the bedroom.

The air-conditioning in the closet was on full pelt and she studied herself, curiously, for a moment. She hadn't had a full-length mirror since leaving New York and she hardly recognised the person staring back at her. She had lost weight in the past few months, she observed, without any particular feeling one way or the other, inspecting the taut lines of her stomach, which had turned a golden brown contrasted against the milky whiteness of her bikini line.

From somewhere downstairs, there was a clatter of glasses followed by the sound of the maid's voice in the distance. Imagining Rory in the kitchen, preparing drinks, Judy thought of the first time she had seen his face, a couple of weeks before the party. People were never the same in photographs, but Rory in particular was nothing like the character she had been expecting. In person, there was a tenderness and sincerity about him that was particularly acute given the stuffiness of the people he was surrounded by; it was almost as if, like her, he was part of a certain world but felt separate from it.

Plus, he was so handsome.

Taking the swimming costume from her bag – the bottoms catching as she rolled them up before clipping the plastic clasp of the bikini-top in place – she took a step towards the wardrobe, running her fingers over the rail of clothes. Hovering over a black spaghetti-strapped dress, she pulled it out and inspected the label – US size 4, silk, dry-clean only – nodding in approval before letting it fall back into place.

Judy knew very little about Caroline, besides what she had read in the papers about the young, tragic wife of Rory Harrington. *The youngest treasurer the International Wine Society had ever known.* According to the reports, she was well liked by all who knew her. Though did anyone really ever speak ill of the dead?

None mentioned the cause of her death, but that wasn't unusual either. Obituaries rarely carried such details.

Moving her attention to the drawers, Judy pulled the circular crystal handle of the one on the left-hand side. It opened with the same gratifying swoosh as when Arlene had opened the drawer below it to find the trousers. This one was shallower, though. Inside, Caroline Harrington's underwear was folded in neat rows.

Judy's fingers ran over a pair of black cotton pants, hovering above a pair made of silk and lace.

'Are you ready to go downstairs?'

Arlene's voice came from just the other side of the door, and Judy winced as she pushed the drawer back into place, moving slowly to minimise the sound of the rollers. 'Just a second,' she called out as she pressed the drawer closed, her heart beating high in her chest as she stepped back and crouched down beside her open bag, stuffing the damp sports clothes inside it, and barely standing again as Arlene opened the door.

Smiling, Judy looked up at her. 'Ready.'

Francesca

Kensington police station is a brown-brick building on one of the borough's less salubrious streets – a street I will always remember from a day I would rather forget.

Pausing in the doorway, I imagine myself in a past life, seated on the bench, my young face pale, sweet tea growing cold in the plastic cup in my hands.

'Can I help?' the officer behind the desk asks as the electric door shifts a millimetre back and forth on its hinges, bringing me to his attention.

Taking a breath, I step inside.

'My name is Francesca Harrington-Talbot.' In my desperation to get here, I haven't thought through properly what I am going to say and I fumble over my words. 'My mother . . .'

Seeing my own exasperation reflected in the police officer's eyes, I lick my lips and start again. 'My mother is in trouble—'

'Is she with you?' The officer casts around for signs of a woman in some form of distress nearby. Briefly following his gaze to the woman in uniform passing behind me, I focus again on the man behind the reception.

Keep calm, I tell myself. Just stick to the plan.

54

'She's in France. She's not . . . She has been falsely accused of a crime—'

His face changes, taking on an altogether different expression – one he presumably reserves for lunatics and timewasters, whichever bill I now fit in his eyes. Casting an eye over my expensive clothes and bag, he continues. 'Have you tried the embassy? Or presumably you've thought of flying out if you're concerned—'

'My mother is Judy Harrington,' I cut him off. 'Ah. I see from your expression you know who I'm talking about.'

'I'm sorry, but I'm not at liberty to talk to you—'

'But the case against her has been reopened? You're not denying it.'

'As I said, I can't—'

'Half of fucking Fleet Street is camped outside my door right now – they're allowed to know what's going on but I'm not? I'm her daughter, Perhaps you could ask whoever in this building leaked the news to the press to send me the memo too?'

'If you want to take a seat and try to calm down, I will ask one of my colleagues to come and see you when they have a moment—'

'I want to see Detective Joy Brown,' I say. 'She knows who I am.'

Judy

Cape Cod, July and August 1985

They arranged to meet the following day, and then the next, the cycle continuing over the subsequent weeks, so that Judy spent most of the time, when she wasn't at the vineyard, at Rory's place, or the two of them going for walks along the beach, talking about everything and nothing.

'Are you OK?' she asked one afternoon, looking up and seeing him pausing over a commemorative plate with the name *Caroline Delilah* just visible from the angle at which he was holding it. Judy had offered to help him clear the decks before the estate agent arrived to take photos for their property listing, and they were kneeling side by side on the kitchen floor organising unwanted crockery, place mats and so on into piles either for Goodwill or to keep.

'I'm fine.' Rory inhaled. 'I'm not sure what I should do with this.'

'Then hold on to it,' she said empathetically, putting down the silver goblet she was placing in an open box marked KEEP. 'It's so soon. You're allowed to feel . . . however you do.'

Judy used precisely the same words Mrs Briscoe had used to her, the first time she'd found her crying in her dorm room. It might have been the first time Judy had cried at all, after it had happened.

'Your brother died. That is a lot for any child.' The teacher had spoken in even tones, settling down next to Judy on the floor – not easy for a woman of her age – pulling up her brown ankle-length skirt slightly, revealing a glimpse of sheer black tights.

As she spoke, Judy had wiped her eyes angrily with the back of her hand. 'I don't belong here. These girls are all snobs. I hate them. Portia laughed me at me because I said hotel rather than 'otel. They're all from country estates and have horses and second homes in the south of France. I'm—'

She was what? It wasn't as though Judy had been dredged from a swamp. But she wasn't one of them, and they could smell it.

Her hands had balled into fists, and Mrs Briscoe had smiled kindly back at her, lowering her voice, laying a reassuring palm on the child's arm. Still, her tone was firm. 'Come, now, Judy McVee. Why would you want to fit in with the likes of Portia Blythedon? You're far more interesting than any of them.' She motioned her head towards the exit, towards the hall where Latin class was still in progress. 'Yes, those girls are sickeningly rich and even more sickeningly entitled. And honestly, they're all the same. But, in all the years I've taught here, I have never met anyone like you. I know I shouldn't be saying this but I don't care any more. You get to an age when you no longer . . .'

The teacher coughed, hard, and then she smiled wistfully.

'Being different is a gift, and I'm telling you that as one who knows. Where you come from isn't who you are.'

There was something about the way she'd looked at Judy that had made the girl sit a little straighter and dry her eyes.

Where she came from. The truth was, Judy wasn't exactly sure where she came from, or how she had got here at all.

Not like her mother, Esther, whose trajectory had been clear if not exactly straightforward. A village in the West Highlands where she'd lived with her two parents, her older sister Susan and a couple of sheepdogs until she'd won a scholarship to the Royal Ballet School in London. Then the accident, and a segue into other kinds of dancing, and a spell working on the markets after being introduced to them by one of the girls she'd met at the tennis club. Then she had met Judy's father . . . Then what?

'I haven't had the world handed to me on a plate, either,' Mrs Briscoe continued. 'Sometimes you have to choose the life you want, and make it happen – you know? If you don't like the person you are, then *become* someone else.'

'How am I supposed to do that?'

'Use your imagination!' Mrs Briscoe beamed. 'If there is one thing I have learnt about you in the months since you joined us, it's that you can do anything you put your mind to. You're clever and smart; you can have any life you want. You just need to reach out and take it. Do you hear me? I wish I'd not wasted so much time . . .' She coughed again, and the sound was interrupted by the ringing of a bell signalling that it was time for lunch.

For a moment, Judy had thought her teacher was going to say something else. But then she'd simply motioned towards the door. 'Off you go – and remember, Judy, you can be anyone you want to be . . .'

'Thank you for being so understanding. You're amazing,' Rory said, his voice interrupting her thoughts, and Judy looked away, wary in case he looked into her eyes and read her mind.

'Yeah, well.' She cleared her throat. 'Caroline was your wife. You're allowed to feel sad.'

There was a silence before Rory stood. 'I think we need a drink,' he announced, pulling Judy up from her cross-legged position on the kitchen floor. 'Enough of this packing up. You're not here as the hired help.'

'No, just the unpaid one.' She laughed, following him into the living room with its uninterrupted view across the bay, happy to be lured back into the present. 'I'm kidding. I enjoy it. What can I say? I'm nosy. And spending time with you is a small price to pay.'

'Ha!' Rory called back to her as he walked into the adjoining room where the drinks cabinet hung on the wall. Once he was gone, she let her eyes drift over the view, at the expanse of blue and gold, her attention eventually returning to an oil painting which hung on the wall ahead. It was of Rory as a boy, with his parents and a spaniel seated in front of them.

Half-smiling at the piece, Judy sat on the sofa, her eye catching on the photo album set on the ornate glass coffee table.

Listening for the sound of Rory pottering around in the other room as he fixed them a drink, she leant forward, cautiously, picking up the leather-bound book and turning the pages. As she did so, she found herself eye to eye with Rory's late wife in a series of reposes: in a demure yellow sundress in front of a blaze of bougainvillaea; leaning slightly to her left, imitating the slant in front of the Tower of Pisa. In one, Caroline's hand was held over her mouth as she laughed, the diamond ring on her finger shimmering in the sunshine.

Closing the pages, Judy placed the album on the table and returned her hands to her lap as she heard him call out, 'See you tomorrow!'

Judy looked up as Rory walked back into the room.

'Sorry, not you,' he said, seeing the confused expression on her face. 'Arlene just finished up for the day. Hey, what are you doing tomorrow?'

'Hmm? Oh, working. The usual.'

'I'll pick you up afterwards, if you don't have plans. Will you have dinner with me? I want to show you my favourite spot.'

'Sure.' Judy smiled as she stood. 'Sounds great. Do you mind if I freshen up quickly before I go?'

'Of course not,' Rory replied. 'You know where the bedroom is.'

The following morning Judy awoke to the alarm in her apartment. She made coffee from the drip-filter and turned on the radio loud enough that she could still hear it as she took off the Hard Rock T-shirt she had slept in and stood under the dribble of the shower. Rubbing shampoo into her hair, she watched the suds running down the drain as she sang along to Dolly Parton's '9 to 5'.

Judy had called her mother the night before from the payphone on the strip opposite the apartment, using one of those little wall-mounted boxes that reminded her of boarding school; they were nothing like the red booths in central London, with their pervasive stench of urine and colourful rows of call-cards. Or the phone boxes in New York, for that matter.

Esther's number had remained the same for Judy's whole life, and she'd inserted the coins into the slot one by one, enjoying the satisfactory thud as each landed in the machine, before dialling from memory.

'Hello?'

Even across thousands of miles, she recognised the sound of ice clinking against glass on the other end of the line as her mother answered. Massachusetts was five hours ahead of England and it was just after ten in the evening here so Judy guessed it was five o'clock in London. Very civilised – though, in her mother's world it was always five o'clock somewhere.

Resting her head against the wall, she smiled. 'Hey, Mum.'

'Judy, is that you?'

'It's me.'

'Christ. Where are you? I've been worried sick.'

'Listen, Mum, I'm on a payphone so I have to be quick. I just wanted to let you know I'm OK. Did you get my letter?'

'It didn't give me much to go on, other than that you left New York – how long ago was it? I've lost track. Honest to God, Judy.' Even now her Scottish accent was soft and comforting.

'Mum, my money's going to run out but I'm fine. Please don't worry. I actually have a new boyfriend. We've been seeing each other for a month or so now.'

'Well, whatever you do, don't get knocked up and spend the rest of your life reliant on a man to look after you. That's my advice, though I know you probably won't take it.'

It was the most lucid thing Judy had heard her say in a while, and she laughed, coiling the phone wire around her finger. 'I keep telling you, you don't need to worry about that.'

There was a beeping sound, signalling that the money was about to run out. 'Mum, I've got to go.'

'Judy, where did you say you were—'

Holding the receiver in front of her, Judy had called out, 'I love you, Mum,' just as the phone cut out.

Smiling at the thought now, she turned off the water, stepping onto the bathroom tiles, which were stained with mildew. Christ, she couldn't wait to be out of this place.

The clock in the bedroom read 7.45 a.m. by the time she got out of the shower. The feeling of the thin-threaded towel loofahing her skin shoved her back in time to the changing rooms at boarding school, the smell of chlorine and teenage sweat turning cold in the air; the whistle in the background signalling three minutes until they had to be dressed and in line.

'And where are you going for Christmas, Judy?' Portia had sniggered, challenging her as she stood between Harriet and another girl Judy didn't recognise. Looking down at her toes, she had felt her cheeks burn, thinking of her mother seated alone in the flat in London.

'The Middle East, I think. It depends on whether my father will be back from his posting in time.'

Portia's pretty little face flickered. 'The Middle East?'

'Mm-hm. Or Tuscany.'

Judy held her gaze as Mrs Briscoe bustled into the changing room, clapping her hands. 'What's going on, you should all be lined up in one minute.'

'I'm dressed.' Portia smiled sweetly at the teacher. 'Judy was just telling us about her plans for Christmas. She's going to be *in the Middle East*, apparently.' Portia bit her lip, the laughter shining in her eyes.

'Judy,' Mrs Briscoe said, turning to Judy, lowering her voice remonstratingly. 'Your mother made it very clear that you're not supposed to talk about your father's government business.'

The teacher's left eye barely flickered and Judy paused, confused, and then nodded. 'Oh, yes. Sorry.'

Turning back to Portia, Mrs Briscoe ushered her and the other girls towards the door. 'Quick, quick!' With another wink, the teacher called Judy's name. 'Judy McVee, you'd better get a move on.'

Back in the present, in the apartment on Main Street, Dolly Parton gave way to Cyndi Lauper, and Judy slipped on her uniform, a short-sleeved white shirt with the words 'Well Springs Vineyard' embroidered on the front, along with a pair of black shorts. Using the tiny mirror propped on the side table – the only other piece of furniture in the room – she ran a comb through her wet hair and pulled it back into a ponytail, using kirby grips to pin back the locks that fell around her face.

The Mustang was parked out front. At this hour, the street was still quiet, with no one around besides an old woman in ostentatious sunglasses with a small poodle on a lead. Mac's Bar, just across the street, was a world away from the kind of dive Judy had frequented in New York, reminding her of the Edward Hopper painting Aunt Susan kept on display in the living room in Bay Ridge. Like the rest of this patch of New England, the bar felt largely like a performance put on for the out-of-towners who descended every summer. And that was fine by Judy – she was happy to be part of the show.

When she thought of New York again, a million synapses went off in her mind. A mid-afternoon movie at the Alpine near Aunt Susan's brownstone. Cocktails in the Rockefeller overlooking that endless skyline; all that smoke and broken dreams blowing between the buildings.

Already, it felt like a world away.

'Earth to Judy,' Marnie whispered in her ear as she passed behind Judy at reception.

'Hmm? Oh, sorry.'

Taking the pile of account books from Marnie's hands, Judy placed them on the desk behind the counter, blinking away the thought of Rory and the coat he had slipped over her shoulders for the walk home the previous evening when she'd resolutely refused a lift.

It wasn't far, she had assured him for the third time, keeping it vague as to exactly where she was living, insinuating that she wasn't up for unexpected late-night visitors. She was a single woman, after all, and he was an older man. He respected the boundaries she was putting in place. He still hadn't tried to kiss her. It was better this way – Judy was in no rush.

'So who is he?'

At Marnie's question, an involuntary smile formed on Judy's lips. 'Sorry?'

'The lucky guy.' Marnie rolled her eyes. 'Come on – I can tell that look anywhere. You're in love.'

'Excuse me?' Judy laughed, making a face. 'I'm afraid you're in the wrong ballpark.'

'Right.' The other woman smiled.

Judy shook her head. Of course she wasn't in love. She and Rory had barely known each other six weeks. And yet, when she thought of him, there was a feeling in the pit of her stomach that she couldn't name. Rory was kind and sweet and self-effacing. He was the antithesis of the entitled rich guy she had been expecting. In a way that should have made it easier, but really it complicated things, setting the whole transaction off balance.

Judy had a plan, and falling in love wasn't part of it.

Unsettled by the comment, she watched Marnie place Cleo in the rocking chair near her feet. Bending down to coo at the baby, Judy tickled the folds at the back of her knee. Cleo was beautiful, with big, serious eyes and pouting lips.

'Oh, listen. You remember that couple you showed around yesterday who were in from the city? She lost her purse somewhere and wanted to know if anyone had handed it in?'

'The older woman?' Judy asked, after a pause, standing again. 'I'm not surprised – she was sloshed before they even got to the bar. What does it look like?' She made a funny face at Cleo.

'Hold on, let's see.' Marnie reached for the notepad by the phone. 'The description is right here: purple leather, two Amex inside and some cash.'

'I'll keep my eyes peeled.'

'Shit.' Marnie looked at the clock. 'I've got to take the baby to a doctor's appointment. Do you think you could put the till money in the safe?'

Judy's back straightened as she cleared her throat. It was the first time Marnie had trusted her with the tills. 'Sure, why not?'

'You're an angel. Here's the key. And you're sure you're OK to open up tomorrow?'

Judy smiled, feeling the tension in her neck ease. 'No problem.'

Judy

Judy kissed Rory on the cheek as she stepped into the passenger seat.

It was an hour after her shift had ended and she had come straight home, to change out of her uniform and into cut-off denim shorts and a white shirt.

Something about Marnie's remark about Judy clearly being in love had left her uneasy, and she fiddled with her sunglasses as they made their way along the coast, feeling Rory's eyes on her from the driving seat. His left arm was resting on the ridge of the open window, the collar of his shirt flapping in the breeze as he took the turn for Sesuit Harbour.

'I know they say Wellfleet oysters are the best in the world but I'm telling you, the lobster rolls on the marina are second to none.' He spoke with remarkable certainty as she kept her eyes on the horizon, her long legs stretched out in front of her on the dashboard, her arm circled protectively around her handbag.

'Judy?'

Turning from the window, Judy met his eye. 'Sorry, I was just thinking.'

'Is it about the job?'

For a moment, she was quiet again, swallowing as she returned her attention to the scenery tumbling past beyond the window. As far as Rory was concerned, Judy worked on reception at a different vineyard on the other side of town, a job that would be coming to an end with the arrival of autumn, which was fast approaching.

Just enough truth.

'Not really,' she said as Rory pulled in a few yards along the road, parking on a patch of dirt track next to a sand dune which gave way to the beach. It was late afternoon and the sunlight danced on the water as Judy gazed at the ocean, trying to determine the exact line where the sea and sky met. In front of them, a series of colourful boats were suspended precariously in mid-air, obscuring the pale blue sky. Just beyond where they stood, a group of kids darted between the reeds, playing hide and seek.

'There's no menu, you just get whatever the fisherman caught this morning. Fresh as anything.' Rory opened the boot, taking out a plastic wine cooler. 'We used to come here when I was a child. Every summer holiday, we'd fly in from New York on vacation.'

Stepping back to make way for a young boy scooting past, his hair sticky with the remnants of a day on the beach, Rory slammed the boot shut again.

'And then, when they retired, they had no need for the city, and spent their time between Wellfleet and Europe.'

'And now?'

'They're no longer with us.'

There was a breeze, and Judy pulled her new silk scarf up over her shoulders. It was so much softer and lighter than the heavy, scratchy material of the mohair one she had dumped after the party. The perfect upgrade. 'I'm sorry,' she said, automatically.

'Don't be – you never met my father . . .' He laughed, sardonically.

'And your mother?'

'She was ill for a long time.' He paused, appearing to gather his words. 'Bone cancer. It was agonising in the end; she didn't leave her room for weeks on end . . . I'm sorry, this is not—'

'No,' Judy replied, holding out a hand and clasping his wrist. 'I get it. My mother—'

It was hard, in hindsight, to understand why she said it. She could have said anything, could have told the truth, even, in part. But instead she squeezed his hand. Already, control was slipping from her grasp.

'My mother had the same.'

Once she had said it, Judy knew she could never take it back. In that moment, the foundation had been laid, and she could never pull it up again without exposing everything that lay beneath.

The way he looked at her, for a moment Judy imagined he might laugh, scornfully, seeing the lie. But who would lie about something like that? It wasn't so far from the truth, and she needed him to see that they were somehow connected, without seeing the whole truth. A truth that was too humiliating and too complicated. She wasn't ready to give him all of herself. It was important to hold something back. At least, that was how she justified it, looking back.

As the words tumbled from her, Judy watched a thousand possible reactions play out in his gaze, and then he took her hand and squeezed it, blinking away the tears that glistened like daggers in the corners of his eyes. 'Well, then, you know how it is. You seem to know everything already; you're almost unreal.'

Before Judy could respond, he changed the subject.

'I'll go and get the food, and you can do the honours with the wine.'

They settled on one of the picnic benches, taking a bottle from the cooler he had brought from home.

'None for me – I don't like seafood.'

There was a pause before he replied. 'Are you serious? But we've just driven all this way so that . . . Why didn't you tell me?'

'You didn't say where we were going. Anyway, bread and wine are basically the food of the gods, I'll be more than happy with that.' Reaching for the corkscrew, she pierced the foil with its sharp point. 'What, why are you looking at me like that – would you rather I pretend?'

'Probably.' He made a face.

'Not really my style. This bottle, on the other hand, very much is.'

Judy felt Rory watching her, as one might a curiosity in one of those tragic little museums in town marking the heyday and decline of the whaling industry. Tearing the foil on the wine bottle and peeling it away in a single practised movement, she filled her own glass and then his.

'You know, I find it hard to trust people. When you're – well, let's just say, in the circles I inhabit, people aren't always honest about who they are. But you . . .' He admired her, inhaling as though sniffing about for the right word. 'I thought the English were supposed to be all buttoned-up and proper. You . . . you're . . .'

'Improper?'

'Refreshing. I think I could fall in love with you.'

'Don't be so silly, you don't even know me.'

Judy could hear the irritation creeping into her voice. But why? Perhaps it was because hearing the words come from

69

him confirmed to her that she felt the same. Because she had to work so hard to stay in control around him.

'I know you hate seafood.'

In spite of herself, Judy laughed and then stopped, searching his face for signs that he was joking. 'Rory—'

'Relax: I said I *could* fall in love, not that I already have – it was hypothetical.' He put his glass down and leant forwards. 'Look, I'm leaving here in a few days. I'm heading to France, to my house there for a while, to sort out my father's estate, and – well, I can't speak a word of French and I'm going to be horribly bored. Come stay with me.'

She put up a hand to stop him. 'OK, you're crazy.' The more he spoke, the less in control she felt.

'Why? You said it yourself, you're living in a dive. Your job here is temporary—'

'I didn't say it was a dive—'

'The house in France is big enough for several guests.' He reached out a hand. 'The weather will be beautiful and I'll be lonely all on my own; you'd be doing me a favour.'

'I'm not who you think I am.'

Her voice was accusatory. She was cross with him for making this so hard. She hadn't come to Massachusetts to fall in love. Falling in love with the man she wanted to marry would complicate things impossibly. Judy thought of her mother as she liked to remember her, in the years after her ballet career fell away. The woman who had made her own life, forging her own path from next to nothing. The beautiful young Scottish antique dealer who haggled like the best of them, who was as soft as a pearl and as sharp as a razor, even when she arrived at the market to pitch up having not yet been to bed.

The woman whose entire life had been destroyed, and who had allowed her entire future to be left at the mercy of a man.

Judy pushed away the image away as soon as it formed.

'What are you talking about?' Rory searched her face, and she felt a pang of longing. Leaning in, she kissed him, feeling a fluttering inside as his mouth responded to hers.

'You're completely mad,' she said, matter-of-fact, after pulling away, the air between them febrile. They still hadn't been to bed together, and the anticipation was electric.

Rory smiled, clearly emboldened. 'No strings attached. Just come stay with me in France for a while. You can talk about the weather as much as you like. And if you hate it, you can leave.'

Judy hesitated. What harm could it do, spending a few months in France, making plans for the next stage? What was the alternative: starting again with no long-term job, in a place she hardly knew? There was no way she could go back to New York, or London for that matter.

'No strings attached,' Rory repeated, and then his face changed. 'Oh, Christ.'

When she turned, following his gaze towards the couple marching towards them from the car park, Judy spotted the woman with the Bette Midler perm from the party a few weeks earlier, charging towards them.

'Jesus, are those people never not five yards behind you?' Judy said under her breath.

'Rory! I thought it was you. And who is this?' Turning to Judy, the older woman continued without pause, in her southern drawl, 'I don't believe we've met, but actually you look familiar. I'm Tamara, an old friend of Rory's family, and member of the International Wine Socie—' Tamara paused. 'How strange. Your scarf – I had one just like it.'

Smiling, Judy held her gaze. 'Really? Well, you clearly have excellent taste. They sell them in the shop in town, don't they?

I should be more careful to choose something less distinctive, in such a small place.'

The woman studied Judy's neck until she felt herself reaching for the horseshoe pendant that hung beneath the silk material. 'That's right. Yes, mine was exactly the same. I lost it at a party . . .' Turning her attention to Rory, Tamara continued. 'We lost you there, too. You don't mind if we join you?' She indicated to her husband who was making his way towards them, a few paces behind. 'I was worried we had missed you. When are you off to the Languedoc?'

'Not quite sure yet,' Rory said, looking over at Judy.

'Actually, please take our seats,' Judy replied, standing as she held out a hand to take Rory's. 'I have packing to do. We're leaving in a few days.'

Judy

It wasn't yet eight o'clock and a golden light crested the tops of the buildings along Main Street. With the last days of summer drawing near, the tourists were eking out their final hours on the beach.

The street outside was practically deserted behind her as Judy let herself into her building. At the top of the stairs, she stepped into the tiny apartment and pulled out a soft-top box of Marlboros from her pocket. It was so hot, and she cracked a window before lighting up, holding the cigarette between her teeth as she dropped her keys and bag onto the counter.

Opening the cupboard, she pulled out a bottle of bourbon. Her last night on the Cape – might as well make it count.

Looking around, she was thankful she had never bothered to do anything to the place. Not that she would have been allowed to, even if she had been inclined to ask the landlord. Both of them seemed equally keen to have as little communication as possible so long as Judy paid the rent a week in advance, in cash, having responded to the advert on the billboard in the grocery store in town, keeping it top-line when he asked about what had brought her so far from home.

But she really had done *nothing*.

Sifting through a series of cut-out newspaper articles and hand-scribbled notes, she scrunched up each piece in turn before walking over to the bin and dropping them in without a backward glance.

The barman at Mac's Bar had his back turned to the entrance, swilling glasses, as Judy stepped inside. He smiled at her as she walked towards him, a single bin bag swinging by her side.

'It's so quiet in here,' she said, looking around at the empty booths.

'Yeah. I guess everyone is still at the beach.'

Inhaling, she leant forward onto the counter, peering behind him at the fridge. 'I'll take two beers.'

'Open or closed?'

'Open.' She watched as he flicked the lids off the bottles and handed them to her.

'That one's for you,' she said and he dipped his head.

'Cheers. Isn't that what you English say?'

She smiled.

'So where are you from?'

'Here and there.' Judy shrugged. 'Listen, I don't suppose I could pop some garbage in your bins? Mine's full, and the landlord—'

'Sure.' The barman took a swig of his beer. 'Just leave it by the bar, I'll sling it round the back.'

'Thanks,' she said, standing again.

'You're not staying?'

When she didn't stop, he called after her. 'Come back in soon.'

'Maybe. I'm leaving town in a while.'

'Oh yeah, where are you heading?'

Shrugging, she turned to him and smiled. 'I guess I'll know when I get there.'

Francesca

It has started to drizzle. For a moment I sit completely still in the driver's seat of the car, a street away from the police station, listening to the sound of the rain. Possibilities spin over the surface of my thoughts, each of them more unnerving than the last.

None of this makes any sense.

Reaching into my pocket, I pull out my phone and press the most recently dialled number, closing my eyes as Judy's line rings out.

For a while I sit like this, thinking of my mother and Lily and all the lies we have told and been told. What the hell is going on? Why is she not answering my calls?

And then I sit straight, and start the engine, beginning the familiar journey across London to Primrose Hill.

Judy

The south of France was still warm in early September, that first trip together – like stepping into a freshly run bath. They had travelled light, Rory carrying little more than the paperwork regarding his father's estate, claiming he already had a set of everything he needed at the house.

Stepping out into the balmy afternoon sunlight, Judy imagined herself as a snake that had shed its old skin – writhing in the grass, exposed but alive, ready to start again. Light-headed as she was after the seemingly endless flight, the solid ground felt unfamiliar, somehow, beneath the same Reebok high-tops she had worn when leaving London, the high-waisted jeans suddenly too warm.

The old caretaker Rory had told her about was waiting to drive them from the airport to the village, propped up in front of an ancient Citroën 2CV. Dressed in navy overalls, sucking on his cigarette without removing it from between his lips, he looked as though he belonged in another century.

'You have to be kidding me,' she whispered to Rory. 'Honestly – why are the French always so ridiculously French?'

He suppressed a laugh. 'Jacques has been looking after the

house for forever, and then, since my father died – well, he's been a godsend. He's wonderful. Or at least I think he is. He doesn't speak a word of English, so he could be a Nazi for all I know. But his son, Patrice, is the new village policeman, so either way we need to be on our best behaviour.'

'No English? How shocking.' Standing back a little to let Rory greet Jacques, she waited before holding out her hand to shake his, his skin rough and leathery from years of hard graft. '*Bonjour, Jacques. Merci beaucoup d'être venu nous chercher.*'

The old man nodded, taking Judy's bag.

'Good job you travel so light.' Rory opened the passenger door, indicating for her to step inside as Jacques placed the cases in the boot. 'You sit in the front; the view is gorgeous.'

'Thank you. I told you I didn't have much stuff.'

'On account of your being on the run?'

'Exactly,' she said. 'And not being a horrible materialist. What time is it in Massachusetts now?'

'We're six hours ahead here, so I guess somewhere around dinnertime. You should try to get some rest.'

'*Vous êtes prête?*' Jacques shuffled into the car beside her, fastening the half-window to its latch.

'*Oui. Je peux . . . ?*' She indicated towards the radio and he switched the dial, motioning for her to find a station. Noticing the specks of dust dancing on the dashboard, she leant forward, scanning the stations before settling on a gentle guitar riff and sitting back, finally at ease, her attention moving to the view outside the window.

She slept for most of the journey, waking up as they arrived at the end of a road which was really more of a track, with only one way in or out. The old abbey was like something from a film, sand-coloured steps leading up from the street to a balcony running half the length of the building towards large, pale blue doors that led into an atrium, with two further doors, on the left and right.

'My parents bought it in the sixties, as a place to stay when they were in Europe, travelling around the wineries. It was practically derelict back then.'

Jacques moved ahead as Rory talked, leading the way up a flight of external stairs that ran along the left-hand side towards the main entrance. At the top, they turned left into the main house, which was cool and dark, the shutters pulled against the beating mid-afternoon sun.

'Jacques lives on the other side of the building. My parents liked to throw big parties – and sometimes friends from the Wine Society would come and stay while they were in town.'

'You don't like to throw parties?'

He shrugged. 'I prefer to go to other people's. Actually that's a lie – I'd rather avoid them altogether. Caroline liked to host.'

There was a peculiarity to his voice when he mentioned his ex-wife's name.

'How did she die?'

When he turned, his expression was full of some emotion Judy couldn't place. He cleared his throat. 'She had cancer.'

'Like your mother?'

'Well, it's not particularly rare,' he snapped.

'Of course,' Judy said. 'You must really miss her. How long were you married?'

'Only two years. But yes, I loved her very much.' He looked away, gripping the side of his trousers. There was an edge to his voice and Judy found herself turning to gaze out at the field that extended towards the road.

'Of course you did. She was your wife . . . Is that your land?' she asked, changing the subject.

He was silent for a moment and then he replied, more evenly.

'I'm afraid so. It's a curse really, having so much space and no one to look after it. My mother wasn't very green-fingered. Jacques's wife used to grow some vegetables and keep chickens, I believe, down there.'

Smiling, Judy nodded. After a long, dry summer it was little more than scrub, but when she squinted she could imagine it as it might be: a plot for growing food; an area for flowers they could pick and display in large pottery jugs around the house; maybe some fruit trees.

'I'm sorry,' he said, suddenly. 'Caroline's death was . . .' His voice peters out again, 'I'd rather not talk about it, if that's OK with you.'

Moving behind her, he placed his hands around Judy's waist.

'I did warn you that it's all very rustic.'

Smiling, unsettled by his sudden change of mood and the rush of warmth she felt, she shook her head. 'It's absolutely perfect.'

Judy

Their first time together, the quiet tension that had grown around them during the previous weeks built into something hot and alive. Briefly, as his skin pressed against hers, there had been nothing left between them – no more lies or half-truths to cushion the space between her body and his – and she felt exposed in a way that was both freeing and terrifying.

Once Rory rolled back onto his side of the bed, Judy had lain with her eyes wide open, fixed on the ceiling, her heart thumping in the aftermath of what she had felt, telling herself it was nothing – that it had just been so long since she had been touched in that way.

It was true, in a sense. She hadn't been with anyone since the boy who worked at the library, on her last day in New York. Practically a stranger, he had taken her back to the tiny apartment he shared with his mother and brothers in Brooklyn, while the boys were at school and his mother slept following her night shift as a cleaner in one of the office blocks downtown. Being sure to keep quiet, they'd had perfunctory sex on the mattress in the room he shared with the younger boys. Afterwards, Judy had slipped out while he dozed, stopping to pull fifty dollars from her backpack and leaving it under a bottle of pills on the kitchen table. Here in Hérault, she felt like a different person, leading a different life.

They woke not long after dawn, eating the croissants Jacques had put out for their arrival while still entwined in the sheets, sticky with heat.

'What do you want to do today?' Rory asked, once they had polished off the pastries, draining the dregs of the cafetière.

'Give me the tour of the village,' Judy said, gazing out towards the endless blue through the window.

It was little more than a few streets that connected the river on one side to the main boulevard on the other. Here, the houses were tall and narrow, with Juliet balconies, lines of washing running between them. They spoke in whispers as they walked below criss-crossed lines of bedding and children's clothes airing in the early morning sun, Judy leaning into Rory, the only other sound a dog yapping somewhere in the distance.

'I can't believe you've never been to France,' he said. 'It's only, like, two hours on the plane from London, right? And you even speak the language.'

'My mother was scared of flying.'

'Really?' His ears pricked up at the mention of the parents Judy barely acknowledged. 'You never talk about her.' He gave her a hesitant look, as if assessing whether this was an appropriate statement. They had already proven equally reluctant to discuss their respective pasts.

'There's not much to tell. Not much that's first date material, anyway.'

'This is hardly our first date.'

Feeling his hand reach for hers, she took a few more paces before continuing. 'OK. Well, she was a ballerina. She left Scotland to train at the Royal Ballet School in London.

She was quite a prodigy, in line to become their principal dancer. But then she was in a car accident, and it ruined her career before it properly began.'

'That's terrible.'

'It is what it is.' Judy sighed. 'After that, my mother was terrified of getting into any kind of moving vehicle. Even trains. So definitely no holidays to France. But we learnt French at school – boarding school.'

After the fact, Judy would wonder if she had been about to continue with the rest of the story before Rory interrupted her.

'Of course. Hard for you, though. And then for her to be so ill—' He stopped himself, misreading the look that fell across her face as she was reminded of her own lie.

Why had she said her mum died of cancer? It had all been so spontaneous, so ill-thought-through. If she had known at the time that this would last more than a few weeks, as per her original plan – to stay around long enough to charm Rory and run off with his money – then she might have been less impulsive with her storytelling; she might have come up with something a little more robust.

'What about your father – how did he and your mother meet?' Rory continued, altering his line of questioning.

There was a moment's pause as Judy pictured the photograph on the mantelpiece in her mother's flat in Marylebone: the black-and-white print of the two of them standing together in Piccadilly Circus. Her mother was young and lithe, with a dancer's physique; her father was dressed in the suit he had worn earlier that day for his various Cabinet meetings.

'I'm not exactly sure. It's funny, the things you don't think to ask. He and I were never close, and after he died my mother didn't really want to talk about him.' Judy paused, changing the subject. 'Do you think we could go and buy some plants at some point this week, if you don't have too much to do?'

'Of course.' He checked his watch. 'It's still early; if we head into town soon we can catch the market, get some supplies in. And then tomorrow we can go a little further afield for plants. Though you know if you plant something you will actually have to stay here to water it? I'll basically have you trapped.'

They parked at the edge of town, passing cafés with old men with blank stares, and teenagers smoking cigarettes. The market was still in full flow and Judy inhaled the smells as they weaved through the stalls, filling a wicker basket with paper bags brimming with figs, cheese and olives, and a long baguette.

'I bought you this,' he said, later, as they strolled back the way they had come, presenting Judy with a wide-brimmed straw hat, which he placed on her head. 'Do you like it?'

'I can't see it,' she laughed. 'But I love it anyway.' Kissing him on the lips, Judy took it off, smiling as she studied the weave.

'You know, apparently a new Mediterranean garden has just opened, about a twenty-minute drive away,' Rory mentioned as they drove home, her hand moving to rest itself on top of his as he shuffled the gearstick in and out of position. 'How does that sound?'

Stretching out her legs in front of her, she watched the sun beat on the fields that passed out of the window and smiled. 'It sounds perfect.'

They took the viaduct over the River Orb, and Judy looked down at the river cutting through swaths of green and smiled as Rory took the turning for the garden, which was set inside a series of dry-stone walls.

'What does the leaflet say, then, Madame Translator?' he asked as they followed the path through an area of cacti and agave, towards an orchard built on a series of terraces.

'It says that there's a microclimate in this area, which is sheltered from the north winds, making it perfect for growing certain grapes as well as a variety of Mediterranean plants.'

'Well, there you go, that's it – our perfect place.' He studied her, curiously. 'If you don't mind my saying so, you don't strike me as the gardening type.'

Amused, she gave him a quizzical look. 'Why not?'

'I don't know. You're not even twenty years old and . . . well, you're really attractive.'

'What can you do?' She rolled her eyes, bumping against him playfully with her hip. 'Anyway . . . if I'm not the "working at the vineyard" type and not the gardening type, what type do you think I am, Rory Harrington?'

Studying her, sidelong, he licked his lips. 'I don't know – I haven't quite worked that out yet.'

They walked a while longer, his hand looped around hers.

'So what is it that appeals about gardening?' he asked as they reached the end of this particular stretch.

Inhaling the scent of pine and orange trees that suddenly suffused the air, Judy relaxed further. 'I guess I like the idea of building something from nothing. I had a teacher at school, Mrs Briscoe. Sometimes she would take me to the garden to do private study. While we were there, she would teach me about the plants. And about life, generally, I suppose.'

'Teacher's pet, eh?' Rory smiled, triggering a memory as they reached an area where cuttings were displayed in pots for sale.

'Not exactly. Some of the other girls were . . . let's just say

I didn't exactly fit in. But apparently Mrs Briscoe saw something in me.'

'I find it hard to imagine, you not fitting in.'

Judy considered this for a moment. It wasn't so much that
she hadn't fitted in as that she'd felt she didn't belong there.
Perhaps it had made them fearful? People were afraid of what
they didn't understand, hadn't she read that somewhere?

'Well, anyway, clearly they were idiots,' Rory said.

With the other, she felt for her necklace as she pictured
Portia Blythedon's tearstained face receding in the wing mirror
of the car, the day she was expelled.'

'Asphodels,' Judy said, running her fingers over the leaves.
'These are pretty; we should get some.'

'Like the Asphodel Meadows in ancient Greece?' Rory
replied. 'A place where ordinary souls are sent to live.'

Shuddering, she laughed. 'Ordinary? Oh, God, anything
but that.'

'I might go for a walk while you finish your writing,' Judy
suggested back at the house, once they had finished decanting
the goods they had bought at the market onto the various
shelves of the fridge and larder. Rory was sitting at the kitchen
table in front of the window overlooking the garden, a pile
of paperwork before him.

Picking up the empty basket and new sunhat, Judy placed
an old battered copy of *Lady Audley's Secret* inside, along with
the packet of Gitanes she had bought in town.

'Do you want me to come with you?' Rory sipped his coffee
as he looked up.

'I'll be fine,' she replied, shaking her head.

'And you know where you're going?'

'Not really, but I like an adventure.'

'If you head along the river, don't go too far beyond the old chapel; it's hunting season, and the local pig farmers aren't exactly cautious.'

'Oh, that's nice to know.' Judy laughed. 'If I'm not back by midnight, send out a search party.'

The river was accessed by a footbridge at the end of the lane, opposite the house. As soon as Judy was off the road and walking alongside the stream where the water was at its shallowest, she slipped off her shoes and let the pebbles massage the soles of her feet.

Following the line of the water to the far bank where the trees at the edge of the woodland created an area of shade, she sat on one of the low boulders that lined the water and pulled out her book.

It had been a favourite of hers ever since reading it at school. While the other girls in the dorm opted for books like *St Clare's* which reflected their own experiences in some way, Judy wanted stories that transported her to another world. She never related to the idea that people turned to fiction in order to be understood.

Judy didn't want to feel understood; she wanted to feel extraordinary.

She was just a few pages in, skim-reading the text she practically knew by heart, when she reached into her bag for the packet of Gitanes. Taking one out, she felt for a match, patting her pockets and coming up empty.

Returning the novel to her bag, she strolled back the way she had come, turning left by the house and heading towards the bar she had noticed on the main strip.

It was a five-minute walk and there was hardly anyone around when she arrived, placing her book on one of the round tables outside the *tabac*. Inside, she took a moment to adjust to the darkness. In the corner a television was playing, otherwise the only sound was the humming of the refrigerator.

The barman barely looked up as she entered.

'*Une boîte d'allumettes, s'il vous plaît,*' Judy said, taking the matches before scanning the bottles behind the counter and ordering a *pastis*.

'You're English?' a voice behind her replied in a local accent.

Reaching into her bag, she pulled out the purple leather purse and took out the exact change, leaving it on the bar.

'Guilty,' she said, returning the purse to her bag and lighting a cigarette as she turned. 'My French accent is clearly terrible.'

'Not at all. It is good that you try.'

The man was around her own age, wearing a policeman's uniform.

'I am off duty,' he added, noting her expression. 'You are safe.'

'*Merci,*' Judy replied with a strained smile.

'You are on 'oliday here?'

'I'm staying in the village with my boyfriend, Rory Harrington.'

'*Ah, oui, je connais Monsieur Harrington.* My father, Jacques, looks after the house.' Fixing his eyes on her, he held out a hand. '*Je m'appelle Patrice.*'

That autumn with Rory unfolded like something out of a fairytale: lazy mornings and late afternoon walks, long shadows chasing them as they wandered along the woods at the edge of the river.

Perhaps it was the hormones, bracing her for the life she never knew she wanted, for by the time she found out she was pregnant, just four months after she and Rory had met, Judy could almost fool herself that fairytales had happy endings.

Francesca

Laura's house stands in a mews on the edge of Primrose Hill, one of London's most coveted neighbourhoods. She answers the door with a baby in one arm, a bottle in the other.

'Fran! Is everything OK?'

Behind her, the house, which my best friend had grown up in, inherited and then lived in with her husband, Johnny, until he went off the rails again a few months ago, is broad and straightforward in its proportions, with huge Georgian windows and high ceilings allowing for plenty of light. Stylish but lived-in, it is both the same as it was, and completely changed. In the hallway, there is the same antique Persian rug that has been here since we were children. On one side of the hall, where as teenagers we once discarded our Buffalo boots and patent wedges, stands a double buggy and a child-sized scooter with tassels on the handlebars, which I had bought Eva, my goddaughter, for her most recent birthday. Laughing apologetically, I had noted Laura's horrified expression as she opened the box and pulled out the hot-pink plastic death trap accessorised with a garnish of shiny silver spray, mouthing jokingly back at me, 'Could it be any more off-brand?'

'Come in. Come in, come in!' she says, her demeanour one of partial relief at the sight of one of her oldest friends, edged with reflexive irritation at yet another unwarranted interruption in a life already overflowing with demands. Even now, in the midst of a divorce and juggling her career with looking after three children under ten, she is so beautiful and poised.

'Hi, cutie,' I say to Leo, touching the child's foot as I step inside. 'Sorry. I should have—'

My voice trails off as Laura closes the front door behind us, nudging a rogue child-sized football boot back into line as she passes.

'What's going on?' Stepping closer, she reaches for my arm. 'Fuck. Is it Hugo?'

'Hugo? Christ, no. Your brother is fine.' Looking towards the staircase, I shiver and look away again. 'Can we go through?'

'Of course. Sorry. I'm – do you want coffee?'

'I need a cigarette,' I say, walking through into an enormous open-plan kitchen overlooking the perfectly landscaped back garden, indecently large for its location.

At once, I am both anchored and unsettled by the familiarity of Laura's home. Always, in one another's presence, we are several people at once: the twelve-year-olds mainlining testers of kiwi lip balm at the Body Shop on Oxford Street after school; teenagers rolling spliffs on the bench at the top of Primrose Hill; bursting into delirious giggles after I mistook Laura's false-nail glue for eye-whitening drops and temporarily glued my eyelids together while on lunch break at sixth-form; twenty-somethings struggling to reconcile our own markedly different lives.

When Laura had returned from her year in New York, where she had bagged an internship at the kind of magazine that featured manufactured indie kids on the cover blowing bubbles, I was already pregnant. By the time Laura had her own first child, ten years later – having left modelling and made a name for herself as a well-respected interior designer – I had just finished retraining as a lawyer.

Our lives seemed to be constantly at odds, and yet we had more in common than either of us might care to admit.

'Johnny's old ciggies are in the back of the cupboard,' Laura says, waiting while I fish out the packet before calling through to the next room, which is accessed by folding partition doors. 'Violetta, could you take Leo for a minute?'

The nanny comes in, smiling at me in recognition, beaming at the baby as she extends her arms and scoops him up.

'Where's Charlie?' The box of Marlboros feels clunky in my hands. I haven't smoked in years, aside from the occasional spliff Hugo rolls after a particularly gruelling day in court and smokes at the table in the garden, beneath the roses.

'Sleeping.' Laura rolls her eyes. 'They're tag-teaming – through the night, as well, just to really keep me on my toes. I'm fucking knackered.'

This is surreal. I feel as if I'm slowly emerging from a bad dream. How am I here, in my best friend's kitchen, discussing her twin sons' sleeping habits? It is impossible to reconcile the banality of Laura's domestic situation with what is suddenly happening in my own life.

Not for the first time, I feel as though we are existing on different planes.

'Here, bring those outside.' Laura pulls open the high glass doors, stepping into the garden and leading me down towards a table decorated with heavy white candles in oversized bell-jars.

Only once we are away from the house does she look me in the eyes. For a second the direct contact stings.

'OK, Fran, what's going on?'

The matchbox is almost the size of a box of chocolates, with a stately lion painted on the outside; the type that is now ubiquitous in every overpriced boutique in England. Laura draws one out and strikes it, holding it out for me, and I watch my fingers tremble as I lean into the flame. Inhaling the first drag of the cigarette, I pull the smoke deep into my lungs and hold it there.

'It's Judy.'

Laura's eyes widen. 'What? Shit. Judy? Oh, my God, is she OK?'

'They're reopening the case. Laura, they're saying she murdered him. My dad.'

And, for the first time, it feels real.

Judy

London, June 1986

London crackled with portentous energy, the promise of summer in the air when Judy returned to England with Rory, the year their daughter was born, the bump of Judy's belly clearly visible under the black peg-leg trousers she had bought in Cannes on one of their final trips to the beach.

'You're not having second thoughts, are you?' Rory asked as they strolled through the West End the day after they landed, the late spring sun bright.

'A bit late for that now.' Judy laughed, adjusting the silk headscarf she had wrapped around her hair in the manner of a French film star.

'Not the baby, that bit's sort of a given at this stage, but the wedding . . . And being back in the city you were trying to escape?'

'I wasn't trying to escape,' Judy replied, too quickly. 'I was just . . . you know, trying something else.'

'Oh, right, is that what I am – an experiment?'

Judy leant into him as they walked under an arched sign reading CARNABY STREET WELCOMES THE WORLD. 'Something like that,' she replied, avoiding eye contact as they passed on towards Chubbies sandwich bar, breathing in the smell of the chimney smoke carrying on the air.

It was a question to which she no longer knew the answer.

They had only been back a few days, staying at a hotel in Hyde Park which was convenient for the private hospital Rory had booked them into. The birth was still six weeks away, but he had been adamant they had to be back in good time to somewhere he could converse with the doctors.

And Judy was excited. If someone had asked her, just a few months earlier, to list the things she saw in her future, motherhood wouldn't have featured. It had never occurred to her before to want a baby. But the moment she'd felt it, it was as if the seed had always been there, just waiting to be watered.

Besides, being a mother didn't have to change anything, she kidded herself.

'You've grown on me, actually – which is lucky, in the circumstances,' Judy replied, straightening her sunglasses. 'I thought we might have a look in Liberty,' she added, casually, as though the thought had just occurred to her. 'What is it they say? Something old, something new, something borrowed, something blue?'

'Well, I suppose you're going to need some new clothes, if you expand any more – and maybe a dress?'

'Expand?!' she scolded him, playfully, placing a hand on her belly as they passed a couple with matching Mohicans, the boom box he was holding playing 'Straight to Hell'.

Stopping at the doorway to Liberty, Rory kissed his fiancée tenderly. 'You know we're keeping the house, whatever happens, so we can go to France whenever you like.' He held open the door to the department store and ushered her inside. 'Why don't you take off your sunglasses? It's really not that bright in here.'

'They make me feel like Joan Collins,' Judy shrugged, keeping them on. 'What about this?'

Pulling out a turquoise lamé dress with ruffled sleeves, she watched Rory's eyes widen in vague distaste. 'I mean, it's definitely *new*. And it would be perfect if you were auditioning for *Dynasty*.'

Laughing, she played with the hem of her grey Jane Fonda-esque off-the-shoulder sweater. 'None of it is very *me*.'

'Well, then, choose something that is you. It's just going to be the two of us on the day, I want you to feel comfortable.'

'You're such a surprise, Rory Harrington.' She turned to him, letting the dress drop back into the rail of clothes. 'I never imagined you would be so . . .'

'*Imagined?*' He looked back at her, curiously, and she felt herself blush at the slip of the tongue.

'You know, in my wildest dreams.' She laughed, covering her tracks. 'I suppose when we first met I had a different idea of the kind of person you might be.'

'It's good to know I make such a terrible first impression.'

'You don't, actually,' she said. 'That's the problem. By the way, please don't think for a minute that I'm the kind of person who likes to be "comfortable". I couldn't think of anything worse. What about something like this?' She held a pale blue suit with slightly padded shoulders and matching elasticated trousers against herself. 'And I saw a nice cream shirt over there that I could wear underneath.'

'I think it's great. You'll look beautiful, whatever you wear.'

'It also ticks off something new and blue, in one. Only old and borrowed to go.'

'I need to use the bathroom,' Rory said, looking around.

'It's upstairs.'

'Right. Well I'll see you back here in—'

'Give me ten minutes,' Judy interrupted. 'I'll meet you by the jewellery counter. It's bad luck, isn't it, to see the bride in her dress before the big day?'

Keeping one hand on her stomach, she moved under the high ceilings, her eyes scanning upwards towards the mezzanine level and then back over the shop floor. A carousel of sunglasses stood next to the jewellery counter and she picked out three pairs in turn, trying on each and checking her reflection in the tilted square mirror stuck to the top.

Suddenly aware of the time, Judy placed the glasses back on the stand and walked over to the jewellery counter.

'Are you looking for something special?' The woman behind the bar was around Judy's age, her hair pulled back in a ballerina-style bun.

'I am, actually. I'm getting married . . .'

'Oh, how exciting.'

'It is. Nerve-racking, though. And trying to find something to go over this—' Turning slightly, Judy showed off her bump.

'Oh, you're pregnant!'

'I know – already. It's sinful.' She laughed, conspiratorially.

'How far along are you?'

The question invoked a sudden image of Marnie crouched over beside the lamppost in front of the entrance to Well Springs Vineyard. 'Seven months . . . Can I see those?'

Pointing to a pair of pearl earrings and a silver bracelet studded with semi-precious stones, she waited as the woman laid them out on the counter. 'Here we are.'

Watching how the stones twinkled under the artificial light, Judy smiled. 'They're beautiful.'

'Bankrupting me already, are you?' Rory said, appearing next to her so unexpectedly that she jumped.

'I'm going to have a think about it.' She winked at the sales assistant, who smiled as the couple walked away.

* * *

There was no queue for the cashier and Judy tried to pay for her own items, but Rory insisted, arguing that as it was tradition for the bride's family to cover the cost of a wedding, and as their wedding was to be intentionally non-traditional, it had to be on him.

Rolling her eyes fondly behind her shades as he signed the cheque, Judy looped her fingers through his as they headed towards the door. They were nearly at the exit when she heard footsteps moving quickly behind her, and a woman's voice calling out.

'Excuse me, madam?'

Ignoring it, Judy walked more briskly, her heartbeat rising as she felt the tag of the pair of sunglasses which was tucked up under her headscarf, leaving the ones she had arrived in on the shelf in their place.

'I think that person's calling for us.'

'I don't think so,' Judy replied, smiling tightly as Rory slowed and turned towards the voice. Bracing herself, she turned too, rearranging her face into an expression of polite enquiry.

'Hello?'

'Hi! Are you – did you used to live in the mansion flats in Marylebone? Yes, I thought it was you! You had a brother. I'm trying to remember the name. Esther, that was your—'

Not a security guard: worse.

Her smile tightening further, Judy squeezed Rory's hand. 'I'm so sorry, you have the wrong person.'

'Really? Wow. Well, I suppose it was a long time ago. I just . . . when I saw you trying on the different glasses . . . Gosh, how strange. You look like someone. Keir, that was it, the name of the boy.' She shook her head as if she might add something else. 'Well, anyway, I'm sorry for disturbing you.'

'That's OK.' Judy nodded, nudging Rory towards the exit, her heart galloping as they stepped out on to the street.

'That was weird,' she said once they were far enough away from the shop that she could be sure no one else was following them.

'It wasn't that weird,' he replied. 'Maybe she was just getting you confused with Joan Collins?'

'Ha ha.' Taking off the glasses, Judy pretended to study a piece of jewellery in a shop window while her fingers worked at pulling off the tag. Moving off again, she put them back on her face and slipped the label into a bin as they passed. 'God, I'm hungry, I don't think I can handle any more of that hotel food.'

'Glad to hear it.' Rory's expression changed in a way that made her study his face.

'What?'

'Nothing. It's just good timing for you to be unable to handle any more hotel food.'

'What are you talking about?'

Before she could say another word, he put his hand out and flagged down a taxi.

Ushering her into the cab ahead of him, he slipped the driver an address on a piece of paper before getting in. Removing her glasses, he placed them on his lap and slid off the scarf tied around her head.

'Rory, what are you doing?'

He looked down, picking up the glasses and studying them. 'Wait, are these the same ones you were wearing when we went in?

Judy tutted. 'No, I just stole them. What the hell are you doing with my scarf?'

'I'm blindfolding you.'

'Rory, this is ridiculous, I can't see a thing.'

'That's the point,' he said, adjusting the silk square he had tied around her eyes so that when she peeked – peering downwards through the slight gap between her face and the material – she could only see the floor of the car beneath her protruding belly.

Tuning in to the huff and puff of the city, she tried to calculate where they might be driving, singling out particular smells and sounds from the route: the hiss of the bus as it slowed on the other side of the window, the number of speed bumps on a particular road. In her mind, she counted out the seconds. *One Mississippi, two Mississippi.* 'What's going on?' she asked again, a while later, a slight feeling of panic enveloping her as Rory opened the door and ushered her outside.

'Keep the change,' he addressed the driver before turning to his fiancée and untying the scarf. 'OK, we're here.'

Blinking to adjust to the daylight, she looked about at the residential street lined with traditional London townhouses hidden behind neat front gardens, feeling strangely nervous.

'Rory, what is going on?'

Holding up a pair of keys, he moved towards the black gate of the house in front of which they were standing.

'Launceston Grove, Kensington,' he beamed. 'Our new home.'

Francesca

'Laura, they're saying she murdered him.'

The words hang between us, and I find myself almost laughing at the absurdity of what I have just told my oldest friend.

In a sort of out-of-body experience, I see myself earlier this morning in my usual running clothes, entering the phone box off High Street Kensington, the hood pulled up around my face.

'What?' Laura's face – her beauty only enhanced by the fine lines that now run along the sides of her eyes as we both creep towards forty – searches mine as if this is where the answer lies.

For a second I think I will tell her. Blinking, I picture myself taking the pound coins from the small zipped pocket on my upper arm that I had taken with me specifically for this purpose and slid behind my iPhone.

Closing my eyes, I hear once more the money drop into the slot with a thud that had echoed my heartbeat.

But then the moment is broken by the sound of Laura's phone vibrating on the table, and I sense the relief we clearly both feel, followed by a renewed tension when I glance down and see Johnny's name flashing on the screen.

Again, I feel myself tip back into another lifetime, a day decades earlier: the sound of smashed glass on the towpath that runs along canal; the throbbing beat of the drum 'n' bass drifting over from Bagley's nightclub.

My mother's voice, earlier this morning: *I can't talk now.*

Fucking hell, I'm losing my mind.

Flustered, Laura shakes her head. 'Sorry. I should probably take this . . .'

'It's fine. Answer. I'll be here.' Clearing my mind of the image of Judy in the hall in the house in France, I sit straight. Whatever happens, I have to stay calm.

Hold it together, Francesca – that is all you have to do. Everything depends on this.

And yet already the plan seems to be falling from my grasp.

Laura holds my eye a moment and then nods, picking up the phone and walking away as she answers.

'Johnny?'

Waiting until she is out of sight, I place my head in my hands, protecting my eyes from the images that flash past, fighting back the tears that rise up again out of nowhere as Laura's voice recedes into the house that screams with memories.

Laura's house, the place where so much of this began.

Judy

There was a six-week stretch between their return to England and the baby's due date at the beginning of August.

Knowing it would be his last opportunity to do so for a while, Rory split his time between London and the Cape, finalising the sale of his parents' house through a local agent. It was odd, Judy thought, that he never took the chance while he was there to catch up with old friends. After Caroline died, Judy gathered, Rory had barely kept in contact with anyone, apart from Wine Society members. From the way he spoke of it, she deduced that the society itself was more of an obligation than a pleasure.

Judy, too, had few friends of her own. But that was different. Judy was much younger than he was, and the girls from boarding school – well, the less said about them, the better. Certainly none of them had lived in London like her.

Now, back in the city she grew up in, years later, it was like starting again. And if there was anything Judy was good at, it was fresh starts.

In the afternoons, when Rory was in town, Judy would make her husband take a break with her before dinner to dance around the kitchen to new tapes she picked out in Our Price, taste-testing a selection of English sweets from the pic 'n' mix in Woolworths: foamy mushrooms and wine gums; Liquorice Allsorts and Werther's Originals. And he seemed so content to fall into this world they had created together that Judy never thought to question what *he* was running away from. She never wondered why he was always so keen to avoid conversations about Caroline and made so little effort to keep in contact with old friends. She never questioned why he, like her, was so keen to eradicate all traces of his past life.

Even if the thought was there, in the background, she never asked why he remained so committed to a society he appeared to have no genuine attachment to.

On those pre-baby stints when Rory was away working on a book, or on one of his trips to the vineyard to meet with a new supplier, Judy busied herself leafing through huge square sample catalogues in Laura Ashley and having in-depth conversations with the ladies behind the desk about the merits of palm prints versus seafoam-green wallpaper. It was fun, she decided, building a stage of her own for the life she and Rory were creating from scratch. As long as she could hold back enough for herself, she mused on those nights when she lay awake in the small hours of the night, the feeling of suffocation sometimes threatening to close in, then it would be OK.

It was possible to be two people at once, to hold two lives in balance. You just had to be careful not to lean too far in any one direction. And, in that respect, she was already hatching a plan.

Looking back, with the clarity of hindsight, Judy found herself wondering why she couldn't simply have told Rory the truth about her mother. Now would be the perfect moment to explain. Rory might not like it, given that Judy had told him that her mother was already dead; worse, that she had claimed she suffered the same agonising condition his own mother had. But he might understand, given the trauma she had gone through. He might choose not to press her harder on how she had come to be in Wellfleet. Even if he did, perhaps Judy could be honest about that, too. Wasn't there something romantic about it all? Judy coming across the newspaper article about Rory Harrington, one of the country's most eligible bachelors. How she had stolen a car – two, in fact – in order to meet him at the party in Massachusetts.

How she had simply planned to wring him dry before moving on to the next con. Until she fell in love, that was.

But that was a hell of a lot of 'mights' for a woman with no savings and no meaningful qualifications, with a mother to look after, and rent and bills to pay.

For a woman who was already carrying a man's baby, and who had already sacrificed so much, taken so many risks to be where she was.

And hadn't Rory already told her how hard he found it to trust people; how he feared those around him weren't always truthful; that they wanted something from him?

Judy was similarly guarded. She didn't want to give herself wholly to a man, even if she did love him, which she was increasingly unable to deny. If she couldn't control her feelings for him, she needed at least to keep just enough chips in her back pocket in case, God forbid, she ever had to play her hand again.

Besides, her way would be a lot more fun, wouldn't it?

So Judy played the role of housewife with gusto, choosing for the nursery a cream-coloured wallpaper with navy and bronze stripes and a duck motif – waiting until Rory was away again before heaving herself onto the rickety A-frame ladder and applying the steamer to bring up the old paper, watching the patch grow damp before peeling back the layers of what lay beneath.

It was a good job she never believed in ghosts on those nights alone in the house. At least not the dead kind.

And yet, whatever past Launceston Grove might have once held, it was theirs now. Hers and Rory's, and whoever it was that was soon coming to join them.

Standing in the half-empty first-floor hallway, listening to the builders fit the new oven downstairs, Judy could picture it just as it would be in the future: the single room just along from the master bedroom illuminated with fairy lights and plenty of books, her childhood favourites, *Pollyanna* and *Robin Hood*, lined up in pride of place.

And, while it might not be anything compared to the one in France, the garden at the back of their new London townhouse had space for a paddling pool and roses growing up a trellis; and the patio area was generous enough that, when their child was a little older, Judy would be able to put out an easel and paints for him or her, along with a paddling pool.

She'd always known she would recognise the life she was meant to have when she saw it; she had just never imagined it would be this – exactly the kind of life her mother had warned against.

The difference was, Judy knew what she was doing, didn't she? And she was making provisions.

Putting aside any lingering doubts, Judy gravitated towards the places her mother had loved when she was a little girl, before Keir died – studying the pieces at the markets in Bermondsey and Portobello Road, only occasionally faltering as she imagined herself and her twin brother weaving through the crowds, laughing as they dodged between the stalls.

In those moments, Judy would put out a hand to steady herself. Because Keir wasn't there. It was a fact that, even all these years later, was still impossible to fathom. Her funny, silly, easily distractible brother – a child with a heart so big he once brought home an injured pigeon; who would divert his sister with made-up jokes when she had nightmares. A boy who never wanted more than he already had; who was always completely present in the moment. Until he was gone.

There was no reason why she should only head to market on days when Rory was out of town, but there was something sacred about these places and their connection to her old life. By the time the twins were born, their mother, Esther, had given up her stall and only took Judy and Keir with her very occasionally. Once he was gone and it was just the two of them, Esther had never been able to face it again.

In spite of, or perhaps because of, those tainted memories, Judy had inherited Esther's love of the market just as she had her looks. There was something almost sacred about rifling through other people's things: the sense of gratification at finding something beautiful and rare, something that no one else would have noticed; and the theatre of it, the call and response of the chorus.

Maybe, in those lost treasures, Judy was looking for traces of herself; of a life that had been suddenly and violently snatched away from her.

Another thing she loved about the market was how easy it was to get lost in the crowd. That was another quality Judy had inherited from her mother. She might not always have been able to fit in, as her time at boarding school had attested, but she shared Esther's ability to either stand out or disappear into the background when she wanted to – using it either way as and when it suited her. And she loved the transience of the place, how something and someone might be there one week and be gone the next, as though they'd never really existed at all.

No, the market wasn't something she wanted to share with Rory. Besides, making contacts required stealth. Show up too often, too quickly, and Judy might start to alert the wrong eyes, for the wrong reasons.

Softly, softly. Her mother had taught her that, too.

It was July, with a bright blue sky and summer blossoms marking new beginnings.

Rory was due home around lunchtime and Judy had woken early, making her way through the streets of west London towards Notting Hill, on foot. The doctors had advised walking to bring on labour, and the world seemed to shine in Technicolor, the smells of the city turned up to two hundred per cent as she made her way through the stalls at Portobello, her cheeks flushed with the late stages of pregnancy.

Pausing in front of one laden with costume jewellery, she scanned through the pieces, the battery-powered radio next to the stallholder hissing the sporting results as he scanned the morning paper.

'Everything in that box is two pounds,' the man said, then his expression sharpened as his attention rested on Judy. 'Well, I never.' As he looked more closely, his face broke into a smile and he closed his paper. 'You have got to be Esther's girl. You're the spit of her.'

Placing a hand on her belly in response to the baby's fierce kick, Judy smiled back at him. 'Wow, good memory. You knew my mother?'

He was around Esther's age, wearing a flat cap, an old blazer and jeans. There was something about the man that Judy couldn't put a finger on, almost as if she understood at once the significance of this introduction, without knowing what it meant.

'Sure did. Fine woman.' He paused. 'I'm closing up in a minute. Fancy joining me for a cup of tea?'

Judy felt a surge of emotion at this sudden connection to her mother. Looking at one of the small plastic clocks on the shelf next to the radio, she shook her head. 'I can't. My husband's coming back from America this afternoon.'

'Next time.' He smiled, holding out a hand. 'I'm Jim Doherty.'

'Yes.' Judy smiled. 'I'd like that. I'm Judy.'

'You're on.' Jim winked. 'Hey, Jude – be sure that you do.'

Judy

'If it's a girl I think we should call her Gigi,' Judy called out from the sofa one afternoon not long after Rory got back from Cape Cod, having completed the sale on his parents' house.

Stuffing popcorn in her mouth with one hand, she accepted the cup of coffee her husband handed her with the other, her eyes remaining fixed on the large wood veneer TV screen to the left of the fireplace. On her lap rested the book of baby names she had brought home a few days earlier, along with a three-pedestal desk that was a welcome home gift for Rory, purchased at one of the antique dealerships on Kensington Church Street.

'We are not naming our daughter after the character in a more than slightly dubious film,' he replied, pushing her legs over to make space and taking a seat beside his wife.

'Oh, come on.' She rolled her eyes. 'Maurice Chevalier isn't dubious.'

'*Thank heaven for little girls?*' Rory quoted, picking up the remote and pressing the mute button. 'It's a matter of days until he or she comes; we need to get serious about this.'

Judy laughed. 'Your French accent is what's dubious.'

'Also, Gigi and Judy?' He shook his head. 'Alliterative family names are just odd.'

'And the name Basil isn't odd?'

She knew what she had said the moment she opened her mouth.

Silence sliced, axe-like, through the air.

'How do you know my father's middle name?' Rory asked after a beat, turning to her, his expression steely.

'What?' She only faltered for a second. 'You must have told me.'

'I definitely never told you that. It's mortifying. I never tell anybody.'

When she blinked, Judy pictured the wall in the apartment on Main Street appearing like the image in a Polaroid slowly taking form. As it did, she saw Rory's father's face looking back at her from a carousel of newspaper clippings.

Taking a tentative sip of coffee, she looked down at the baby name book as some form of distraction from her husband's searching expression. 'Well, I'm sorry but you clearly did. Otherwise how would I have known? Honestly, there are some truly mad options.' She read some names aloud, trying to keep her voice even. 'And look at this – did you know that *Murder* was a popular Scottish name until it fell out of fashion in—'

'When did I tell you my father's middle name?'

'Rory, why are you asking me this?' Judy met his eye. 'What do you think? That I would make it up?'

Rubbing his head, he turned away. 'Sorry. Sorry, Jude . . . I don't know, I— I'm tired. I keep losing things lately. Maybe I'm going mad.'

'You shouldn't joke about that kind of thing,' she said, leaning forward and kissing him softly. He smelt of Old Spice and shampoo. She had never met a man with better personal hygiene. He was so careful, so ordered. She loved that about him. Yet, at the same time, he never cared what others thought, or tried to be someone he wasn't. Well, what did they say: you seek out people who have the things you lack?

Rory did things because they were the right thing to do, whether anyone was watching or not.

'What have you lost?' she asked.

'Hmm?' His comment had already slipped his mind and she kicked herself for bringing it up again. 'Oh, an old silver goblet that belonged to my grandfather, which is worth nothing apart from sentimental value – and a ring, which belonged to Caroline.'

'What sort of ring?'

'A diamond ring.'

'Why do you never talk about her?'

'Who?'

'Caroline.'

Clearing her throat, Judy took another sip of coffee, sensing danger in the air again as Rory stared back at her. His silence was a challenge, and she decided she didn't want to pursue the question. What did she have to gain from hearing about her husband's late wife, or indeed opening lines of reciprocal questioning? There was a distinct benefit to their mutual aversion to personal history.

But there was something about the icy silence around Caroline's death that was disturbing. It was a scab Judy knew would be best left to heal, but that she was compelled to pick, nonetheless.

'Is it insured?' she asked, backing down first. 'The ring, I mean.'

Rory licked his lips and looked away. 'That's not the point.'

It sort of was, though she didn't say so.

'Well, I'm sure it will turn up. We've barely unpacked; things have probably just got muddled. Unless the moving company lost them in transit . . .' Judy waited a moment, looking up from the page and smiling. 'Hey, what about the name Francesca?'

'Hmm?'

Reading on through the etymology, Judy continued aloud. 'It derives from the Latin Franciscus, meaning from France or free one.'

'Francesca,' he replied, his expression finally softening. 'Yes, it's perfect.'

The arms of the cherry tree waved gently in the breeze in front of the house on Launceston Grove the day Judy and Rory brought their daughter home.

'Could you take a photo of us?' Judy asked the taxi driver who dropped them off, the engine still running as she passed him the Polaroid camera and moved in beside Rory, Francesca eyeing the world warily through puffy eyes from the Moses basket they had picked out in the market in Bédarieux before they left France.

Waiting patiently, she felt something expand inside herself as she watched the image form from nothingness – the three of them on the front step, the first-floor veranda and the ornamental cherry tree in the background. It all seemed brighter in the photograph, the colours saturated. But otherwise it was all real: her family, her life.

Judy had made this happen, and no one would ever take any of it away from her.

Judy

It was late autumn when she saw Jim Doherty again.

She had been pushing three-month-old Francesca around the market in her buggy when the older man in the flat cap looked up from his stall, nodding at her and then the sleeping child.

'I remember you. Esther's girl. What was your name?'

'Judy.'

'Judy. That's right.' Smiling down at the baby, Jim made a cooing sound that was at odds with his gruff appearance. 'And who's this?'

'Francesca,' Judy replied.

'Francesca, beautiful name,' Jim Doherty said.

'How much are the pearl earrings?' she asked, idly casting her hand through the jewellery on his stall.

'They're not real pearls.'

'I know.'

'Two quid. So will you join me for a cup of tea this time? You always seem to catch me when I'm about to close up. Must be fate.'

'Must be.' Judy nodded. 'Sure, why not?'

* * *

112

A few days later, she returned to the jewellery counter at Liberty department store for the first time since the afternoon Rory had first taken her to Launceston Grove. The day outside was bright and fresh and she smiled as she approached the rows of jewels laid out on a bed of velvet, adjusting her sunglasses.

'I don't suppose you remember me? Probably not. It was almost half a year ago – time seems to be whizzing past right now!' Judy laughed, reprimanding herself for such stupidity. 'I'm so tired, with this one keeping me up all night, I can't think straight. Luckily, it's sunny enough that I have an excuse to still be wearing my sunnies. No one needs to see *these* eye-bags.'

Judy's accent was the same soft Australian twang she had used in the bar near Rhode Island and she felt a sudden pang of nostalgia. 'Anyway, I came in with my husband and was looking at some pearl earrings . . . I think I'm just going to go for it.'

Adjusting the fastening of the silk headscarf at her chin, she jumped as the baby cried out from the buggy – *Oooh!* – and Judy and the woman behind the counter both laughed, marvelling at the child in the pram. At three months old, Francesca was dressed in dungarees and bundled in a blue woollen blanket.

'Well, he approves. Don't you, Sammy?' Biting her lip at the extravagance of the pearls, Judy carried on. 'I don't know which size to go for – what do you think?'

'Why don't you compare them?'

'Sure.'

She waited patiently as the woman brought out three boxes, each containing a slightly different sized set, and laid them out side by side on the counter.

'They're all so beautiful. Do you mind?'

'Oh, no, go ahead . . .'

The woman watched on, vaguely, as Judy picked up each pair in turn, studying the detail.

'I'll ask my son. What do you think?' Turning to baby Francesca, she held the medium-sized pair up to her ears, the cashier's eyes lighting up as the child cried out again in glee, clearly delighted by her mother's new trick.

Meeting the shop assistant's eye, she made an apologetic face. 'I'm so sorry. What a shriek! At least it's a happy cry, right?'

'He is gorgeous.' The woman leant over the counter to smile at Francesca as Judy returned each of the earrings to their rightful box.

'You wouldn't say that if you were sitting next to him on a twenty-hour flight. We just came back from visiting my folks in Sydney. Hmm, OK . . .' Making a final expression of indecision, Judy ran a finger over each box, picked one up and shut it. 'Right, no more deliberations, I'm taking this one!'

'Excellent choice.' The woman smiled back at her, taking the box from the young mother's extended hand.

'Could you keep that here for me? I'm just going to get my husband with his cheque book.'

'They will be right here, waiting,' the shop assistant replied, stowing the box safely behind the counter.

'Perfect,' Judy said, pushing the buggy towards the exit. 'See you in a second.'

Judy

Judy indicated left off Commercial Road, chattering to Francesca in her car seat, as she pulled into an alley cast in shadow. Parking outside the unit signposted *East London Storage*, she lifted her daughter out of her seat and into the pram, and strapped her in.

'Didn't we do well?' Stroking the child's perfectly plump cheeks, she planted a kiss at the end of her nose before standing upright. 'One last stop and then home. OK?'

Francesca grizzled, clearly tired from a day of driving around London, Judy comforting her over the top of the buggy as they set off down the cobbled street, the sunshine of earlier in the day having disappeared.

Believing the street was otherwise empty, Judy jumped when a young man with a sleeping bag pulled over one shoulder approached. She felt for the earrings in her pocket, in case they were to once again magically disappear.

It was impossible to know how long it would be before anyone noticed that the pearls in the box the shop assistant had put aside until her customer returned to pay – but never did – were in fact fakes. Likelihood was, once she realised her customer wasn't going to return, the shop assistant would simply have returned the box to the locked cupboard, without checking the contents. It must happen all the time: people changing their minds at the last minute and not going through with their purchase. It could be weeks before anyone noticed. By that point, the camera tapes would have been wiped clean, or put in storage. Even if they had found the right tape, who would have been able to identify the woman in a scarf and sunglasses? The pretty Australian with the adorable baby boy.

Ringing the bell at the entrance to the shop, Judy waited to be buzzed inside.

'Imran,' she said when the shopkeeper answered.

'Lucy. Nice to see you again.' He nodded to Judy, making a kindly gesture at the child from across the bulletproof glass that lined the entrance. 'How is the little one?'

'He's perfect,' Judy replied, then, her tone turning business-like, 'I want to put a few things in my safe, if that's OK?'

'Come round.'

It was a moment before she was buzzed inside, and Judy waited while Imran double-locked the door behind them and led the way into a back room, where several safes were stacked on top of one another.

'I'll turn my back,' he said, respectfully, as she approached the iron safe marked 'Lucy Graham' and input her code.

As she pulled open the door, Judy felt a pang of guilt at the sight of the silver goblet and diamond ring. The ring was insured, and honestly what use would it have been to anyone, sitting in a box gathering dust for the rest of eternity? In a way, Rory might have understood, had she been able to tell him, to explain that this was about building the nest egg she needed in order to feel safe setting up a life with him. A big 'might', admittedly.

But the goblet was different. If she had known its senti-mental value at the time, as they'd sat side by side in the kitchen sorting between boxes marked BIN, CHARITY and KEEP, she would have chosen something else to act as a decoy. As Rory said, the goblet probably wasn't worth much – and it would have looked suspicious if the only things that had gone missing from the KEEP boxes was something valuable.

It was a shame, though Judy could hardly put the thing back now. To do so would undermine the whole reason for taking it in the first place. Besides, he seemed to have forgotten about the missing items. That was what happened when you had so much. You could afford to lose the odd thing here and there.

Judy hadn't expected to need to cash in so soon, but perhaps part of her had always known that this nest egg wasn't just about creating a Plan B; perhaps Plan A and Plan B were always inextricably linked. If she was to continue to help her mother out with her rent and bills, without disturbing the life she was building for herself with Rory, she needed money. And, as she said, she didn't want to rely on handouts. If she needed something, Judy would take it herself. It was the one promise she had made to her mother: she would not rely on any man.

Placing the pearl earrings on the bed of treasures, Judy pulled a fifty-pound note from the bundle of cash and locked the door. 'Thanks, Imran. I'll see you soon.' She waved as she pushed the buggy back onto the dusky street.

The boy with the sleeping bag was slumped against the wall opposite the car when they emerged, the sky turning dark, and Judy took the cash from the pocket of her jeans and slipped it into his hands as she passed. His eyes were still wide with disbelief as she buckled Francesca into her car seat and drove away.

* * *

Jim was seated on the same foldaway chair behind his stall, fiddling with the aerial of his radio as he struggled to find reception, when she returned the next day.

Around them, the market traders were beginning to pack away their wares, and Jim must have sensed something in Judy's expression, because he put down the radio when he saw her walking towards him, Francesca asleep in the buggy.

'Hey, Jude, everything OK?'

She stroked her daughter's head as the child stirred, then looked about them before leaning in. 'Sure. I just . . . do you have a time for cup of tea?'

'I tell you what: I have to go back to the lock-up in King's Cross straight after this, but if you want to jump in . . . ?' He turned the radio off.

Looking down at Francesca, Judy made a face. 'What kind of van do you have?'

'One that will fit us two plus the wee one, no bother.'

'OK,' she said, brightening. 'Then let's do it.'

The smell of lead pumped back into the van through the air vents as Jim's old Transit took the Westway, eastward-bound.

'This is where your mother lived, isn't it?' he asked as they joined the Euston Road, and Judy nodded, any elaboration she might have provided interrupted by Francesca wriggling on her lap.

Only once the baby had settled again did he continue.

'You said there was something you wanted to ask me.'

She knew from her mother's stories that some of the old-school traders weren't wholly puritanical in their approach to how they acquired their stock. For some, selling on the market was a useful front for more lucrative trades; hence the need for the lock-up, should the police come sniffing round.

Last time Judy had had tea with Jim, a few days ago, he had dropped enough hints that she knew he was someone who preferred to keep his revenue streams broad, and delineated. Still, broaching the subject outright was a risk.

'I have some jewellery,' Judy said before she lost her nerve. 'I want to sell it.'

'There's Dawson and Briant on Kentish Town High Street,' Jim replied, quick as a flash, as they turned left at King's Cross, taking the road that ran towards the old railway tunnels.

'I was thinking of something more . . . personal.'

Her words hung there a moment.

'Oh, yeah?' Raising an eyebrow, he glanced at her and then back at the road ahead. 'What sort of thing are you talking about?'

'The sort you don't necessarily want people looking into too closely.'

'You mean stolen?'

'Well, I mean, when you're talking about jewels, everything's stolen somewhere down the line. Just look at the crown jewels,' she joked. 'Not to mention blood diamonds . . .'

'Diamonds?'

He slowed the van as they turned into a cobbled lane, which led down towards a series of arches.

Biting her lip, Judy waited as Jim considered his next move. As if coming to a decision, he turned and studied her, looking from Judy to Francesca and back again.

'OK,' he said, finally. 'I might be able to help, or, rather, collaborate.'

'Collaborate?'

'Come on, now, Jude. You don't think anything in life comes for free?'

Francesca

'Bastard,' Laura mutters under her breath as she walks back out onto the patio, placing her phone on the garden table. Her face is flushed with a range of emotions that once upon a time I would have had no difficulty in reading.

'So you and Johnny are talking again?' I ask, at a loss for what else to say.

'Actually that was the first time we've spoken in a while. He tried to get in touch a couple of months ago as part of his Narcotics Anonymous process . . . you know, the usual bullshit: trying to absolve himself of his guilt by offloading onto other people. But . . . I don't know. He's still their dad, isn't he?'

Taking a drag on my cigarette, I see that my fingers are trembling. 'Is he still clean?'

'How the fuck should I know?' Laura replies, taking one of the cigarettes and absent-mindedly tapping the top of the packet against the edge of the table just as she used to when we were teenagers. 'I'm just glad I don't have to deal with him any more. If he wants to see the kids and I can be sure that he's not high then he can come over when I'm not here. Obviously I'll lock up any valuables first. Where is your mum now?'

I flinch, aware of the brief respite of listening to someone else's problems – even if my and Laura's problems have always been a shared entity.

'I don't know. She was at the house in France this morning but she said she had to go, and hung up on me, and now she's not answering the phone.'

And none of this was part of the plan. Focusing on my oldest friend, I try to contain the dark thoughts lurking at every turn.

'Have you tried her mobile?'

'She never has it on, keeps it in a drawer. You know what she's like about technology.'

'Fran . . . wasn't she already questioned and ruled out?'

It's a rhetorical question, but what else can she say? Laura is one of the few people who knows exactly what happened in the aftermath of that evening, or most of it.

Laura and I always knew everything about each other's lives – until we didn't.

PART TWO

Judy

London, July 1999

Last call for passengers travelling to Palma—

It went against every mother's instinct to watch their child walk away from them like this, Judy thought, leaning forward to get a final look at Francesca as her daughter passed through the barrier. Still, she was almost thirteen years old now, she reminded herself as she watched her only child being eclipsed by a sea of strangers – a flash of dark hair pulled back in a half-ponytail, strands pulled down on either side of her face; the *Have a Nice Day* record bag they picked out together in the Lipsy concession in Oxford Circus slung sideways over her steadily maturing body. No longer a baby.

When Judy was the same age that Francesca was now, she hadn't seen her own mother from one term to the next.

Pulling a cigarette from her pocket and remembering not to light it – you couldn't even smoke in airports any more, except in designated areas – Judy rolled the butt between her forefinger and thumb, focusing her mind. Francesca would be fine. She was only going to stay in a villa in Mallorca for a month with her best friend, Laura, and Laura's family. It was hardly leaving home. And it was 1999, not the fifties; children no longer had to walk three hundred miles to school, with only rainwater and coal to survive on.

At that, Judy smiled, picturing herself and Keir squished together on the sofa watching re-runs of the Monty Python sketch in which the four Yorkshiremen recounted, with increasing competitiveness, the various hardships of growing up in their day. Keir had roared, not really understanding why he was laughing but in stitches nonetheless, as their mother chuckled between them, the ice clinking against her glass.

But Judy hadn't laughed. She had felt baffled, not understanding, even then, why someone might apologise for ending up somewhere better than they started out.

Last call for passengers travelling to Palma.

Yes, it went against every instinct in a mother's body to watch her child walk away from her; but, as she stood there watching the sea of bodies building a wall between herself and her only child, Judy felt a sting of excitement, too, followed by a twinge of hunger. It was well past lunchtime and she hadn't eaten since breakfast.

Picking out a limp ham and cheese baguette from Upper Crust on her way back to the car park, she took a few unpleasant bites before dropping the rest into a bin next to the pay-and-display machine.

The sky out here was bright, the air fresh as Judy inhaled, triggering a rush of adrenaline, that surging thrill she recognised as the promise of possibility as she ran through what she had to prepare for her own journey to Somerset.

She had to go home and pack, for one – not that she had much to take. Judy preferred to travel light, at least on the way out. The same, alas, could not be said for Francesca. They had spent all of Saturday shopping for 'last-minute bits and pieces', running through the list of so-called essentials as they circled Hyde Park towards Marble Arch in their Volvo estate, Francesca simultaneously scanning through stations on the car stereo – from Kiss 100 to Capital FM and back again.

Ordinarily, Judy didn't like spoiling her daughter like this – it did a child no good to have life handed to them on a plate. On this occasion, though, she had relented, smiling to herself in amusement as she watched Francesca self-consciously try on outfits in the changing room in Topshop and Miss Selfridge, being made to leave before she tried on a bikini, which seemed a little confused given that her daughter was presumably planning to wear it in public.

Who could truly claim to understand the mind of a teenage girl?

Her heart had dropped a little when, passing a Waterstones and proposing that Francesca might like to choose a new paperback to keep her company on the flight, she had watched as her daughter's hand hovered over the latest in her favourite *Pony Club* series before self-consciously picking out the newest instalment from *The Boyfriend Club*.

Still, for all her pretence at adolescence, Francesca had taken no persuading when her mother suggested they take a detour back to the car via Benjy's on Regent Street, and wander, with their pints of hot chocolate in takeaway cups, through the piazza in Covent Garden to look at the doll's house shop that had moved there a few years earlier from the quiet corner of Marylebone where Judy would pass by with her own mother, as a child.

It was here, too, where three years earlier Rory had commissioned a miniature rendition of the house on Launceston Grove, as a birthday present for Francesca's tenth birthday. Judy had gasped when he'd brought it home in all its three-dimensional glory, squirrelling it away in the attic, where they had sat and marvelled at the intricate replication of the life she and Rory had built together.

As a child, Judy had never been allowed to buy from this shop, only to look in from the street – she and Esther standing on the other side of the glass, observing other people's lives recreated in miniature so that the imperfections were no longer visible.

Now, that life was hers; all the joins neatly plastered over. Or so Judy had thought.

Part of her wished she could show Esther the life she had made for herself. Another part relished the separation: this was her world, preserved and untainted, just like the models behind the glass. Much as she needed to keep something for herself away from her husband – a nest egg all her own – she also needed to keep any trace of him and Francesca away from Esther. Cross-contamination could only lead to trouble.

Not that it mattered any more what she told her mother.

About a year ago now, Judy had made her weekly call to Esther from the phone box on Kensington High Street and found herself slightly taken aback when her mother's neighbour, Irene, answered the phone. Irene worked as a carer, and when Judy had gone to America she had taken it upon herself to keep an eye on Esther; for the past two years, since she'd noticed that the fridge was often empty and Esther was losing weight, Judy had been paying her a small amount to go in every day.

'Hi, Judy,' Irene had said, in her usual unflappable tone. 'Are you in France for the summer?'

'Yes,' Judy had lied. She'd wanted to tell Irene the truth, but couldn't risk it. There was value in keeping certain things separate, partly so as to avoid unwanted questions from either side.

Or maybe she was just aware of how easily things might fall apart, if she didn't maintain the barriers between her two lives. If one thing gave, everything else might collapse, too.

'I'll be there in a second,' Irene said. Her voice was muffled as she held the phone away from her ear and spoke to Esther. It went clear again as she re-addressed Judy. 'Listen, love, when do you think you'll be back? Only your mother—'

'Yes?' Something about her voice put Judy on edge.

'She's not well. She misses you. It's confusing for her—'

'Yes, well—' Judy replied, defensively. 'I want to, I just—' She cleared her throat. 'I'll be back as soon as I can. Probably in a couple of months.'

'Right,' Irene said, brightly. 'Well, that's great. As I said, she misses you.'

'But she's OK?'

There was a pause. 'For now. Just come back when you can, yeah?'

Esther hadn't been OK at all. That was what Irene had been trying to say, in her practised, tactful way. A week later Judy had worked up the courage to visit, in the early afternoon when she knew Irene wouldn't be there. And, for all that the other woman had tried to prepare Judy, her mother's decline had come as a shock. She needed more care. More than Judy could afford.

Reaching for Francesca's hand now as they crossed Covent Garden, she inhaled, thinking how lucky she was. Not that it was all down to luck. Judy was a grafter. She had worked hard for what she had. Not like the trophy wives she dodged at the various Wine Society events she frequented with Rory, which saw them taking weekend trips to Paris and Vienna and Rome. Gold-diggers who would have nothing if their husbands left them; no getout if for any reason they decided they wanted something else.

More fool them.

Judy McVee would never be trapped. At least that was what she told herself, to justify what she had done and what she was about to do. But honestly, she couldn't be sure. Why did anyone do half the things they did, besides eating and sleeping and fucking? When it came down to it, for all their pretence and affectations, people were just animals. Sometimes they did what they wanted simply because they wanted to – and because they could.

A group of bystanders had gathered to watch two sopranos singing '*Io t'abbraccio*' at the edge of the square as Judy and Francesca approached the doll's house shop. Pushing aside thoughts of Esther, Judy had taken her daughter's arm and interlinked it with her own as they walked across the cobbles. Steering the girl inside, she had spoken to the woman behind the counter and then watched with delight as the sales assistant presented Francesca with the miniature Picasso pencil drawing Judy had secretly commissioned, to match the one that hung on the stairs in the downstairs hall.

Leaving the airport's departures area, Judy made her way across the car park, picturing the smile that had broken across Francesca's face in that moment and feeling herself buoyed once more. Their daughter was happy. She was on her way to the holiday of a lifetime – and now it was time for Judy to concentrate on her own endeavours.

It was a warm summer's day and despite the energy building inside her, Judy reminded herself that she was in no rush. Moving unhurriedly across the tarmac, she lit a cigarette and leant back against the bonnet of the car, watching the clouds change formation as she smoked.

Blowing perfect circles, she played with the scarf at her neck and found her mind wandering to another day with a perfect sky. An evening sky, in fact, though it had still been perfectly clear; the sound of violins and glasses clattering in the distance – no sign whatsoever of what lay on the horizon.

* * *

At 2.25 p.m., Judy looked up at the plane cutting through the sky and pictured her daughter in her aisle seat, her spongey headphones blaring out Destiny's Child as she soared towards an unforgettable summer.

They had heard all about the recently completed renovation of the Deià house – Casa Salas – in excruciating detail from Laura's parents at a recent dinner at Launceston Grove. Laughing into her glass, Judy had enjoyed the way poor Rory had bristled as Laura's father, Paul Talbot, dressed in a cravat and white trainers, sporting tortoiseshell glasses, wandered through the house they had lived in for thirteen years without any thought of remodelling, and asked what they were planning to do with the place.

Opening the car door, Judy took a final glance up at the sky before ducking into the car and turning on the radio.

For all his social graces, Rory simply didn't know what to do with men like Paul, and it was amusing to see how easily her husband was wound up by the other man's comments about things Rory cared so very little about. For someone who spent his whole life surrounded by pompous arseholes, Rory could be remarkably intolerant. Perhaps it was simply because the pompous arseholes Rory was used to interacting with belonged to a world that her husband understood and therefore could more readily ignore or forgive.

This reminded her of Tamara and Edward de Burgh and the weekend ahead, and Judy sighed, blowing a kiss towards the sky where the plane carrying her daughter to another country disappeared into the clouds.

Turning the key in the ignition, she braced herself. There was no point putting it off any longer: home to London for the night, and then on to Somerset.

Francesca

Deià, Mallorca, July 1999

When I look back on my friendship with Laura, that summer is where my mind always snags.

1999: the year that started with the impeachment of President Bill Clinton and ended with predictions of a devastating Y2K bug that never really materialised; the year Kurt Benson left *Hollyoaks*.

Tucked in the middle of it all, the summer where it all began.

The smell of driftwood and rope. The feel of soft moss and dry stone. The taste of honey and lemon, the bitter and the sweet.

Sunlight danced on the surface on the swimming pool like jewels scattered across glass, that first morning in Deià. The scent of pine and last night's citronella was still ripe in the air, and as I leant back in my lounger, letting the sun kiss my face, I listened as the birds called out to one another above the gentle chords of Morcheeba oozing from wall-mounted speakers.

Squinting against the brightness of the day, it was possible to picture the thirteenth-century monks Laura's mother had spoken of the night before, the ones who had built their monasteries around Deià after the Crusades, sweat prickling their backs, their robes trailing through the scrub as they worked.

By the time Laura's mother, Marcia, was growing up, the Christian pilgrims had been replaced by writers and artists attracted by both the rugged scenery and the magical properties the poet Robert Graves claimed were held within the walls of the Teix, surrounding the picturesque village.

Their own *finca*, Casa Salas, was tucked deep within the Deià hills, a short walk away from the village, hidden within acres of trees in the Son Salas valley. Laura's mother had reeled off the names of film stars who had since bought up land on this part of the island. She spoke in a Spanish lilt that seemed to have become more pronounced in the two weeks that she and her family had been back here, but I had only been half-listening. The truth was, I had already heard so much about the place, both from Laura, who had been coming here every year since she was born, and from Laura's father, Paul, who spoke of little other than his ongoing renovation project on those evenings and weekends I had spent at my best friend's house in Primrose Hill. Originally three stone cottages, the new house had been built on an area of secluded hillside that had belonged to Marcia's family for generations. I could have written the estate agent's brochure – not that Marcia and Paul would ever have sold the place. This hadn't stopped Paul getting a valuation, the outcome of which he'd dropped into conversation the evening he and Marcia came for dinner at my parents' house after it was decided I would be allowed to go on holiday with the Talbot family.

Seeing my own family home through Marcia and Paul's keen eyes that evening – the mahogany Victoria furniture and outdated cushions – I'd felt ashamed. And then, immediately, I'd felt doubly bad for feeling embarrassed by my parents' more old-fashioned tastes. If houses were wine, my home on Launceston Grove would no doubt be considered old world: heavy and cloying and full of character.

But even if I did sometimes wish my dad, in particular, could be a little less formal, I adored my parents, and could see that Judy – though perhaps less obviously gregarious than Marcia, and less concerned with material things – was fun and beautiful and smart.

Still, when you lined it up – the prospect of spending the holiday in London with my parents, or a summer at Casa Salas with Laura and her family – it hadn't been much of a contest.

The night I'd arrived, the moment we'd reached the gates, via an unassuming turning leading off the mountain road and along another path deep into the countryside, I had finally understood the magical quality Laura had struggled to describe. The road from the mountain was lit by strategically placed cat's eyes, leading past a series of A-frame *cabanas* and a separate outhouse for guests. My chest had expanded with a fluttering anticipation as we snaked towards the house, the crunching of gravel and the chorus of the cicadas growing louder as flashes of it came into view: stone and glass rising from a sweeping terrace that ran all the way around the front of it.

It had been dark then. Other than a glimmer of sky and sea just visible through Marcia's car window, I had been unable to see what lay beyond the roaming grounds. Now, in daylight, it was clear that the area was lined with woods, the air steeped in the scent of lemon trees.

Sipping from a glass of ice-cold orange juice, I shifted position on the sun lounger, blushing as Laura's brother, Hugo, stepped outside, his hair still messy with sleep. He was just a year older than us girls, which meant he had been almost thirteen when Laura and I had first met, in line for lunch on the first day at our private girls' secondary school in central London. We had almost instantly become inseparable. Two years later, Hugo seemed like a different creature entirely.

'What time is it?' he asked, stretching so that his fingers trailed the vine woven along the pergola that stood between the pool and the house, creating an area of shade. He wore Stüssy shorts and a gold chain, the grooves of his lean back lightly defined.

'How should we know? Check the clock.' Laura spoke with an inflection picked up from watching endless episodes of *Blossom*. She had a pink, purple and yellow hair-wrap braided through her long blonde hair, which she chewed the end of, absent-mindedly.

'Where's Mum?' Turning slightly, Hugo glanced at me as if he had only just noticed that I was there, nodding in casual acknowledgment. 'Oh, hey, Fran.'

'Hey.' I sucked in my belly. It was already two weeks into the summer holidays and Laura and her family had been on the island for the duration. Compared to Laura and Hugo, I felt pale and bloated.

'She's out,' Laura said, and Hugo sighed, giving no warning before running and bombing into the pool without taking off his shorts. Cascades of water circled out around him as he re-emerged, shaking his head like a wet dog, his hair whipping his face one way and then the other.

'Such a fucking nerd,' Laura muttered under her breath, rolling her eyes and putting down the copy of *Just Seventeen* I had bought at the lounge in the airport once Mum had left. 'Fran, I'm going to get more juice. Come with me?'

Laura led the way, past the outdoor seating area and through the large glass doors into the open-plan kitchen, which was lined with the original beams. Her long legs crossed the tiled floors with a casual stride that hinted at the model she would briefly become.

'Did I mention that the house was originally three cottages?' Laura asked, adopting a deep voice in imitation of her father. '*Mark my word, girls, hemp is going to be THE big thing by the time you're my age.*'

Rolling her eyes, she stopped at the silver American fridge-freezer. 'Dad says it's naff as fuck but my mum insisted.'

'Shit,' I said, picturing my parents, who would be unsure of whether I had arrived safely. 'I better call my mum and tell her I got here OK.'

'Go for it. Phone's through there. Dial 0044 for England.'

Following the direction of Laura's hand, I turned the corner before stopping abruptly. The boy blocking my path had dark hair and a deep tan that emphasised the green of his eyes.

'Did you find it? Oh, hi, Johnny,' Laura said, her voice changing slightly as she addressed the boy, who must have been around the same age as Hugo. When I turned to my friend, I could see that her cheeks had flushed pink.

Of course it's not possible, but looking back now I could swear I felt it then, the moment I set eyes on him; a feeling I can only describe as a twisting in my gut.

We spent the day on the beach, taking a shortcut through the woods, the boys walking ahead, their dusty footprints forming a faded path as the trees gave way to an opening, and acres of sky.

'Oh, my God, I love him. Don't you think he's fit?' Laura whispered as we laid out our towels and applied each other's sun cream, the smell of coconut lingering in the air.

Following my friend's line of vision to where Hugo and Johnny were bombing into crystal-clear waters from the craggy rocks that lined the cove, I shrugged nonchalantly. What was I supposed to say? He had clearly been marked as Laura's territory.

'How do you know him? By the way, I don't think you have to whisper – unless he has supersonic hearing.'

'He lives in Deià. His parents are, like, fucking movie stars. They moved here a few years ago from California. Johnny goes to school with some kids our family has known since forever, and Mum's such a shameless social climber she invites him over whenever we're here. I'm pretty sure she wants to fuck his dad.'

'Laura!' I blushed, focusing on the froth on the surface of the water, lapping back and forth.

'What? It's true. So embarrassing. I wish she was more like your mum. Judy is so cool.'

'Mum, cool?' I laughed. 'She's really not.'

'Er, are you joking? She looks like an old-fashioned film star or something and she is like so composed and cool, and smart. I feel like she's always thinking.'

I snorted with laughter but, as I rolled on to my back, I also felt a swell of pride. 'Oh, my God, Laura, you sound like such a dumbass. *Always thinking.*'

She stopped applying her lip gloss and made a face. 'I can't believe I just said that. Err, anyway, why do your tits look so massive?'

'Shut up.' I batted at her, embarrassed, but she was right. They seemed to strain against the seams of the bikini Mum and I had bought in town, just last weekend. And they felt tender.

'Come on, Pammy,' Laura said, standing. 'Let's go for a swim.'

* * *

It was late afternoon by the time we got back to Casa Salas from the beach and headed to the A-frame *cabanas*, which stood a little way from the pool. Each had its own private changing area, with terracotta tiles on the floor and a wooden hanging rail layered with sand-coloured towels that looked as though they had never been used.

'This is insane,' I said as Laura showed me inside the one that would be mine.

'The shower's in there,' she replied, pointing towards a door leading out into a tiny courtyard made of soft grey concrete, with a large circular showerhead at the centre.

Setting out various miniature creams on the shelf, alongside a bottle of Impulse, I stripped off my bikini and let it fall to the floor before taking a towel and walking towards the shower. The water was blessedly cool as it rushed over my hair and shoulders. Would Mum be in Somerset by now? I wondered, rinsing the salt and sun cream from my skin as I gazed up at a canopy of trees, which appeared like holograms against the blueness of the sky. It was less than twenty-four hours since we had parted ways at the airport, but my mum and I had never been apart this long before. It seemed ridiculous, but already I missed her.

It had been heartening to hear Laura's comments on the beach, especially as I'd always considered my parents boring compared to hers. But in the absence of any siblings or grand-parents, or really any other family at all, we were a unit. Perhaps I should have resented how often my dad seemed to travel for work, but our life, whether he was home or not, never felt lacking. Mum knew how to have fun, and it was contagious. She was completely self-contained, never needing anyone or anything. My mother knew herself in a way that I'd never otherwise witnessed; she didn't need people's approval or even their company. She was always there for me, if I needed her, and she gave me my freedom, too. If I thought about it, it was hard to fathom a better mother.

Back in the changing room, I noticed the lines like slap marks running just below my neck where Laura's fingers had circled my shoulders with the sun cream. My skin began to burn as soon as I was out of the shower, and I let my towel drop to my feet, appreciating the soothing slick of wet hair against my upper back as I wandered towards the concrete counter and picked out a pot of aloe vera that Judy had insisted I pack, along with half the contents of Boots. Scooping a handful of the jelly from the green plastic tub, I felt the skin goosepimple under the cool of the gel, which was tacky beneath my fingers as I rubbed it into my neck.

On the far wall, above a square concrete sink, was a round mirror edged with a woven frame. Taking a step forward to check the precise areas that were turning a golden red, I heard a noise and turned, finding Johnny standing in the doorway.

Naked and stunned, an animal caught in headlights, it was a moment before I was released from my position, and then I bent down, grabbing the towel from the floor.

'What the fuck?' I called out as I stood straight again. 'Can you close the door, please?'

His reply was casual and unapologetic.

'I didn't realise you were in here.'

Judy

The day after Francesca left for Mallorca was one of those glorious English summer days when even the sun-beaten west-bound lanes of the M4 seemed to brim with promise.

Taking the exit for Longleat as per Rory's directions, Judy pulled over in a layby, winding down the driver's-side window and lighting a cigarette.

Typically for them, Tamara and Edward de Burgh's country home was too obscure to be found with only the help of the old *A to Z* that lay abandoned in the footwell. It was the very same atlas Rory had bought thirteen years earlier when they'd moved to England together, its outdated lines and curves still favoured over the Tom-Tom Francesca had insisted they buy him for Christmas the previous year, which neither Rory nor Judy had ever used.

Scouring the hand-scrawled directions provided by her husband, who had gone on ahead to discuss International Wine Society business with Edward, Judy took a moment to clear her mind, not letting herself dwell too much on what came next.

* * *

Irene had been waiting for Judy at the flat, three days earlier, aware that Friday afternoons were when she tended to visit. At the sound of the key in the lock, she had greeted Judy in the hallway.

'We need to talk.' She smiled in such a way that Judy had braced as she let herself be guided to sit on the top step. Irene had that power, to make a person succumb; to make you lose your front, which, when you spent as much time censoring yourself as Judy did, was a relief.

'Your mother – she needs more than I'm giving her right now. Me coming in once a day, you once a week if you can . . . it's not enough. She hasn't washed her hair for weeks, and the other day I came in and the hob was left on.'

'What?' Judy tensed. It was hard to think of Esther in another part of the city, in danger, and not feel ashamed.

'Judy, I don't want to scare you. I just think I need to be here morning and evening, and stay for much longer. If I could afford to do it for free you know I would, but—'

'Don't be silly,' Judy replied. 'You're a care worker, not a charity.'

'And I found these.' Irene sighed, handing over a bundle of envelopes marked with warnings. UNPAID BILL ENCLOSED. DO NOT IGNORE. 'I opened some of them. I hope you don't mind. There was no one else—'

'Shit,' Judy muttered.

'They run back months.'

How had she not thought to check that her mother was collecting her state pension, and using it to pay her bills?

'What's this?' The final statement was a phone bill with certain numbers showing up again and again, the cost of the calls amounting to hundreds of pounds.

'I think they're game shows, quizzes, that sort of thing. They tell her to call in, and she does.'

Judy held her face in her hands, the paper scrunching against her skin.

'It's not your fault,' Irene said. 'Unless she can come and live with you . . .'

More quickly than she was proud to admit, Judy shook her head. 'It's not possible.' Quickly pasting a smile on her face, she patted Irene's knee. 'Don't worry, I have the money. Give me a few days? We're going away tomorrow.'

We.

'*I'm* going away for a week or so. But as soon as I come back.'

When the newsreader started her hourly update, talking about the tragic death of John F. Kennedy Junior and his wife in a plane crash, Judy leant forward and turned off the car radio. Listening instead to the gentle hum of insects and birdsong in the hedgerow, she thought of Francesca, who had called earlier to say she had arrived safely in Mallorca, talking in that slightly sassy voice she reserved for when other teenagers were around; in the distance the indeterminate sound of teenage flirting or squabbling.

Oh, to be young again.

Cutting the engine, Judy closed her eyes and let her thoughts drift somewhere meditative, imagining the low seat of her old Mustang anchoring her as she headed along the coastal road, the wind blowing through her hair. There was nothing like the feeling of driving without a destination in mind, never quite knowing where you might end up. The possibility of youth, of what might still be; of looking forward rather than in the rear-view mirror.

With a final inhalation of smoke, she opened her eyes and smiled to herself as she restarted the engine. She might not be as young as she was, but she was as young as she would ever be. And she wasn't dead yet.

The narrow lane opened up exactly as described in Rory's directions. The roads and fields leading back towards Bath and London, far beyond, were steeped in sunlight, the colours shifting from green to blue where the river cut its path.

Someone must have been watching through the window and spotted the car as, before Judy had even arrived at the gates, Tamara was outside, waving her in.

'Judy!' the hostess beamed. 'Every time I forget just how beautiful you are, and so thin! You can't even be forty – it's sickening.'

Thirty-three, actually, Judy thought but didn't bother to correct her. 'Tamara, lovely to see you. The house is looking glorious.'

'Do you think?' The older woman looked about as if the thought had never occurred before now and then she shrugged. 'Well, I suppose you're right. At this time of year, at least. Such a *shame* you couldn't bring Francesca, but no doubt she will be having the time of her life without us grown-ups to ruin her fun.'

Tamara's Texan twang seemed so out of place here, like a character from *Dallas* on one of those occasional special episodes where a handful of actors went on holiday to some wildly incongruous destination, never to mention the experience again. Though Tamara had always seemed out of place wherever Judy had seen her, first on the Cape, and then, over the years, back in London and at various international events.

Somehow hugging Judy without really touching her, Tamara pulled away again, studying her guest's face with the same intensity as she had the first time they'd ever properly met, on the beach the day Rory had invited Judy to go with him to France. For a moment, she stood there, simply looking at the younger woman standing in front of the fountain. Not for the first time in Tamara's company, Judy felt as though she were a jigsaw the American was determined to figure out or, failing that, one she might be compelled to smash to pieces.

Brightening suddenly, Tamara pointed to the boot of the car. 'Now, just leave your luggage there, we'll send someone to bring it in later. Unless you want to freshen up after the drive? Not that you need to. Let's go and see what those men are up to, shall we? Talking shop, no doubt. Are you hungry? I'm on a diet, but I've had the staff stock up on snacks ahead of the party.'

She led Judy across the gravel drive, past an ornamental fountain and up the front steps. Beyond the portico, the house was gloomy in that special way of English country estates, having sat in the same spot for centuries, the cold seeping into their bones.

'Your bedroom is up there, but I'll show you in a minute,' Tamara said, her face fixed in a smile.

'Gosh, that's an extraordinary room.' Judy pointed to the door on the right, which was ajar, revealing original black oak panelling and a needlework tapestry lining the length of one wall. Along a low table, there stood a series of oversized glass bell jars.

'That's the principal hall,' Tamara replied, breezily. 'If by *extraordinary* you mean *creepy as hell* then I'd have to agree – it feels more 1800s than 1999. Some of the paintings are worth a fortune and Edward, the dear fool, refuses to open the curtains to avoid light damage. The moths are having a field day. I've tried telling him we should get all the artwork put in storage, like normal people, but he would rather have them out on display and take his chances with starting a fire—'

Judy took in the various shapes and textures of the room.

'The house has been in Edward's family forever and he feels a sense of duty to keep certain rooms just as they were, but honestly, the whole damned thing is just a money pit. Sometimes I'm minded to burn it down. Obviously I'd have to take all the valuable stuff out first.' Laughing, Tamara turned back towards the hall. 'Anyway, it's all a bit jollier through here. I insist on keeping all the drab old stuff in one place. All the modern pieces are upstairs. This room is that sort of "country casual" look you English seem so fond of.' She winked, leading Judy into a smaller living room, where Rory and Hugh were sitting in armchairs in front of an open fire, deep in conversation. 'Here you are, boys! We thought you were hiding from us, didn't we, Judy?'

'Judy!' Rory jumped up and held her close, whispering in her ear, 'Thank God you're here.'

'How was the drive? Not too frightful, I hope.' Once Rory had let her go, Edward leant in to kiss her on the cheek, lingering a moment too long as he squeezed her arm.

'Not at all.' Judy smiled back at him. 'And how about you two – how long have you been down here?'

'Just since yesterday, arrived a few minutes before Rory.'

'And the staff only got here the day before so I'm afraid it's all a little chaotic,' Tamara added. 'It was so *cold* when we got here. In July! We hadn't been to the house for a month, and you know how a house like this needs bodies; one measly caretaker just isn't enough – but of course keeping staff when you're in the city costs a fortune.'

'I thought you lived here most of the year?' Judy asked, taking Rory's hand and squeezing it affectionately.

'Oh, God, no. There is a reason why it's called Somer-set. We only really pop in during the winter, and then stay for parts of the summer. At this time of year, with the gardens and the light, it's magnificent. But we're off to the Hamptons to take my parents' cottage soon. Now, let me show you to your room and then we can have drinks. OK?'

'Sounds perfect.'

'Rory, will you join us?'

'We just need to finish off here, and then he'll be free.' Edward smiled, revealing a set of too-bright teeth to match his wife's.

Rory stifled a smile, giving a discreet salute only Judy would notice. God, how did he put up with these people? Though, with the de Burghs, Judy always had the feeling it was less that he put up with them and more that they simply refused to let him go. Their sense of entitlement was bewildering.

'I do hope it will be to your satisfaction,' Tamara said as she led Judy towards the stairs.

'I'm sure it will be lovely. It's so good of you to invite us; Rory has been so looking forward to it, and I'm sure the party will be great fun.'

'I hope so,' the older woman added, wistfully, 'We've put you in here. Rory doesn't like being in the room where he and Caroline slept – too many memories . . . Such a tragedy. I know he still feels guilty—'

'Guilty – what do you mean?'

There was a hint of triumph in Tamara's expression at knowing something Judy didn't. For a moment Judy thought the other woman might continue, but then, appearing to shake the thought away, Tamara smiled, her voice instantly brighter. 'Anyway, now he has *you*, and I can see he's completely bewitched. You're, well, so *different* from Caroline. So different from all of us, really.'

Judy was struck by a wave of *déjà vu*. Lifting her fingers to the horseshoe chain at her neck, she regarded the older woman. Of course. Judy knew exactly who Tamara reminded her of: Portia Blythedon.

She smiled back at her hostess, her fingers scrunching into fists.

No, she wouldn't give Tamara de Burgh the satisfaction of knowing how desperate she was to understand; of exposing her fury that there was something this awful woman and Judy's husband shared that she, Judy, would never be party to.

'The Hamptons?' she said, changing the subject. 'I've always wanted to go.'

'I bet you have!' Tamara laughed. 'Where did you holiday when you were young?'

'Oh, here and there,' Judy replied, picturing Portia's tear-streaked face. Matching Tamara's smirk, she continued, 'Will you be away long?'

'Not as long as I'd like. Our live-in man here has a wedding so he'll be away in the first week of September and then – well, long story short, we can't leave the house totally unmanned for more than a few days so we'll have to be back by the fifth.'

'What a shame.' Judy's smile was genuine now. 'But I'm sure you'll have a wonderful time.'

Francesca

Early evening, Laura's parents arrived home with a boot full of supplies for the barbecue, as well as several boxes of my favourite cereal, and my favourite flavour of crisps and iced tea.

I wasn't sure why I didn't mention the incident with Johnny as Laura and I helped prepare for the evening meal, but maybe I was scared of upsetting anything, given how much effort everyone was putting in to make sure I felt part of the family; or maybe I was worried that my friend might think I'd in some way orchestrated it.

'Help yourself; the proper food will be ready soon.' Marcia smiled as she moved towards the outside bar, ruffling my and Laura's hair as she passed, the gentle strumming of Spanish guitars playing over the speakers. The terrace was illuminated by flares pitched into the ground, which hummed below the sound of the cicadas. Smaller candles on the terrace had also been lit, casting pools of flickering gold across the table, which Marcia had laid with a beautiful linen cloth and bowls of olives and almonds and slices of chorizo.

Taking a handful of crisps, I ate half and brushed the rest into a napkin. My stomach ached in a way that I put down to my unease at the thought of seeing Johnny again. And yet, when I thought of him, there was a bristle of excitement too.

'Fran?'

'Hmm?'

When I looked up, I saw Marcia pouring a large glass of wine for herself and another for Paul, who was lighting the barbecue in readiness for the *dorada* his wife had prepared with freshly pummelled *mojo verde*. Beside her now stood Hugo and Johnny, both sun-kissed, shadows flickering across their faces in the candlelight.

'I asked if you would like juice?'

'I'm OK,' I said, my cheeks burning as I felt Johnny watching me. 'I'll have water when we eat.'

Marcia paused before filling two smaller glasses, which she handed to each of the boys.

'You know what? I think I'll take a beer instead,' I heard Johnny say.

'Grab one for me too?' Hugo called after him, and Marcia laughed as her son's friend headed into the kitchen.

'We'll have their wine?' Laura brightened and her mother tutted, shaking her head.

'Laura! You're thirteen.' She pronounced her daughter's name in the Spanish way, *Low-ra*.

'Hugo's only fourteen!' Laura protested.

'Not you, my babies,' Marcia replied with a look that confirmed the conversation was over. 'Now, everyone sit. Francesca, I hope you like fish?'

Marcia served the salad using large wooden-handled tongs, scooping a tablespoonful of tomatoes drenched in olive oil alongside.

'It all looks amazing, thank you so much,' I said, taking

my plate and spotting Johnny returning to the patio with two bottles of cold beer.

'Doesn't it just?' He caught my eye, the sage green of his own illuminated against the candlelight, his tongue moving over his lower lip as he took his seat.

Looking away, I focused on my food.

'So how are your parents, Johnny?' Laura's mother asked, and when I looked up again I noticed Laura watching her brother's friend from her side of the table. 'We were hoping to catch up with them next week, but I hear your dad's filming might still be ongoing?'

'They should be back soon but – I dunno. My dad's starring and my mum's exec-producing and something's come up so they're both stuck out in Arizona until it's done.' Johnny spoke with the sort of transatlantic drawl that presumably came from spending half of one's teenage life in California and the other half at an international school on a Balearic island, surrounded by the children of rich expats largely from Russia and Germany.

'Well, you give them our love when you speak to them. Tell them to come and stay with us – any time – in London. And you too. You are always welcome.'

Marcia turned her attention to Francesca.

'And how about you, young lady? I have hardly met your parents but I find them intriguing.' She was on her third glass of wine and her eyes twinkled as she considered me. 'Your mother is so beautiful – was she a model?'

'No.' I smiled.

'But she grew up in London, correct? Not like Paul, who says he grew up in the city but it turns out is actually from a place called Buckinghamshire. You have ever seen it?' Her accent had grown stronger since they had been here, or maybe it was the alcohol.

Across the table, Paul cleared his throat.

Laura winced. 'Ouch, Dad.'

'There's nothing wrong with the Home Counties.' He gave a forced smile, lifting his glass to his mouth. The wine had stained the inside of his lip a dark red.

'Yeah, my mother actually grew up near our school,' I continued.

'Oh, wonderful, and where did she go?'

'She boarded for a while . . .' My voice trailed off, embarrassed by how little I knew of my parents' past. 'My dad's American, as you know. They met there.'

Johnny looked up. 'Whereabouts?'

'Cape Cod. East Coast,' I said, pretending to focus on my plate.

No longer interested, he looked back at his food.

'My dad's family were in the wine business and lived between places that had particularly good vineyards, I guess.'

'This I respect.' Marcia winked, lifting her glass to her mouth. 'And what about your mother's family?'

There was a pause while I scanned my memory for the scant details Judy had told me about my grandparents. My maternal grandmother had been a dancer for a while and my grandfather had been wealthy. What else had I needed to know? They were dead. Like most children, I believed the world started the moment I was conceived.

Paul intervened. 'Marcia, is this the Spanish inquisition again?'

'What?' His wife shrugged. 'It's interesting. You know I am fascinated by all this stuff.'

'You mean you're nosy.' Laura dumped her knife and fork on her plate. 'I'm done. Can we leave the table?'

'Don't take it with you,' Paul replied and Laura and Hugo both rolled their eyes.

'We're done, too,' Hugo said, standing.

'Thanks for dinner, it was delicious.' Smiling politely, I followed suit.

'It is my pleasure.' Marcia beamed back at me. 'I hope you don't think I was interrogating you.'

'Not at all.'

I paused, an image forming in my mind. It was of an old piece of newspaper tucked inside the pages of a novel belonging to my mother, which I had stumbled on years earlier at the house in France while looking for a suitable book to read; an obituary detailing the life of a recently deceased Cabinet member. Henry Porter. The single word 'father' was scrawled in the top right-hand corner in pencil.

'My grandfather,' I continued. 'I think he was a politician.'

There was a cramping pain in my stomach, and I reached a hand to the table to steady myself. I was wearing the white sundress my mother had picked out for the trip and, as I turned, Laura pulled on my arm, leaning in with a conspiratorial whisper.

'Fran, you're bleeding.'

Judy

After they returned from the West Country, Judy kept the windows in the house in London open, making the most of summer. The sound of lawnmowers and the distant hum of traffic from the nearest main road drifted in as she rushed into the kitchen, wincing in her attempt to manoeuvre a silver hooped earring into the hole in her ear, a cigarette pressed between her lips.

Rory was seated at the breakfast table.

'I wish you would stop smoking,' he said, without looking up from his copy of the day's *Times*, continuing to scan the crossword clues.

'Have you seen my shoes?' she replied, ignoring his comment. She didn't usually smoke in the house these days, especially at this time of year, when there was nothing more sublime than a single cigarette taken whilst seated under the roses. But with Francesca still in Deià, what was the harm? Besides, she was in a rush, keen to get going before the bus that would shunt her along the Euston Road turned into a slow cooker, as they did at this time of year, and she needed something to soothe her nerves.

'Are they where you left them?'

153

'Hilarious,' Judy said, picking an apple from the fruit bowl and taking a bite before moving to the sink and running the tap over the butt of her cigarette, enjoying the hissing sound as the embers died away. 'Right, I'm going.'

Dropping the soggy butt in the bin, she headed back towards the hall to continue the search for her shoes, glancing down at Rory's crossword as she passed.

'Number nine, UTOPIA,' she said. *Posh patio type is out of this world.*

'I hate it when you do that,' Rory shouted out, and she called back at him.

'I know . . . Love you, bye!'

It was nearly midday by the time she arrived in King's Cross, the faded bassline still reverberating across the cobbles outside Bagley's as she passed over the footbridge.

Turning right, away from the club and the canal that ran alongside, she stood a moment in front of the sliver of shop fronts where, between a deserted Irish pub and a newsagents, stood the spot where she and Jim Doherty had met up, intermittently, over the years.

As he never trusted her to use his contact directly – or rather, as he was unwilling to lose his substantial cut – it was here that Judy would come on the occasions when she had something she wanted to trade in.

He was seated at the back of one of those increasingly rare London caffs – two 'f's – where Mary, the owner, served coffee two ways: black or white. Or occasionally, as Jim liked to joke, in reference to the centrist political stance adopted by the New Labour government, the third way: with a fly in it.

She saw him lick his thumb, turning the corner of the pages of the *Racing Post.*

'Jim,' Judy said, taking a seat opposite, the small laminate table wedged between them.

'Hey, Jude,' he replied – the same quip every time. 'How's your ma?'

'My mother's fine,' she lied, above the hiss of bacon in the pan a little way away from where they sat.

'Good. She could have sold the wind back to the sky, that one. Give her my best.'

Judy swallowed, keen to change the subject, and Jim closed his paper, entwining his fingers on the table in front of him. They were fine, pianist's hands, Esther might have said, though she couldn't imagine Jim Doherty having been near a piano in his life other than to nick or to sell it.

'So, what you got for me today?' he asked, moving straight on to business.

'It's big.' Judy paused. 'I'm going to need cash up front.'

Narrowing his eyes, he lowered his voice. 'What sort of thing are we talking about?'

'Paintings, mostly. Antiques, too.'

There was a buzzing noise and he reached into his pocket, pulling out a pager. Frowning, he looked up again as though trying to figure something out – whether he could trust the woman sitting in front of him, probably. But this wasn't seriously in contest. As far as Jim Doherty was concerned, he knew who and what Judy was. He had no reason to doubt her.

Apparently arriving at the same conclusion, he necked his cup and stood slowly. 'I've got to go to the lock-up. Walk with me.'

They talked logistics as they crossed Goods Way and headed towards the disused railway arches, passed a burger van blasting Mussorgsky, an older man in glasses serving bacon rolls to workers in high-vis jackets, and the final dregs of those leaving the club.

Judy kept a slight distance from Jim. The area around them was growing dark as they headed below ground level.

'And you're certain of this?' Jim patted the head of the collie who emerged from one of the open doors.

'Absolutely.' Leaning down to pick up the saliva-sodden tennis ball, Judy lobbed it deeper into the darkness, watching as the dog charged away after it. Jim grappled with the padlock that separated his arch from the outside world.

When the stark overhead light came on, the lock-up was illuminated to reveal boxes brimming with the kind of bric-a-brac Jim sold on his stall.

'Load of crap in here – sentimental bollocks, mainly.' He spoke as if to himself, indicating towards a series of shelves next to a Page Three calendar.

'Do you want me to write down the address or dates?' Judy asked, vaguely noting the old mugs and the jar of broken Zippos, wedged up against an abstract bronze statue.

'You've got to be joking.' He shook his head. 'First rule in our job? Never leave a trace.'

Francesca

London, September 1999

'I called into Dad's study to say dinner's nearly ready; he'll be here in a minute.'

I was slouched on a chair in the kitchen in front of my homework, the radio on quietly in the background, my mother standing at the counter chopping vegetables for dinner.

'Thanks, darling. Are you OK? You seem tired.'

Yawning, I shook my head. It was my first week back at school after the summer holidays and the initial burst of excitement at joining Year 9 had already begun to wear off. After Mallorca, where I had grown used to going to bed at midnight and sleeping until mid-morning, lounging by the pool for hours or at the beach, the early mornings were taking their toll. Back in London, the turn towards autumn was already making itself apparent, the tips of the leaves visible through the window of my bedroom already turning brown.

But I was glad to be home. Though I would never have admitted it, the first couple of days away from my mother had been tough. Especially after the incident with Johnny and the shower, followed by the horror of my first period starting like that in front of everyone at the dinner table. Not that Laura's family had been anything other than lovely about what happened, Marcia ushering me up to the bathroom and ordering Laura to find a change of clothes while Marcia soaked the bloodstained dress in a bowl of cold water.

By the time I had come back outside, dressed in a pair of black shorts and a pyjama T-shirt with Minnie Mouse on the front that Laura had lent me, the boys had already scarpered. At Marcia's suggestion, I'd tried my mother on the house phone, momentarily forgetting she had gone to stay with my father at Tamara and Edward's place in Somerset, and the line had rung out. Back in the kitchen at Casa Salas, I had tried not to feel embarrassed as Laura's mother stirred two heaped spoons of Cola Cao chocolate powder into a saucepan of warm milk.

The next day had been even hotter than the first and Marcia had taken us girls into Palma to look at the shops. We had just walked back through the door when the phone rang and Marcia called out that it was Judy. My mother, who had left London at eighteen to travel to America alone, didn't even think to ask me if I was missing home. But, when she heard the news about my period starting, she had gasped.

'Being a woman is the best and worst thing,' she'd said, simply, and I had pictured her, a shock of red lipstick, her curls pulled back from her face, standing in the wood-panelled hallway of the de Burghs' Somerset home. 'Now listen, I've got to go, as people are arriving here, but I love you so much and I'm so proud of you.'

She repeated the same words now as she stood at the counter, her back to me as she chopped vegetables. 'So proud, and just so happy that you're home. It's never the same without you. We should do something to celebrate, just the two of us.'

'To celebrate me starting my periods? That is the weirdest thing imaginable.'

'Well, then, young lady, you need to improve your imagination.'

I made a face. This was classic Judy.

'I wondered if you fancied going to the cinema this weekend. That new Hugh Grant film is showing at the Coronet,' she continued, seamlessly, and I shook my head.

'It's always so smoky in there.'

My mother turned, rolling her eyes. 'Whose daughter are you? Or there's a new show in the West End. *Mamma Mia!* – it's supposed to be fun. Fancy it?'

'Sure.'

I paused, thinking of Marcia's question about my grandparents that night in Deià. Now was as good a time as any.

'I've got to do this family tree thing for history this term,' I said. 'Can you help me at some point? I've got most of Dad's line but not yours . . .'

Glancing up, tentatively, I saw the knife my mother was using briefly suspended in the air before she returned to slicing the pepper at her previous speed.

'I can try,' she said finally. 'But you know what a mess it all is. Your grandmother hardly told me anything.'

'You must know some stuff. Like, your dad worked for the government, right?'

When Mum turned towards me, there was an expression in her eyes that I didn't quite recognise. 'Why would you say that?'

'I just—'

We were interrupted by the ringing of the house phone. My parents didn't believe in having one handset in each room, and aside from Dad's separate work line, which he kept in his office just along the hall where he was working now, there was also a phone on the counter outside his half-open door, and another in the main bedroom.

He must have been halfway to the kitchen already when the phone rang, as I heard him call out, 'I'll get it.'

Neither of us said anything for a moment and then Mum broke the silence, her voice light again as she turned back towards the supper she was preparing, the water boiling in the pan signalling that it was time to add the pasta. 'I'm sure we can find a way around it. Are you thirsty? I bought Ribena at the supermarket.'

Pushing back my chair, I stood. From the hallway, I heard the strained sound of my father's voice as I moved to the cupboard. Dad never lashed out, and the harsh note I detected in his voice caused me to listen harder.

Turning towards Mum to gauge her reaction, I saw her pouring dry fusilli into the pan, the clattering sound of the cascading pasta shapes obscuring any trace of the conversation taking place in the hall. Picking a glass from the shelf – one of the tankards my mother had come home with a few week-ends ago – I poured two fingers' worth of cordial and went over to the sink to add the water.

Taking my first sip, I turned and found my father paused in the doorway. He was tapping the side of his leg, absent-mindedly, as he sometimes did when he was agitated.

'That was Tamara – the house in Somerset has been burgled.'

His voice was still strange, I noted, but different from how it had been during the concealed argument of a few moments earlier. It didn't make sense. Why would he and Tamara have been fighting?

'Burgled?' Mum turned towards my father, setting down the knife. 'When?'

'I don't know, I didn't ask. She was beside herself. The paintings, jewellery . . . all of it.'

The brief silence that followed was disturbed by the tinkling sound of glass against plastic as Mum went to the fridge and pulled out a bottle of wine from the shelf in the door. 'Jesus, that's terrible. What did the police say?'

Dad didn't answer for a while and then he shook his head. 'Edward won't let her call them. I've told you before, people like us don't involve the police. Far more sensible to sack the staff and start again.'

The silence was jarring, and lasted a little longer than one would expect.

'The staff? But—' My mother, when she spoke next, sounded genuinely upset. 'Why did they do that?'

Loosening the tie he wore even when working from home, Dad took a step forward and took a wine glass from the cupboard. 'Well who else could it have been? The house was only empty for four nights. There was no way anyone else would know the place would be unguarded for that specific period apart from those in their inner circle. You know Tamara and Edward are careful about their property.'

'But don't they need to tell the police in order to claim insurance?'

'Why do you care, Judy?'

There was silence, and my father took another long sip of his drink.

'Terrible shame for the people who had to lose their jobs, but there you have it.'

My mother lifted her drink to her mouth, her hand trembling slightly. 'Yes. A terrible shame.'

Judy

The rains came thick and fast the following winter, storms battering pockets of London.

It was no longer possible to drive into central London, and Judy dodged puddles as she made her way across the lights at Marylebone Road towards Esther's flat. Part of a mansion block running above a series of shops, her mother's home stood directly opposite a Catholic church that had been built not long after Esther moved in.

Esther, who had been raised by Presbyterians, used to joke that living there, under the constant disapproving eye of God, was her punishment: the Fallen Woman, forever condemned to judgement.

'Mum?'

Judy kept her eyes averted from the pavement as she rang the bell, her stomach still turning whenever she saw that patch of concrete.

'Who's that?' a voice called.

'It's me, Judy. I'm coming up, OK?'

Placing her key in the lock, Judy heard the music even as she made her way up through the stairwell, wondering what the neighbours made of the endless rotation of Joan Baez and the Rolling Stones.

'You in the bedroom?' Judy asked as she stepped inside and was met by the familiar scent of Pears soap tinted with musk, picking up the post gathered by Irene and stacked on the hallway table for Judy to deal with – paying the bills on Esther's behalf and discarding the junk mail.

'I'm in the kitchen. Your father isn't here so I'm making a drink,' Esther called out as Judy stepped inside. 'Will you join me?'

When Judy and Keir were children, there had been a train set permanently set up in the corner of the room below the curtains that matched those in Aunt Susan's apartment in New York. In those days, the table had been partitioned with one half for Esther to sit at and the other half for the children, with a pile of books her mother kept on permanent rotation from the library; only a couple of favourites were owned outright. Those chosen few were proven to be a favourite by virtue of the fact that Judy – rather than Keir, who was too flighty to hold any interest in books – had borrowed them more than twenty times.

Esther had particular ideas about collecting things. For a market trader specialising in jewellery, she had remarkably little time for possessions. But, once something had earned its place, it stayed: the ballet pointe shoes displayed beside a framed postcard of the Isle of Skye; the bronze bust Esther had been given by the children's father. There had been two originally; one he had given to her and the other he kept for himself. It was the only thing she still had of his.

'Are you coming in or have you already run off again?' Esther's voice retained its old mischievous spirit, which seemed to reveal itself when Judy least expected it. From the record player, Joan Baez sang of staying forever young and Judy's eyes prickled with tears that she blinked away as she passed the old sofa, neatly covered in a creamy yellow blanket, towards the galley kitchen, with its familiar Formica table.

'Coming, Mother, before you finish all the Campari without me,' Judy laughed, her good spirits falling away again as she spotted her, this once glamorous figure, now with her feet bare, toenails uncut, standing opposite her on the lino floor. There was a wildness about the woman before her now that stopped Judy short.

'Is your brother not with you?' Esther asked, wide-eyed, taking down another glass.

'Not today, Mum,' Judy replied, righting herself. 'Here, let me help you with that. Go and put on your slippers and a dressing gown. It's freezing in here. Are your nail-clippers still in the bathroom?'

'You have enough money to give Irene for your shopping?' Judy asked a while later, as they sat side by side on the sofa. Esther was wrapped in the blanket she'd brought to London with her the day she'd left Skye for the ballet school.

'Your father sends plenty,' she huffed in response, giving the blanket a tug. 'It's all over there on the dresser. Why, do you need some?'

'I'm OK, Mum.'

Judy stood, making her way over to the diminished pile of notes she had left on her last visit.

'Good. Never let yourself get to a point where you rely on a man, Judy. It's no good, mark my words.'

Judy picked up the framed black-and-white photo of her parents, taken at Piccadilly Circus in the 1960s, nine months before she and Keir were born, and studied them: her mother was so young and lovely; the father Judy had never known, with his arm around her, neither of them appearing to have a care in the world.

'He had one of those cameras with a timer,' Esther pronounced, wistfully, after a moment. 'We took it ourselves. He had to be so careful, being seen with me in public, with his job and everything. We might have been a target, if anyone had known. I hope he's safe wherever they've posted him now. Middle East, I imagine. He'll call soon, anyway.'

Feeling her cheeks burn, Judy returned the photo to the shelf and placed five twenty-pound notes beside it, securing the cash with a paperweight. 'OK. I'm putting another £100 here. It's for this month's food shopping. You will be sure to give it to Irene?'

'Don't be so ridiculous, your father will sort it all out.'

'Right,' Judy said, taking the empty glasses through to the kitchen, rinsing hers out and drying it with a tea towel before hanging the towel over the rail of the gas oven.

Refreshing her mother's glass with a splash more Campari, Judy added as much soda as she knew she could get away with before walking back into the living room. Esther's eyes widened a little at the sight of her daughter.

'What are you doing here?'

They were the same pale blue Judy knew so well, but with a dull milky quality now that made it appear as though she was somewhere else.

'I just popped in,' Judy said, working hard to cover up her unease. Esther was worse, so much worse. Every time Judy came, something else seemed to have fallen away. 'I got you a drink,' she said, settling it on the side table.

'Oh, you angel. Is it Campari?'

'It is.' Judy leant down and kissed her mother softly on the forehead. 'Will you ask Irene to call me when she comes tomorrow?'

As she said it, she realised the ludicrousness of asking Esther to remember anything and made a note to call the carer herself, later, from the phone box near the house in Kensington.

'Your brother's not been to visit,' Esther said, clearly smarting, as Judy stood straight again.

Picturing Keir's beaming face as he arrived home from the market the last time she saw him, proudly holding the yellow vase with the hand-painted red flowers that he had bought for his mother's birthday, Judy wiped away tears with her wrist.

'What's wrong, love? You look upset. Is it the girls at school?'

In a way Judy wished she could stay longer, but Rory was away, and she had told Francesca she would meet her and Laura in Cavendish Square after school.

In another way, she couldn't run out of there fast enough.

'Mum, please look after yourself,' Judy said, with a sigh, blowing her a kiss from the door. 'Love you. I'll be back soon.'

Judy

London, January 2000

The girls gossiped non-stop on the bus journey home, distracting Judy from her own thoughts as they got off at Gloucester Road and walked the rest of the way.

Shrieking at the rain, Francesca and Laura ran ahead towards the house, dodging the puddles, Francesca throwing open the door and answering the phone as her mother made her way up the front steps a minute later.

'It's for you,' Francesca said, leaving the receiver on its side on the hallway table.

'Could you tell them I'm—' Judy replied to no one as Francesca and Laura tore off their matching puffa jackets and thundered towards the kitchen in search of snacks.

Peeling off her long coat, Judy rolled her eyes. She lifted the phone receiver and held it in the crook of her neck. 'Hello?'

'Judy?'

It took her a moment to compute who the voice belonged to, though the Southern Belle accent should have made it instantly obvious.

She cleared her throat as the penny dropped. 'Tamara. How lovely to hear from you. I'm afraid Rory's not here—'

'I know. But Edward and I are in town for a couple of

nights, on our way back to the States from Somerset. Will you meet us for dinner?'

Judy could almost feel the electricity running from one end of the line to the other and, momentarily, she faltered.

'I'm sorry, I can't,' she replied, gathering herself. 'Francesca's here with a friend—.'

'So she said. But she also mentioned she has a sleepover somewhere else tomorrow night and that you would be free.'

'I—'

'Edward's booked a table at the Ivy at eight. Don't be late.'

Judy loved taking the tube at this time of the evening, a certain anticipation taking hold in the space between the shoppers on their way home, overloaded with bags, and the pre-theatre crowd, freshly done up on their way into town. It was a time when the day was old and the night was young and anything might still happen.

In the relative stillness, Judy closed her eyes. As the carriage swayed from side to side, she imagined herself back in the dormitory at school, regaling her dorm-mates with tales of travels in Tuscany and the Middle East; offering tantalising snatches about her father's job, which was so hush-hush that they weren't allowed to invite friends over during the holidays or even give out their address.

'You're such a liar, Judy McVee.'

Even in her memory, Portia's voice was as clear and sharp as if she was there, on the next seat, tutting in that way of hers, her keen eyes boring through Judy. Stripping back the layers until she could see her victim laid bare. What was it that had made this girl hate Judy so much, to want to expose her as the fraud she clearly suspected her to be? It wasn't a question worth asking, Judy conceded. Some people were just nasty.

When Judy thought of her now, she pictured Portia, hand on hip, on the periphery of Judy's vision, positioning herself a little way back from the crowd. Next to her stood her sidekick, Harriet. Their faces were poised in matching smirks. *I asked my mother and she said she's never heard of a government minister with the name McVee. Isn't that strange?* Harriet had giggled beside Portia and Judy had felt the girls in the circle pull away from her slightly, her face burning with shame and anger as Portia stared at her triumphantly—

Tottenham Court Road. The sound of her destination being read over the Tannoy brought Judy to and she jumped up so as not to miss her stop.

Pushing through the crowd and stepping onto the escalator, she thought of the girl again, weeks later, feeling lighter as she remembered the words Portia had cried out as they pulled the stolen necklace from under her pillow. *It wasn't me! It was Judy. She set me up!* Mrs Briscoe had glared down at the child, along with the headmistress, who had been summoned immediately. Mrs Briscoe's face had been set in a look of disappointment, but Judy had also sensed a hint of satisfaction that she couldn't be sure she hadn't imagined. The teacher's response was curt. *Oh, Portia, you and your tall tales. You've been caught out, just accept it. You're not as clever as you think you are.*

Reaching the top of the escalator, Judy took a step onto solid ground and smiled.

The de Burghs were seated at a table in the middle of the restaurant – best for seeing and being seen – as Judy pushed aside through the heavy curtain and walked through into the dining hall, the high ceilings and Art Deco furnishings giving a sense of performance.

Monitoring the entrance, Tamara spotted Judy and waved an arm, as if she wasn't immediately obvious despite her relatively demure outfit: a stiff satin box-dress and pearl earrings.

Edward, dressed in suit and tie, was in the process of grilling the waiter on the wine list as the new arrival approached.

'Judy. Do sit.' Tamara spoke through gritted teeth which shone unnaturally white. She did not stand or attempt to kiss her dinner companion on the cheek. Whatever work she had recently had done gave her a look of quiet alarm, and she had gained weight, Judy noticed. In all the years they had socialised with the de Burghs, she had never known Tamara not to announce herself to be on a diet; conversely, she had also never not known the woman to be several pounds heavier than the previous time they met. Not that Judy could care less how big or small a person was.

'It's good to see you both,' Judy lied, making no attempt to sound earnest.

'Well, I'm glad to hear it. For a moment I thought you were avoiding us. We haven't seen you since Somerset.'

'No,' Judy replied, tensing as she pulled off her coat. 'I suppose not.'

'No scarf tonight?'

'I'm sorry?'

'The silk scarf you always wear.' Tamara's eyes were trained on her as Judy settled into the chair next to Edward.

'Christ, Tamara, the woman hasn't even been given a drink yet!' Edward interrupted. 'How are you, Judy? You look wonderful as ever.'

Grateful for the distraction, Judy turned to Edward with her best smile. She cleared her throat. 'I'm fine.'

As he filled her glass, she fiddled with the horseshoe chain, aware of Tamara's gaze still fixed on her.

'Are you ready to order food, or do you need more time?' The waiter appeared in what might have been a strategic attempt to stymie the tension that was rising from their table.

Taking a large gulp of wine, she felt Tamara still watching her over the edge of her glass.

'Tamara?' Edward said loudly.

'I'll take the chicken salad. No dressing,' his wife replied, finally, with a brisk smile that fell away as soon as the waiter turned his attention to Edward.

'I'll have the steak,' he said. 'And another bottle of the Château La Tour de By,' adding, under his breath, 'I think we might need it. Judy?'

'Thank you. I'll have the same. With fries. And minus the wine – I'll just have a glass of his.'

Judy's joke hung, uselessly, in the air, and there was a moment's silence after the waiter left, the acoustics in the high-arched ceilings bubbling in her ears.

When Tamara spoke again, her tone was different. She was drunk, her movements out of sync with her words. 'You haven't asked.'

'I'm sorry?' Any wariness Judy had felt was fast turning to irritation.

'The break-in at the house, a few weeks after you and Rory visited.'

'I've not been here more than a minute.'

'No. You're right.'

The waiter returned with the bottle of wine, but before Edward could thank him his wife barrelled on. 'You know, I'm so glad you came tonight. We've known each other for years and yet you know everything about us and we know nothing about you. I remember the first time we met. It was like you appeared from nowhere – poof.'

'I'm not sure that—'

'And you know, I've asked around and no one seems to know who actually invited you to the party.' There was a dangerous edge to Tamara's voice, her eyes glistening as she stared. 'Isn't that odd? Who was it again—?'

'Enough!' Edward slammed his open palm on the table, and the couple at the next table turned towards them.

Finally, Tamara stopped talking.

'That is quite enough,' Edward repeated, steadily, as the waiter receded, the restaurant seeming to have grown quieter.

Judy stood and pushed back her chair. 'Well, this has been lovely. But you know what? I seem to have lost my appetite.'

'Judy—' Edward spoke quietly, possibly more alarmed by the public scene than the risk of offending the wife of an old friend.

'Perhaps you'd better order your wife a coffee.' Smiling to reassure Edward that she wasn't unduly upset, Judy leaned towards Tamara and smiled, sympathetically. 'Best of luck with the diet.'

'I'm on to you,' she called out, and Judy's cheeks burned as she strode across the dining room, the voice ringing in her ears. 'I'm going to find out who you really are. I'm on to you!'

Francesca

Fiddling with the bracelet Tamara de Burgh left me in her will, I chew the inside of my mouth and watch as Laura disappears inside the house to fix us a drink.

Sitting here now, it's impossible not to remember my mother and father dancing to Prince at the New Year's Eve party where, for me, all of this started. My mother. Johnny. And yet, that wasn't true, was it? The trouble with Johnny hadn't begun until later – and I would spend the rest of my life trying to atone for it.

Is it a coincidence that I spend my working days trying to fix other people's broken families? If Hugo understands the irony of this then he never mentions it. But then that's how we operate. If something doesn't fit the version of the events we have constructed, we simply ignore it.

Even after we tried, and failed, to have a baby together, Hugo never resented Lily. At least not openly.

Looking up, I watch as Laura returns, holding two heavy crystal tumblers loaded with oversized ice cubes in a pool of dark rum, and, not for the first time in my best friend's company, I feel a rush of guilt.

With a weak smile, I take one of the glasses from her

extended hand. 'I'm going to use the loo,' I say, putting down the tumbler and standing without waiting for a reply, feeling my friend's eyes on me as I make my way up the garden steps and into the house.

It is strange, I suppose, both of us fast approaching forty and still living in the same houses in which we grew up. But when your family homes are as exceptional as ours, it is hard to give it all up, to know where to go next. In spite of the painful memories these spaces might contain.

Besides, in my case I need to remember. I will never let myself forget.

Standing in the ground floor hallway, I try the door to the bathroom and hear the nanny's voice calling out from within. 'Sorry, we'll be a minute! There's another upstairs . . .'

As if I don't already know.

'No problem,' I reply, hesitating before continuing towards the staircase.

Looking at it, I can't remember the last time I went up there, and it is peculiar but perhaps fitting that, today of all days, I find myself drawn upwards with a sensation I can only describe as one of foreboding after the fact.

The sound of Violetta cooing as she changes one of the twins' nappies recedes as I put one foot in front of the other on the sisal treads. Structurally, Laura has done very little with the house since she took it over from Paul and Marcia after they relocated permanently to Spain, in protest against Brexit, a few years ago. The telltale signs that this is now their daughter's home sit side by side with Marcia's tastes: interiors magazines neatly stacked along the top of a G Plan sideboard; a faux zebra-hide thrown over the sofa in the first-floor guest bedroom, the door to which is open. I reach the top, smiling at the framed poster-sized image of Laura on the front of *Just Seventeen* from her modelling days, printed and hung on the wall.

From a room on my left emanate the faint artificial strains of a mechanical lullaby. Slowing down, deliberately quietening my movements, I find myself again thinking of Judy, and the threat of tears rises once more.

The bathroom is at the end of the hall. Stepping inside and pushing the door closed behind me, I lean back against it, my eyes drifting over the features of the large bathroom. Laura had it refurbished ahead of a magazine shoot at the house, a few weeks before Johnny walked out – a piece hailing the golden girl of interior design and her perfect family. Laura had been pregnant with the twins and Johnny's affair must have already been going on for months but there he sat, cool as a cucumber, posing alongside his beautiful wife and their firstborn child.

Despite all that has passed since then, the room remains just as it was in those painstakingly curated magazine shots: any trace of the mess of everyday life concealed behind brushed ply units; the terrazzo counters clear and sparkling; matt black taps without a hint of limescale.

But in this moment, as I close my eyes, holding on to the sink for stability, I can still picture this room exactly as it was years earlier. How easy it is to strip away the layers and find myself in another lifetime, the sound of the party pulsing below, the white square tiles cool against my cheeks.

Blotting out the scent of bergamot and eucalyptus from the oversized candle at the edge of the bath, I can almost smell Hugo and Johnny's weed drifting down from the upstairs room as I fall back through the tunnel of memory; the familiar voice in the hallway outside, my fifteen-year-old self sobering up in an instant.

New Year's Eve, 2001.

Judy

Judy was distracted as they drove, Rory at the wheel, Judy beside him in the passenger seat, her dancer's back partially exposed in the black Donna Karan dress that Rory had brought home from a recent trip to the States. It was New Year's Eve and London was in the throes of celebration as they made their way to Primrose Hill.

They had been due to spend the evening with Tamara and Edward at their London home in Barnes on the other side of the river. But the party had been cancelled at the last minute and Judy couldn't say she wasn't relieved.

She hadn't seen the de Burghs since that dreadful night at the Ivy, almost two years earlier, which she had never mentioned to Rory. Edward had called the next day to apologise for Tamara who, he explained, had been drunk. She had recently been diagnosed with Type 1 diabetes, he had confided with uncharacteristic openness, and it was proving hard for her to adjust to the significance of her condition.

Judy had been shaken by Tamara's performance – the look on her face as she delivered her threats was imprinted on

176

Judy's mind, and, in the days that followed, the memory of it had woken her in the night.

But, once the shock and anger had worn off, she had felt her nerves ease.

It wasn't possible that any of the stolen items from the de Burghs' estate could be traced back to her. Jim was careful like that. Besides, since her most recent conversation with Irene, her mind had been elsewhere.

'Bets on how long it is before Paul brings up his near miss with the RIBA awards, please?' Rory said as a Catherine wheel went off somewhere in the distance, offset by the clicking of the indicator as they turned past the zoo, the aviary rearing up on the left against a black sky.

'Oh, come on, Rory, play nicely.' Glancing at Francesca in the rear-view mirror as she pulled a piece of Hubba Bubba from the packet in her handbag, Judy caught Francesca's eye and winked. Paul, Laura's father, had recently appeared a handful of times as a friend-of-the-presenter on a popular home makeover TV show that neither Judy nor Rory ever watched. This brush with fame was enough to make other parents suddenly keen to make conversation, smoothing their hair with their hands when he passed them at Parents' Evening with that ready smile and easy charm. And the sudden swell of attention certainly appeared to have gone to his head, judging from the last time they had bumped into him.

But who cared? Francesca had been so happy when Judy had announced that she and Rory would be joining her at Laura's family party, which they had originally declined to attend because of the previous engagement. It wasn't the first time they had socialised with Marcia and Paul but it had been a while – and it was clear that Francesca was excited at the thought of the adults all becoming closer friends. While Judy and Rory might have little in common with Laura's parents and their Primrose Hill set, she didn't want to hurt Francesca by saying so.

Turning right, they skirted Primrose Hill and pulled into a space by the park. Christmas trees sparkled in the windows of the detached pastel-coloured houses that lined the pavement opposite, silhouettes moving back and forth as the city revved up for another night on the tiles.

Stepping out of the car, Francesca tugged at the hem of her dress, wobbling slightly on the wedges she and Laura had bought in Topshop on Oxford Street on their lunch break before they broke up for the school Christmas holidays. The shoes were cork with a black suede toe and strap, and the dress silver and iridescent in a way that she overheard Laura describing as Slutty Mermaid, and frankly it would be difficult to improve on the evaluation.

Watching her daughter through the gap in the half-open door to her bedroom earlier this evening as she posed in front of the mirror, Judy had smiled to herself, seeing Francesca so confident. But now, shivering in the street next to her parents, she looked more than a little uncomfortable, every inch the little girl she still was beneath the fifteen-year-old exterior.

'Here.' Judy held open her long black felted wool coat and waited for her daughter to tuck herself in like she used to. 'Now do you regret not bringing a coat?'

The sound of laughter and shattering glass rose in bursts from the pub on the corner as they walked towards Laura's house.

'I'm fine.' Francesca wrinkled her nose, feigning nonchalance as a gust of winter air wrapped itself around her bare ankles, causing her to shiver. When she succumbed and leant in closer to her mother, a moment later, Judy noticed a smile form at the edges of her mouth and she filled with pride.

Since the money from the burglary had begun to dwindle – at least as much as she would allow herself to touch, ring-fencing the rest – there were moments when Judy had found herself questioning her life choices. Wondering if the adventure had run dry. But of course it hadn't. She was exactly where she was supposed to be. Perhaps this was not where nineteen-year-old Judy McVee might have imagined she would end up, but what did she think, that day in the library, Rory Harrington's face staring back at her for the first time: that she would simply empty his bank account and run off into the sunset?

Taking on a new life meant living it. And that was exactly what she was doing, while keeping enough back that she could jump into another one if this version went pear-shaped. Besides, this wasn't the end, was it? In a few years Francesca would leave home and Judy would be freed up to travel the world and try on the countless lives she hadn't got round to yet. Rory could come with her, when he wasn't working. Or not.

Either way, right now she was part of a life with love and comfort and fun, and she wasn't trapped. At any point, she could spread her wings.

Except there would always someone she would have to come back for. Unless she could make proper provision.

Pushing aside the image of her mother's wan features, Judy drew Francesca closer until she resisted.

'Jesus, Mum, are you trying to strangle me?'

'You could try wearing some clothes, and then she wouldn't need to cover you up,' Rory chipped in with uncharacteristic snippiness, coming up behind them as they reached the place where Laura's house overlooked the park.

For all his outwardly traditional persona, Rory never batted his daughter away when she knocked on his office door; he was never too busy to help with homework or watch her practise dance moves she had learnt from music videos she devoured on The Box or MTV. Judy adored him for that. But there was a tone in that last comment that she didn't recognise or like.

'Ignore him, you look gorgeous,' Judy whispered, pointedly, pulling Francesca in closer. 'And he knows it – that's why he's so upset.'

'So do you. I hope I'm as beautiful as you are when I'm old.'

Mock-gasping, she tickled Francesca, who shrieked with laughter. 'No, no, please – mercy!'

Judy stopped, reaching into her handbag and pulling out a Chanel lipstick in frosted pink. 'Come here,' she said, blotting a layer on Francesca's lips. 'Let me look at you. Oh, yes – fifteen going on twenty-five. What have I let myself in for?'

After she pressed the doorbell outside the large white terrace that ran along a private road opposite Primrose Hill, Judy watched as a silhouette emerged through the stained-glass panels of the door. Laura squealed as she threw it open wide, wrapping her arms around Francesca.

Even from where she stood, Judy could smell the peach schnapps on the girl's breath. But it was New Year's Eve. Teenagers would be teenagers. At least Judy and Rory were here to look out for them.

From somewhere inside, calypso music blazed over the sound system. 'You look fucking amazing,' Laura shouted, placing her hand over her mouth as she looked up and saw her friend's parents following Francesca into the house. 'Sorry! I'm just so excited you're all here . . .'

'So are we!' Judy laughed, taking off her coat as Marcia rounded the corner in a red kaftan. 'It was so lovely of you to reinvite us all, last minute.'

'Of course!' Marcia opened her arms and embraced the other woman with two kisses before turning to Rory, who softened, slightly, in her presence. 'We were so pleased we could steal you away for the night. Next summer we're getting you to the house in Mallorca, it's my mission.' Dark and curvaceous, Marcia was physically the opposite of her daughter but she had the same easy charm, men and women both turning to putty in her presence. 'You look gorgeous,' she said, and Judy tossed her head in gratitude.

'As do you.'

'Louisa will take your coats. Where is she?'

As Marcia spoke, the housemaid, dressed in white shirt and black trousers, appeared behind her in the hall. Marcia would never openly have called her that, but it was evident that a housemaid was what she really was. According to Francesca, Louisa's family had looked after Marcia's place in Mallorca when Marcia and Paul weren't there, and Louisa had come back to London with them one year, to learn English and help at the house, when the children were small. She had never learnt any English, and she had never left.

Blowing a kiss to Francesca, Louisa nodded as Marcia spoke in rapid-fire Spanish, taking the coats and heading to the cloakroom.

When the doorbell rang again, Marcia positioned herself between Judy and Rory and led them towards the kitchen. 'Now, what will you drink? Go and help yourselves and I'll be with you in a minute to make introductions . . .'

Marcia led them inside, Paul placing a hand on Rory's back and guiding him away from the open-plan kitchen towards the adjoining sitting room where an oversized disco ball was at odds with the restrained Georgian features.

It was unusual for Rory to drink heavily, especially when driving, but he had already had two large whiskies before they left the house. He seemed different tonight, in a way that Judy struggled to place. Over the years, she had noted with a degree of amusement the varying expressions of discomfort registering on her husband's face at social occasions. But she had never before seen him grit his teeth as he did now, standing mute in a circle of guests that included a tall, skinny man in a self-conscious pork pie hat and a woman in lace negligée worn beneath a green palm-print silk kimono.

Was it surprising? Although he was only fifty, standing there in front of the stuffed polar bear that Marcia had rented for the Christmas season from a taxidermy shop on Essex Road, Rory belonged a different generation; to a different world. Raised by older parents in New England, to him, Paul and Marcia's faux-Bohemian set might as well have been from another planet.

It was partly what had drawn Judy to him in the first place.

Accepting the cocktail Marcia handed her, she sipped, thinking of the way Rory had looked at her that night of the party in the Cape, Elgar's 'Nimrod' swelling from the violins.

'Georgia and José work in fashion,' Marcia said, leading Judy towards a couple standing in front of a wall-hanging made of neon lights, the words *You're the love of my fucking life* in joined-up handwriting.

'And what do you do, Judy?' the tall willowy woman asked.

Judy shrugged. 'As little as possible.'

They all laughed, and Marcia put an arm around her. 'Isn't she just the best?'

Francesca

It was two years after that summer in Deià when I finally saw Johnny again.

Laura's house. New Year's Eve, 2001.

'This way.' Laura grinned as she opened the door to the party. She wore a mauve halterneck top and low-rise jeans held in place with a studded belt, her mid-length hair twisted into sections and secured away from her face with plastic butterfly clips.

'I thought you were wearing a skirt?' I whined, pulling self-consciously at the hem of my mini dress which suddenly felt way too short.

'Oh, my God, he's here . . .' Laura confided in a whisper, looping her arm through mine as she led me upstairs, my parents heading in the opposite direction, towards the kitchen with Marcia.

'Who?' I asked, not knowing why we were whispering but thrilled by it nonetheless.

The banisters were entwined with firs and fine glass baubles. When we reached the first-floor landing, Laura paused and squeezed my hand, indicating towards the top-floor attic room that belonged to her brother. 'Johnny!'

At the sound of his name, I felt a fluttering in my chest. 'What do you mean?'

'You know: Johnny? The fit one from Mallorca . . .'

'Really?'

'He was expelled from his international school in Palma and his parents went apeshit and sent him to one of those crammers in west London.'

'Wow, he must be really stupid,' I said, trying to make a joke as Laura squeezed my arm.

'He's actually really clever. He just smokes too much,' she replied, her tone self-important as she guided me into her bedroom, crossing to the double bed decorated in fairy lights and pulling out two bottles from underneath it. 'I've got vodka and peach schnapps – I'm going to get so fucking wasted. How do I look?'

'You look amazing.'

'You're just saying that 'cause you're my best friend.' After turning the cap and taking a swig, Laura handed it to me. 'You look amazing too.'

'I look like a slut.'

'Hugo is going to wet himself.'

'What?'

'Oh, come on, he's like completely fucking in love with you. Come on: drink.'

Hugo? I drank, counting the beats: one, two, three. And then I shook my head.

Gross.

'Fuck, that tastes disgusting.'

'I know.' Laura laughed, holding out her hand. 'Let's go and ponce a ciggy from Johnny.'

The atmosphere changed as we made our way up the steps to Hugo's room, the parents' New Year's Eve celebrations receding as we reached the attic.

Even from outside on the staircase I could smell the weed drifting out from under the door, Ghostface Killah and Mary J. Blige blasting from the speakers as Laura pushed it open.

Inside, the boys were talking in that way certain private school boys did, as though they had grown up in Compton rather than the illustrious streets of north London. Though to be fair, Johnny had grown up all over the place, and Hugo never seemed to talk like this when it was just the two of us.

Remembering Laura's comment about her brother, I found myself wondering. The thought had genuinely never occurred to me before. After the summer in Deià, I felt more confident in the presence of the older boys. Despite his and Laura's fiery way of speaking with each other, Hugo had always been sweet to me, letting me have the last can of Coke from the fridge or the final say on the film we were going to watch. And Johnny, clearly, was already spoken for.

'Laura, what the fuck do you want?' Hugo said, his expression softening when he saw me move reticently out from behind his sister. The dormer window was open and I shivered, wishing I had heeded my mother's suggestion that I bring something to go over my dress.

'Give us a smoke, then,' Laura said, picking up a box of Marlboro Lights from one of the records strewn across her brother's bed. Next to it was a packet of silver Rizla papers and a plastic grinder like the ones they sold in Camden Market.

'Hey, Fran.' Hugo smiled at me as I hovered just inside the doorway, unsure where to put myself. 'You remember Johnny?'

'Yeah. Hi.'

His tan had faded but he still had those piercing green eyes.

'Sit.' Lowering herself to the floor, Laura folded her long Bambi legs underneath her and beckoned for me to do the same. Leaning on one arm, she took a half-smoked spliff from the ashtray and lit it. 'What you guys doing?' Her voice was already slurring.

Perching on the edge of the bed, I pulled at the bottom of my dress.

'Nothing much,' Hugo said.

At the same time, Johnny replied, 'We are flyyyying.'

When I looked again, I noticed his pupils were black and wide, his face tilted in an unnatural smile.

Laura squealed. 'Sharing's caring . . . What you got?'

'Nothing, I already said.' Hugo's voice was pointed this time.

He gave Johnny a look that his friend ignored as he opened his palm, revealing three tiny white pills, each embossed with a rainbow. 'We've got magic beans.'

'Should I chew it or swallow?' Laura asked over the music, placing one of the pills in the centre of her tongue.

Already lightheaded from the booze and the weed, I said nothing, wishing I were back downstairs with the adults where the sound of Prince raged from the living room.

'Swallow,' Johnny replied, the morphing shapes of the lava lamp on the table next to him reflecting on the surface of his skin.

'Laura, you don't have to,' Hugo addressed his sister but she ignored him, taking the bottle from my hand. Tipping her head back, she sipped and winced, her eyes wide and already a little bloodshot as she handed me the bottle.

'It tastes gross. Quick, neck it.'

Any uneasiness I felt soon slipped away as the minutes or hours passed, my face softening so that when I pictured myself I imagined one of those pink squishy mushrooms I would load into my bag of pick 'n' mix at the Odeon in Leicester Square.

Laughing, I looked about in wonder at the details of Hugo's room, the alien on the poster above the words TAKE ME TO YOUR DEALER seeming to move a little until I blinked, giggling harder for no discernible reason as I caught Laura's eye.

At some point, the boys left and Laura took over control of the CD player, skipping through Destiny's Child and Missy Elliott. 'I fucking love this one,' she shouted, turning up the volume and swaying precariously by the speakers.

'Laura, I need a drink,' I called out, filled with a rush of love for my friend who was still dancing when I attempted to stand. 'Oh, my God, Laura, I can't get up.'

Creasing with laughter, I half-crawled to the door, Laura leaning on the one of the eaves in an attempt to control her hysteria. 'You've forgotten how to walk . . . You're a slug!'

'Don't, please, I'm gonna piss myself. Stop—' I held my stomach to control the laughter.

As I clung to the banisters, the shift in atmosphere on the top landing sobered me slightly. The beat of Eminem's 'My Name Is' receded as I turned the corner and took the flight to the landing below, where the bathroom stood at the far end of the hall.

Blinking, I attempted to move in a straight line, aware of laughter from downstairs as the music from Hugo's room gave way to the smell of Laura's mother's cooking drifting up from the kitchen.

Turning left, past the print of Laura's recent photoshoot for *Just Seventeen* which her mother had had framed, I remembered the stab of envy when Laura was approached by the scout as we tried on sunglasses in Topshop on our lunch break. I had felt myself turning invisible as the woman handed Laura a card for her modelling agency and suggested her parents bring her in that weekend to have a chat about putting her on their books. Laura, who was wearing no make-up, had made a non-committal gesture, returning her attention to the sunglasses when I asked whether she would go.

It was Marcia who had insisted.

Now, any jealousy I might have felt melted away.

Trailing the glass with my fingers as I passed, I reached the door to the bathroom just as I heard the front door to the house close on the floor below followed by Johnny and Hugo's voices in the hallway.

Closing the door behind me, I slid the lock across and moved to the sink.

Judy

London, December 2001

Swallowing her drink, Judy cast around for Rory, who, at Paul's insistence, had been chaperoned out into the garden for a Cuban cigar and had never re-entered.

It had been a strange day, dominated by her meeting with Irene ahead of what was supposed to have been an evening at Tamara and Edward's pied-à-terre in Barnes. They hadn't seen the couple for so long – and Judy had begun to hope their forced friendship might have come to a natural end. But when Rory had returned home from a Wine Society event in Florence a few months earlier with an invitation for their New Year's Eve *soirée* it had somehow felt like a test.

Of course Judy had said that she would love to go. Part of her was intrigued to see how Tamara would perform with Rory present. But that was the reckless part of Judy talking. The other part, the part motivated by self-preservation, had been utterly relieved when Rory had announced that the plan had been jettisoned, even if the short notice was a little off.

Honestly, by then she had been too distracted to question the possible reason for the de Burgh party's last-minute cancellation. The journey home from her mother's beloved flat in Marylebone to the house in Kensington had passed by in a blur. How could she not have realised sooner that this was coming? Esther's condition had been deteriorating for a long time, at first slowly and then at a pace that could only feasibly have ended with the pronouncement that she needed to go into a home.

Irene had done everything she could for Esther, but even with her dedication it wasn't enough. Esther needed round-the-clock care, and there were only two ways in which that could be achieved. Looking out at the Christmas window displays from the top of the bus, Irene's words had rung through Judy's mind. *A place has come up in the care home I work in part-time. It's not cheap but it's one of the best, and it's sought-after, so if you want the place you'll need to act quickly. If I loved someone, it's where I'd put them.*

But it wasn't that simple. The flat was where she and Keir had taken their first steps – Judy, the first one to master walking, apparently pulling her brother up after her and half-dragging him across the carpet. Where she had chipped a tooth while chasing her twin during a heated quarrel, and Judy had told Keir jokes to make him laugh when he cried at what he had accidentally done to his sister.

The place where she had watched her brother die.

There was little time for nostalgia, though. Irene's parting words had been a reminder that, if she wanted to go ahead with the care home, the deposit would need to be laid down by the first week of January. The numbers she had given had made Judy's eyes widen. But it was the best place, Irene had assured her. You got what you paid for.

'Judy, why are you not dancing?!'

When she looked up at the sound of Marcia's voice, Judy realised she was squeezing her glass so tightly it might break.

'I'll be right there,' she replied. 'I just need to freshen up.'

'Don't run away!'

'I promise.' Judy winked in reassurance as Marcia retreated back to the dance floor, leaving her guest to slip from the party through the kitchen door and into the hallway where the giant station clock that hung on the wall read ten to eleven. Esther would be asleep by now, she figured as she took a step towards the stairs, turning away again as the front door opened, followed by the sound of male voices.

Walking towards the downstairs bathroom, she tried the handle and felt resistance from the other side. 'Busy!' a woman's voice called out, followed by sniggers and the sound of sniffing as Judy moved back cautiously towards the stairs.

A little way ahead of her, Laura's brother Hugo and his friend had clearly returned from the off-licence and were heading upstairs accompanied by the telltale swishing and clinking of a bag of booze. She sighed. Francesca would be sixteen in a few months. While she didn't love the idea, Judy was hardly naïve enough to think her daughter wouldn't be having a drink on New Year's Eve.

Marcia and Paul's home wasn't a million miles apart from their own Kensington townhouse, albeit this one was bigger and showier. Whatever Judy wanted, she had always wanted it for herself, not for show – and she acknowledged the hint of disdain she felt as she walked up the stairs, running her fingers along the banisters which were swathed in greenery and glass baubles.

At the top of the hall was a framed poster of Laura on the cover of *Just Seventeen*.

Smiling, Judy shook her head. Laura had always been a sweet girl but she knew how different teenagers could be among their peers, and she couldn't help but wonder if the girl would be a good influence on her daughter. Especially since she had started modelling and seemed to become thinner with every day that passed.

'Is anyone up here?'

Taking the final step onto the landing, her heartbeat quickening, Judy noticed that the bathroom to her right was occupied. Figuring she had a couple of minutes to kill, Judy followed the light towards the room at the other end, like a moth to a flame.

Francesca

London, December 2001

Oh, my God, I was so thirsty. And everything was so . . . fuzzy.

In Laura's upstairs bathroom, I turned on the tap, downing the water in gulps, drinking for a few seconds before having the presence of mind to tell myself to stop; I was the perfect age to remember the tragedy of the teenager who drowned herself after taking Ecstasy and consuming litres of water.

It was OK, I told myself when a flicker of anxiety reared up. Things like that happened to other people, not me. My life was boring. But right now I was someone else. I looked and felt different. I felt good. Sexy. Fun.

Enjoying the altered version of myself staring back at me, I stood in front of the mirror, listening to the clatter of bottles rustling in plastic bags as Hugo and Johnny passed on their way back towards the upstairs room.

A goofy smile had fixed itself to my face and I enjoyed my own reflection, taking in the details I had always been so quick to dismiss: the large dark eyes and thick brown hair that felt soft now that I stroked it. I looked like myself except for my pupils, which had turned large and black and hollow, as if I could lean forward and fall in through them and land in another universe entirely.

From below, the party vibrated through the floor. Clearing my throat, I placed my hand on the door handle and then froze at the sudden voice on the other side.

'Is anyone up here?'

My heartbeat seemed to speed up and fall away all at once as I peered through the frosted glass, watching my mother's silhouette headed away from the bathroom and down the hall. I stood, petrified, caught between the desire to run out and hug her – the mother who had come to my best friend's house for New Year's Eve, even though I knew she didn't want to; the mother I loved, and trusted to always love me back – and the insurmountable fear of her looking at my face and seeing what I had taken.

The mist finally clearing, I realised she must have come up here to use the bathroom because the downstairs loo wasn't free, which meant there was no way of getting out without being seen. Moving slowly towards the door, I strained to hear. Besides the muffled sound of music converging in the hallway outside, I couldn't make out any noise. Perhaps, having realised this bathroom was occupied, my mother had gone back downstairs. There was a chance she would come up and try again in a minute, or that some other adult would.

Either way, I was seized by a sudden need to get out unseen.

Pulling the door open a crack, I looked out and, with a sigh of relief, saw the coast was clear. Suppressing a giggle, I moved on my tiptoes, the music from Hugo's room starting to dominate as I moved across the landing towards the safety of Marcia and Paul's bedroom, which guarded the stairs to the next floor.

Just as I was about to call out to my friends, I turned and paused, aware of a figure through the crack in the door.

Freezing instinctively, I struggled to focus, to understand quite what I was seeing, my feet glued to the spot.

The picture emerged in pieces after that, the soft lighting of the master bedroom making the make-up compacts and stones in an open jewellery box on Marcia's dressing table glisten, my mother's face in profile disappearing from view as I pulled back and padded as carefully as I could towards the stairs.

Francesca

London, 17 September 2024, 12.30 p.m.

Bile rising in my stomach, I lurch forward, reaching the toilet just in time, retching as Laura's voice calls again through the door. 'Francesca, are you in there?'

Lifting my head from the bowl, I wipe my mouth before answering, willing myself into a sitting position and taking a moment to adjust.

The bracelet comes into focus once again. It was the only thing Tamara had left me in her will, along with a note. *Don't worry, everything will come good.*

'I'm fine.' Calling back to my friend through the bathroom door, I stand and move to the sink, turning on the tap and splashing my face, watching the water stream down my cheeks before I reach for the towel and press it to my mouth, holding it there a beat longer to suppress the scream.

Downstairs, I hear the nanny cooing to one of the twins. Hanging the towel back over the rail before flushing the toilet, I take a final look at myself in the mirror before moving to the door, and open it, shaking my head apologetically.

'Laura, I'm so sorry.' A single tear runs down my cheek.

'Fran, listen to me.' She speaks slowly, as though to a child. Part of me feels as if I am somewhere else, being dragged back into the past, and Laura is the hand anchoring me in the safety of the present. Except it is no longer safe.

'Whatever has happened, whatever Judy has done, you need to protect yourself and your daughter. Above everything else.'

I nod, trying to clear my head. What is she saying?

'Fran, are you listening?'

'Yes.' I fumble for my phone, no longer sure of anything. Except— 'I need to call Hugo.'

My fingers tremble as I dial. He answers after one ring. 'Fran?'

'Are you at the house?'

'Yes,' my husband replies, his voice soothing. I can do this. 'Are you—'

'Wait there, and gather the reporters,' I tell him. 'I'm going to give a statement.'

Francesca

London, January 2002

'Fran, what the hell? I was trying to get your attention all through registration. Are you blanking me?'

I was wrestling with the can of Lilt lodged in the vending machine when Laura found me, the day we started back at school.

'Of course not.' There was another pang when I spotted on her wrist one of the matching friendship bracelets we had bought together at the market in Palma, three summers earlier. Two leather thongs each with half a silver heart, split in two.

'Why would you think that?'

'You haven't answered my calls either. I left two messages on your answering machine, and I've paged you like a hundred times.'

'Sorry. We had to go to stay with my parents' friends in Somerset straight after New Year,' I lied.

Laura's expression changed, and she linked her arm through mine, heading for the stairs. 'I've got so much to tell you. Wasn't the party amazing?' She lowered her voice. 'Johnny kissed me.'

Waiting for my response, Laura nodded furiously and I let out the requisite squeal.

'I know. I know, I know, I know. *Fuck*. I really like him.'

'I know you do . . . It's so great. I'm really happy for you.'

'Why don't you look happy ?'

'I am.'

'Fran, are you OK? Wait, do *you* like him?'

'Me?' I shook my head. 'God, no. I mean he's fit, but . . . honestly, I'm so happy for you.'

'Oh, shit, I meant to tell you – the necklace my mum inherited from her aunt was nicked at the party. It was worth a fucking fortune. My dad is livid.'

'What?' The blood drained from my cheeks. Stumbling around for the right words, all I could come up with was, 'Are you sure?'

'My mum is so upset; the police were basically like it's going to be impossible to find out who it was because there were so many people there and anybody could have gone into my parents' bedroom at any time. So they can't, like, prove it with DNA or whatever.'

I swallowed, shaking away the image of my mother. It didn't mean anything. She could have been in Marcia's room checking the time, or just giving space to the person using the bathroom.

So why did I feel so fearful?

'It's so fucked up.' Laura shrugged. 'I mean, at a party in our house: what kind of psychopath would do that?'

Judy

London, January 2002

The days after Marcia and Paul's New Year's Eve party were deceptively bright, the sun fooling Londoners into believing that it was warmer than it was.

Drumming the fingers of her left hand against the steering wheel, Judy lit a cigarette with the other, winding down the window of her old Volvo estate in a practised movement and letting in a gust of cold air. Passing sari shops and Turkish restaurants that eventually gave way to Victorian workers' cottages and abandoned playgrounds, she relished the occasional sound of the riverboats cutting through narrow alleyways that led down to the water in this familiar corner of east London.

As the traffic moved in fits and starts along the main road, she blew into her hands, her thoughts moving between where she was going and the morning she had already had.

It was the first day of term and Judy had dropped Francesca off at school on her way to Marylebone. Her daughter had been behaving strangely ever since Laura's family's New Year's Eve party the previous week, and she hoped nothing had happened between Francesca and her friend.

In any case, Judy had almost been pleased by the return to school. It wasn't that she didn't want Francesca around – and what fifteen-year-old girl wasn't a pain in the arse at times, especially having been subjected to so much time with her parents over the Christmas holidays? But on this morning's drive to school she had pushed her mother's buttons in a way that Judy had pointedly refused to rise to, breathing in through her nose and out through her mouth as she waited for the lights to turn green on Euston Road.

'Dad's away tonight, we could watch *Gilmore Girls*?' she had tried again, after twenty-five solid minutes of frosty silence.

'I hate *Gilmore Girls*,' Francesca had responded, without looking up at her mother. As they pulled onto Harley Street, Judy forgot to check her inside mirror and had to brake quickly to avoid an office worker charging past on his bike.

'Since when?' Truthfully, she was secretly pleased that Francesca hated the show too, though she was equally unsure whether she was being genuine or just being wilfully disa-greeable. 'All right,' she continued, when no reply was forthcoming. 'What about *Yes Minister* – it's being repeated. We could hold a vigil for Nigel Hawthorne . . . light candles, maybe say a prayer?'

That was the first time Judy had seen a flicker of a smile from her daughter since the party.

'And chicken tikka from our favourite curry house?' she babbled on, buoyed by the reaction. 'Nice and bland, completely devoid of any vegetable-type substance?'

As they pulled up in front of the school, Francesca had instantly closed up again, and Judy had watched as her child disappeared inside without a backwards glance.

Twenty-five minutes later, the car radio crackled, the turgid tones of Radio 4 giving way to ragga and back again as the stations bled into one another. The Prime Minister's notorious

'Tough on crime and the causes of crime' speech was being discussed in relation to the imminent trial of four youths found guilty of murdering a young black boy in Peckham. Judy sighed. Slapping the dashboard with the palm of her hand, she waited as the radio connection became clear again, the end of the *Today* programme signalling it was nine o'clock.

What kind of world was her daughter growing up in? Not the same one as that poor child, Judy reasoned, leaning out to check the queue of traffic. London was as infinite a city as the number of people who inhabited it. Her daughter's version was one of plenty: a cushioned life that she sometimes worried she had made too cushioned.

But there would be time for adventure and independence – she would insist on that.

For the moment, Judy was happy to give Francesca as wide a berth as she desired. Christ, she had been so grumpy recently. But that was what they said, wasn't it? Fourteen or fifteen. That was when a parent lost their child to the world of adolescence. It was inevitable, and given that it couldn't be prevented, only ridden out, surely the worst thing Judy could do was to play up to it. Besides, she had her own concerns.

Hitting the horn, Judy slipped a tape into the machine as the lights ahead turned red again, any movement from the cars in front grinding to a halt. Rory thought she was mad insisting on driving a car so old that it still possessed a cassette player, but she told him she loved it and this was true, in part. It also suited her to get around in a vehicle that would not draw attention, in certain quarters – also, she didn't want anything nice enough that her husband might be tempted to borrow it. Especially now that things were getting a little more serious.

But she didn't want to think about that yet.

Instead, Judy closed her eyes as Cindy Lauper sang of having fun, and imagined herself back on Main Street. There was no way she could have known then the sequence of events she was about to set off. Or perhaps by then it had already been too late.

In the present, the lights turned green, and Judy pressed her foot on the accelerator.

About bloody time! She couldn't afford to be late.

The shop stood at the end of a mews street off Hatton Garden, a single road lined with jewellers on both sides. Following the curve of the pavement, Judy pressed the buzzer and waited for the tiny woman on the other side to let her in, just as she had seen Jim Doherty do when she'd followed him here the last time he had offered to act on her behalf, for fifteen per cent of the profit.

It had been so easy that Judy could hardly believe she hadn't thought of it earlier. All she'd had to do was wait until she knew he was going to cash in a load, and then follow him.

When the door opened a crack, the shop's proprietor hovered in the doorway, looking Judy up and down through thick-lensed glasses. 'Can I help?'

'You must be Edda. Jim Doherty recommended I speak to you. I have something you might be interested in.'

There was a pause while the slight figure considered the woman before her.

'I'm Judy. My mother was friends with Jim from Portobello . . .'

That much was true.

Was Judy worried about any kickback from Jim? No. Edda would have no reason to mention it to her original client, Judy assured herself. Or, rather, she had chosen to assure herself. She couldn't, after all, afford to let self-doubt kick in. What did it matter to this woman whether or not Jim Doherty got his cut?

Besides, even if Edda did tell, Judy wasn't too concerned about any come-uppance. Jim knew her mother; they were connected through that. And she had plenty on him to make sure that, if she ever went down, he would too.

Sure enough, Edda opened the door, shooing Judy inside and locking it again behind them. 'Come on, come in.' Moving across to the counter, she pulled out a loupe from her pocket and waited. 'So can I see it or what?'

Smiling, Judy reached into her pocket and pulled out a satin pouch, wrapped in a matching navy ribbon. Opening it on the counter, she watched the woman's face as the necklace was revealed, the pearl-shaped emerald and smaller sapphire stones set within a gold solitaire pendant.

'Where did you get this?' Edda asked, looking through the magnifying lens.

Judy shrugged nonchalantly. 'It belonged to a friend.'

The lights were off in the hallway by the time she got home. A tiny puddle of red oil formed at the base of the knotted plastic bag she had collected, as promised, from the Indian takeaway on Kensington Church Street.

'Francesca?'

Flicking the light switch so that the paper lantern overhead dimly illuminated a line of shoes strewn along one wall, she scanned the floor for signs of her daughter's schoolbag and coat, which were usually discarded in a heap at the bottom of the stairs.

Satisfied they weren't there, Judy peered through the door on the right, finding the living room empty, the remote control on the arm of the sofa. Otherwise the house was exactly as she had left it that morning, the answering machine flashing the number zero, confirming that there were no new messages.

Taking the stairs slowly, listening for signs of her daughter in some distant part of the house, Judy called her name again as she reached the first-floor landing, sighing in relief at the sight of the telltale crack of light emanating from under the door.

Knocking once without waiting for an answer, she opened up and found Francesca lying on her bed in her pyjamas, facing the wall, the pages of the book she had been reading lit up with a torch. She turned on the main light and, checking her watch, saw that it was 8.45 p.m. Shit. She'd had no idea it was so late. With Rory away again and with the care home issue, there had been so much to sort out.

'Darling, I'm so sorry,' she said, uselessly. 'What's that you're reading, *Northern Lights*?'

Her daughter didn't answer, but her body language said it all as she pulled the duvet up around herself, and Judy felt a surge of guilt quickly replaced with irritation as she thought of all she had done that day.

'I tried calling. You should answer the phone, I was worried.' Moving towards the bed, Judy took a seat on the corner.

'You said you were coming home early.' Francesca's voice was flat.

'I'm really sorry—' She pressed the palm of her hand against her daughter's forehead but the girl pulled away. 'I've got our curry . . . I'll bring up a couple of plates. We can eat it in here if you like, pretend we're having a teddy bears' picnic, like we used to.'

Francesca stretched the T-shirt she was wearing – one of Judy's old ones, from the Hard Rock Café, which Judy had bought in her first week in New York, decades earlier – over her knees. 'Have you spoken to Laura's mum since the party?'

'No. I should call and say thank you,' Judy replied.

In hindsight, she should have recognised what a strange thing it was for her daughter to say in the context of that conversation. But it didn't register at the time. Why would it? And she had been distracted, thinking of the day she'd had: the drive from school drop-off on Harley Street and east to Hatton Garden before heading north, making it to the care home in Barnet just in time, with the deposit in hand.

She was thinking of how tired she was, of the bath she was about to take; of her own mother's face as she'd left her for the last time in the flat she had lived in for more than forty years. She was thinking about the tickets to the show she was going to book the following day – one ticket for her, and two more for Francesca and Laura.

Judy wasn't looking in the right direction, and she didn't think to press harder to get her daughter to open up; to make her sit with her and eat the takeaway that was growing cold in the bag.

If she had, perhaps everything that followed would have been different.

Instead, Judy simply stood and walked back through the doorway, turning and noticing the trail of red oil from the leaking bag as she looked back at the room and, switching off the main light, saw the space between them turn black.

Francesca

Hérault, Languedoc, July 2002

The last of my GCSEs fell on a Tuesday, by which point Laura
– who had chosen to study art instead of music, and therefore
finished her exams several days earlier – had already left on a
family-only holiday to Mexico.

My mother's eyes had lit up at the mention of where they
would be staying, on the North Yucatán Peninsula before
moving on to an island called Isla Mujeres.

'Ursula!' She laughed out loud and I gave her a look,
wondering if she had been drinking or was reaching the
menopause.

'What, do you know it or something?'

'I knew someone from there, once.' Judy sounded amused.
'She ran a monkey sanctuary. Can you imagine anything
better? In another life, that's where I would have liked to live.
If things had been different . . .'

There was an almost wistful edge to her expression. I rolled
my eyes, returning my attention to the Motorola Flip she and
Dad had bought me for finishing my exams. But there were
no new messages.

Already, I was bored out of my mind, the summer stretching
out before me like an elastic band waiting to snap.

The newspaper my father wrote for had been in touch to say a publisher wanted to make an anthology of his column. This meant him writing an extended foreword on the history and future of the wine industry, for which he needed to spend a month doing the rounds of vineyards in Europe and North America, interviewing growers and distributors. It was work that – much as he made it clear his family would be welcome to tag along – would probably be better off conducted alone.

At least that was what had been decided. With Laura gone, I might actually have enjoyed the adventure of travelling across continents, if anyone had bothered to ask me. Especially given the alternative: a month at the house in France with only my mum for company, and nothing to distract us from all the things I had been unable to say.

The day we arrived in the Languedoc, straight off the back of my final music theory test, the heat prickled my skin as we dragged our suitcases up the external stairs.

The air in the village was thick and dry, but inside the house was always cool. I had hardly been here in years, always finding an excuse not to come. When I looked at the door to Jacques's old place, to the right of the main entrance, I felt a tug of regret that I hadn't seen the old housekeeper before he died. I didn't remember much about him at all except that he had always been kind to me.

'Was there a funeral?' I asked, once we had left our bags in the hall and headed downstairs for a glass of water with ice cubes and slices of a lemon Judy plucked straight from the tree.

'Hmm?' My mother looked up from the kitchen counter, where she was running the tap.

'For Jacques?'

'Last spring, when I came here alone for a week to check up on the place. It was very sweet: most of the village was there. Everyone asked after you.'

When I didn't answer, she continued filling the glasses.

'How's his son – the policeman, what's his name?' I asked, after a while.

'Patrice. I haven't seen him in a while.'

'Dad thinks he's in love with you.'

'What?' Judy laughed as she turned to remove a tray of ice from the freezer, turning it upside down and cracking a few cubes on to the wooden counter. 'That's ridiculous. I hardly know him.'

'Yeah, well, you can think you know someone more than you do.'

The words came out before I could stop them.

Feeling a switch in energy, I watched my mother pause before resuming her work, picking up a single ice cube and holding it in her hand.

'I suppose that's true.' Clearing her throat, she let it drop into the glass. 'He used to come over quite a lot, after his wife died. I think he felt a connection to your father.'

'Because of Caroline?'

'I suppose.'

'Tamara said he felt guilty.' I watched the effect of my words on Judy, checking for her reaction, which was to stop quite still in her tracks.

Clearly, my mother didn't know.

'What do you mean?'

'She said he wasn't there for her when she was sick. That he went away and left her.'

'She said this to you?'

I swallowed. Not exactly.

'When?' Judy plundered on.

'At her house, last year some time. I dunno.'

I wished I hadn't said anything. The truth was, I remembered exactly when it was. A couple of days before Laura's parents' New Year's Eve party. My mother had been out again, doing one of her disappearing acts, and my father and I had gone for tea at the de Burghs' house in Barnes. I was surprised when Dad had asked me not to mention it to Mum but given what I'd heard, and his subsequent mood, I had no desire to argue with him. There was something about the way he had lowered his voice when I'd caught him and Tamara in the hall, my mother's name on her lips, that had made me want to forget the whole event.

Handing me a glass, Judy lifted her own to her lips and drank. 'She died of cancer. I don't know much more than that. Your father doesn't really like to talk about it.' A strange look passed over her face and then she fell silent, briefly, turning her back to me. 'I thought I'd pop into the market later, pick up some supplies for lunch,' she said, changing the subject in that breezy way of hers.

'I think I'll stay here,' I replied, taking my bag with me as I walked up the spiral staircase towards my bedroom.

'Right,' she called out. 'Whatever you like.'

My old bedroom stood on the second floor. As I passed my parents' room, I could still see my mother, lying back on the bed balancing me on her feet, holding on to my arms as if I were an aeroplane. How old would I have been: four or five? It was the same summer I had slipped away unnoticed through the back gate and been found by the local policeman, Jacques's son, wandering along the river and collecting twigs before I crossed the bridge to play Poohsticks. There was a photograph of that day, which had been taken by Patrice not long after he returned me to the house, framed on the mantel-piece. I could picture the image perfectly: my mother's blonde curls scraped away from her face with a scarf, the gardening gloves beside her on the table under the battered parasol where we sat. My dad, next to her, with the sleeves of his shirt rolled up, his parting as always pushed to one side. Between my parents, my younger self grinned at the camera, a heavy dark fringe framing my face, smears of chocolate ice cream streaming down my chin and across my OshKosh dungarees.

The perfect family.

Grinding my teeth, I heard Judy call up from below. 'Are you sure you won't come with me?'

I turned away from my parents' room and moved along the hall.

'I'm sure,' I shouted down in reply, and then headed towards my old bedroom. With the shutters of the windows on each wall open, the room was bright. Perched at the edge of the bed, I waited until I saw my mother through the window, driving away in the old Citroën, rounding the corner and disappearing along the road on the other side of the garden.

When she was out of sight, I stood and went to my suitcase, reaching into the side pocket and pulling out a packet of Camel Lights. Coughing a little as I inhaled, I wandered back down through the house and into the kitchen, pushing open the door to the garden. It was impossible to experience this kind of silence in London, even inside our house, where the sound of nannies shuttling children back and forth along the pavement to the prep school around the corner and the fawning of tourists cutting through from Gloucester Place to Kensington High Street would leak in through the windows.

Finishing my cigarette, I headed back into the kitchen,

drinking a second glass of water from the tap and pocketing a few coins from the table.

My mother didn't believe in air-conditioning and, cool as the inside of the abbey was compared to the outside, it was still uncomfortable at this time of day. Taking off the velour cropped hoodie I had borrowed from Laura, I tied it around my waist.

The kitchen was at ground level but, because of the configuration of the conversion, I had to walk up a flight of steps to get back to the living room. Running my hand along the rail of the banister, I mounted the stairs and turned into the sitting room. Going over to the shelf, I paused a moment before pulling out my mother's favourite novel, *Lady Audley's Secret*, and felt inside for the folded-up newspaper article. Opening it, I let my eyes take in the features of the person staring back at me, along with the headline 'Politician Dies Leaving Wife and Two Young Children'. The single word written in pencil in the top-hand corner. *Father?*

I was sitting in the window in the living room smoking my second cigarette when I heard my mother's car in the street outside, returning from the market.

Tucking the book and its contents into the back of my shorts, obscuring it with the hoodie, I leapt up and cast around for somewhere to stub out the butt. Heading for the open window, I crushed the embers against the external wall just as Judy peered through the doorway.

'What are you up to?' She was holding several carrier bags, a baguette and a lettuce poking out of the basket held over her elbow.

I stared back at her, blankly. 'Nothing. I think I'm going to go for a walk along the river.'

'OK,' she said, and I was briefly relieved that she hadn't spotted me smoking in the frame of the window as she drove up the road. 'Hey, can I have a piece of that gum?'

'Sure.' I offered her a piece of the Wrigley's I had quickly pulled from my pocket to obscure the taste and smell of the smoke.

'Thanks,' she said, looking me in the eye. 'We'll eat at seven. Have fun.'

Francesca

The page of newspaper had been folded, several times, to resemble the shape of a bookmark. Perhaps that was simply what it was, I told myself as I walked along the river, reading the article for what seemed the hundredth time, trying to make sense of any potential significance.

Below the headline, the obituary reported that Cabinet member Henry Porter had died suddenly at his home in London, leaving behind a wife and two grown-up children.

Once again, I looked at the date in the corner. The year was 1983. It was impossible that my mother had been one of the two children mentioned – a boy and a girl, aged 19 and 21, respectively. My mother didn't have a brother. Besides, she was born in 1966 – the numbers didn't add up. She would have been seventeen, not twenty-one.

So why was the word *Father?* scribbled in the corner of the page? The most rational conclusion I could draw was that it might have been a possible answer to a clue in the crossword that she had been trying to solve. It was something I had seen her do countless times, writing out letters and working to rearrange them in order to solve some riddle or another.

Finally satisfied, if a little deflated to accept that it was most

214

likely merely a piece of paper that had been used for years as a page-marker, rather than anything more interesting, I stopped and placed it once again between the pages of the novel. Putting it back in my bag and pulling out a can of iced tea, I noticed the old shepherd's hut in the field, which I recalled from afternoons spent walking along here with my parents, as a child.

As I cracked open the ring-pull, I paused, another sound echoing somewhere in the near distance.

Taking a sip, I heard the noise again, suddenly closer. A gunshot, and then another, clearer this time. Following the sound to its source. I saw the pig farmer in a high-vis vest, a little way away through the clearing. In his right hand he carried a rifle.

'*Qu'est-ce que vous faites?*' I heard myself shouting in school-girl French, anger flushing through me. 'You can't fucking shoot here – there are people walking!'

'*Quoi?*' Seemingly amused, the young man muttered something else I didn't understand as I marched the perimeter of the fence between the common land that ran along the river and the field towards where he stood in front of the stone hut, the door cracked open revealing a row of rifles along the wall.

'*C'est dangereux!*' I shouted, seized with fury once I was close enough to see the amusement on his face.

Laughing, he held the gun towards me. '*Ah, oui?*'

Making a cocking sound with his tongue, he turned and walked away, back towards the hut, leaving me shaking at the edge of the fence.

It was barely six by the time I returned to the house, still shaking, the door slamming behind me with such force that my mother heard it from where she sat in the garden.

'Fran?'

My cheeks burned as I stormed through the kitchen and outside to where she sat.

'Is everything OK?'

'There was a fucking pig farmer, shooting just next to the river, like two metres from where I was sitting. How are they even allowed to do that? I fucking hate these fucking inbreds!'

Pouring herself a glass of wine from the carafe on the table, my mother took a cigarette from the packet and lit it. Frustratingly calm, she smiled. 'You sound just like your father. Don't worry, they know what they're doing.'

'Really? He looked pretty bloody brain-dead to me . . . And he had a hut full of rifles. Anyone could get in there. Kids, anyone . . .'

When my mother didn't answer, I huffed.

'Right. Well, thank you for your concern. I'm going to have a shower before dinner.'

Judy

Hérault, July 2002

Exhaling a line of smoke, Judy watched her daughter reappear in the kitchen at two minutes past seven, her hair freshly washed, skin slightly glowing with cream.

'You look nice.' Judy smiled, taking the plates from the cupboard and placing them on the counter. 'Sorry about earlier. I was being silly. You're right, it's extremely reckless and I'll speak to Patrice. Although you know what they're like about these things. Especially when the complaint comes from those English bastards in the old abbey.'

It was another perfect evening, the sky a still and uninterrupted blue.

Francesca picked up the plates along with the cutlery and followed her mother out to the table, where she had spread a white tablecloth, weighted down by a vase filled with delicate freshly cut flowers.

Judy waited for her daughter to speak and when she didn't they sat in silence, the intermittent sounds of birds calling overhead and the motorbikes passing on the road on the other side of the garden. It was something Francesca had inherited from her mother, the ability to withstand long silences: a stubbornness and self-possession that Judy equally admired and resented.

They ate in silence too, the usual first-night meal of ham and cheese and salad, served with torn pieces of baguette and plenty of butter.

'How was the walk, otherwise?' Judy asked, resigning herself to be the one who broke the impasse.

'Good. I read, mainly.'

'Oh. What were you reading?'

'*Lady Audley's Secret.*'

Francesca held her mother's gaze and Judy stared back at her. 'I love that one.'

'I know you do.' Francesca took another bite and chewed thoughtfully. When she had finished, she continued, 'What do you love about it?'

It was an unexpected question and Judy thought back to her conversations with Mrs Briscoe, the day she'd placed the copy in her hands for the first time.

'It's ahead of its time, for one thing,' Judy said. 'It was written in the 1800s and yet Mary Elizabeth Braddon wrote the character of Lucy Audley in such a way that she could exist now.'

Francesca put down the knife she had been using to cut off another piece of cheese, pursing her lips. 'I suppose so. A beautiful young woman who ingratiates herself into a wealthy widower's life in order to take his money? I suppose it could still happen.'

There was a moment's silence as Judy processed her daughter's interpretation, leaning back in her chair. Placing down her cutlery, she reached for her cigarettes. It was an irritatingly banal assessment, and Judy couldn't keep the disappointment from her voice. 'That's not really what it's about, though.'

'No?'

'Not at all. It's about how society treats people. About what women are forced to do to make a life for themselves.' Judy pulled out a cigarette and lit it, pausing a moment before offering the box to her daughter. 'About what happens to women of a certain social standing when they try to make a better existence for themselves.'

Francesca made a face. 'Why are you offering one to me?'

'If you're going to smoke, I'd rather you do it openly than lie to me about it.'

'Excuse me?' Her daughter looked at Judy with daggers in her eyes. 'You're going to talk to *me* about lying?'

Judy stayed very still, not attempting to push back the curl that had fallen in front of her face. 'I have never lied to you, Francesca.'

'Oh, please.' The girl was shaking.

Wiping her mouth, delicately, Judy continued, her voice perfectly contained. 'There is nothing I won't tell you, if you ask me. Ask me. Anything you like. There is nothing I will keep from you if you don't want me to.'

The silence between them seemed to hum with the million ways in which this might go, but, as Judy searched her daughter's face, Francesca simply looked back at her mother, unblinking.

'Well, if you ever want to ask me anything, you know that you can,' Judy said, finally. Stubbing out her cigarette, she sat forward. 'Actually, you're right. I don't believe Lucy Audley – or Lucy Graham, whatever you want to call her – did what she did just because she had to. I think she chose the life she lived. And that's a wonderful thing that should be celebrated. She put her child first. The people she took from had more than enough. Or do you think she should have gone on living at the mercy of the men in her life, letting everyone else behave immorally because . . . why, exactly? Because it was unbecoming to take what wasn't hers? Even if the man she married – who by the way, was old enough to be her grand-father – seemed quite willing to be deceived?'

'So she didn't even love him?' Francesca's voice was small, the threat of another question lingering just below the surface.

'That's not the point, Fran! She may well have loved him. Why do things always have to be this or that, either or; why can't they ever be both? Maybe she was using him for what she needed in order to survive, *and* she loved him . . .'

Suddenly aware of how loudly she was speaking, Judy stood, her legs uneasy beneath her. For a moment she hovered, picking up their plates. Then, with a lick of her lips, she inhaled.

'I bought figs for dessert. I hope they're still your favourite.'

In the reflection of the patio doors, Judy saw Francesca's eyes following her as she walked away, her legs threatening to buckle.

Inside the kitchen, Judy placed the plates on the counter. Her hands shook as she poured herself a glass of water from the tap. Closing her eyes, she pictured herself and Francesca in this very spot, the year Patrice found her daughter down by the river. The realisation of how close they had come to losing her – of how fragile their lives were – had reignited something in Judy, and she had felt herself physically vibrating with love for her child as they sat pouring water from one colourful plastic cup into another, her daughter's face full of wonder.

Putting down her glass, Judy opened her eyes and turned back to the garden. On her way out, she picked up a bowl of figs and a copy of the *Times* crossword which she had printed that afternoon.

'I'm going to teach you how to do a crossword,' she said as she approached the table, putting the bowl on the side and placing the sheet between them.

Her daughter didn't speak as the evening grew old around them, and Judy scanned through the questions, automatically underlining those that could be solved by anagrams.

'I wonder how Laura and her family are getting on in Mexico?' she said after a while, without looking up. 'We should go there one day. The Yucatán Peninsula – I've always wanted to visit. Apparently there's a road along one stretch where at a certain time of year you hardly see the sky for yellow butter-flies. Isn't that gorgeous? And there's an island.' Judy paused, reaching for the name.

'Yes, you said,' Francesca replied, her tone unreadable.

Unperturbed, Judy continued. Based on all that she had read in the library in Prospect Park, she could picture it: the teal blues and yellows of the painted wooden huts that lined the beach. Butterflies flitting on a gentle breeze. The horizon a stretch of aqua and gold, unimpeded by people or buildings or any of the walls she had built around herself. The future still ahead of her, unmapped.

'Isla Mujeres. The island of women. Doesn't that sound fabulous? One day, I'll take you there. That's a promise.'

Francesca

The double shot of rum Laura and I had nursed on the patio fails to soothe my nerves as I make the drive home from Primrose Hill, through central London.

Hugo is waiting in the front garden, the journalists huddled beside him, as I requested. Turning off the engine, I take a moment to gather myself. The silence that permeates the air as I open the car door and step out onto the street fizzes with anticipation. How do they do it, day in, day out: feeding off other people's misery?

In a strained show of respect, the reporters wait as I lock the car, taking a moment before stepping around to the pavement. One of them snaps as I enter the gate, unable to contain himself any longer. 'Is it true, Francesca, that your mother's a murderer?'

'Enough.' Hugo talks like the lawyer that he is, his voice firm and protective. 'Francesca has said she is going to give a statement – you need to be patient. When she is finished, there will be no questions. And you will be asked to leave the house so that we can try to pick up the pieces of our lives.'

'Thank you.' I squeeze my husband's hand, grateful for his steadying presence. And then I turn to the group of reporters at the bottom of the front steps.

'This morning I was woken to the news that my mother, Judy Harrington, is being accused of murdering my father, Rory Harrington, in the early hours of the morning of the 16th of July 2004. We have heard nothing from the police to confirm this and I have absolutely no reason to believe this is true. As you can imagine, this development is deeply traumatic, and at this time I would request space and privacy as our family comes to terms with what is unfolding.'

My voice hardening, I turn to the camera.

'Judy, if you're watching this: please, come forward. I know you're innocent. We all do. We just need you to . . .'

My words fall away and, as I look at the faces of the journalists, I freeze up.

'Thank you, that's all,' Hugo intervenes as I turn and run up the front steps towards the house, gasping at the hallucination of my father's body splayed across the tiles, my mother's face looming above him.

PART THREE

Judy

The annual International Wine Society gala was planned for mid July, a week after Francesca finished her A levels.

In the short term, the plan was that she would stay here in London enjoying her first summer of freedom and the new flatshare she was due to take up in Hackney, while Judy and Rory headed to France for the event. After that, provided she got the right grades, their daughter would head to Bristol to study law, of all things; talk about children rebelling against their parents. But Judy bit her tongue. At least as a lawyer Francesca would be set to make her own money.

The gala was poor timing. More than anything what Judy wanted was to stay in England in these precious final moments before her baby spread her wings, but Francesca had insisted that she wanted to spend the summer in London, not actually using the word 'alone' but not having to in order for the meaning to be clear.

Judy understood. At seventeen, she had been on the first plane to New York. Besides, while Rory would never insist that she come with him, she sensed that he desperately wanted her to. As treasurer of the Society, it was part of his role to oversee the budget, as well as keeping a copy of the guest list, which he stored, along with the rest of the correspondence relating to the Society, in the drawer of the three-pedestal desk she had bought him when they moved to London, giving one key to him and keeping the other for herself, just in case.

The Saturday before they were due to leave, Rory was in his study, overseeing the final arrangements, when Judy popped her head round the door.

'Fran's upstairs revising. I thought I'd go and get some of those éclairs she likes from Maître Choux. Want anything?'

'No, no.' Rory placed a hand on his waist to indicate his restraint.

He was fifteen years older than Judy, and in his early fifties he remained every bit as handsome as the day they had first met. More so. There was something heartbreakingly honourable about his dedication to the Society that he had inherited. He was loyal to a fault; but quietly so, without ever expecting recognition. It shouldn't have appealed to Judy the way it did, she thought, or perhaps it was precisely because this part of his character was so at odds with her own that she admired this nobility in him.

And yet, thinking this now, Judy was reminded of Francesca's comment the night of their bust-up in France, two years earlier. Judy had never mentioned it, either to her daughter or to Rory. But the memory had surfaced every so often. Why would Tamara have told Francesca that Rory felt guilty about Caroline, that he hadn't been there when she died?

The question was on the tip of Judy's tongue when Rory continued, and she lost her moment.

'I'm just finishing this off.'

He didn't look up and Judy stood there in the doorway, watching him as he kept his attention on his work, this man whom she had accidentally found and completely adored.

'Bugger off, then,' he said, steadily, still without looking up, and Judy smiled, retreating from the room, further comforted by the sound of Francesca at work in the upstairs bedroom, the iPod she had asked for last Christmas playing softly in its dock.

It was hard to believe that this time next week their daughter would be living instead in a flat on the other side of London, no longer a schoolgirl.

By this time next week, everything would have changed.

The thought struck Judy as she opened the front door and stepped out into the perfect July morning. It had all crept up on her, and she felt herself drifting into uncharted territory as she turned the corner towards Kensington High Street and heard a voice call out from a car on the road next to her.

'Hey, Jude.'

Turning, she stopped walking as Jim Doherty leaned over and opened the passenger door of his white Transit.

'Hop in.'

'I can't,' Judy said, wrongfooted by his unexpected appearance near her home, and he grinned.

'Course you can. You live just there.' He pointed back towards her street, his eye flickering.

How the hell did he know where she lived? Though, if she could so easily have followed him unnoticed, who was Judy to think he couldn't repay the favour?

Her stomach turned over.

'Don't worry, we won't be long,' he said brightly, the engine idling in the parking bay as Judy reluctantly climbed inside. 'Judy McVee. Well you're a tricky one to track down. Sorry, Judy *Harrington*.' Before she could reply, he pulled out a newspaper. It was the one Rory wrote for, and in the centre fold of the 'Food and Wine' section there was a photograph of herself and her husband, taken at one of the most recent International Wine Society galas.

Swallowing, Judy spoke. 'What are you doing here, Jim?'

'That's not very nice. I thought you might have missed me. It's been so long since I saw you. I mean, *I've* missed *you!* And I didn't have any way of knowing where you might be. You just vanished on me! Tut tut. But then – you've gotta love the serendipity – the other day I went to see a man about a dog. A lady, actually. Called Edda. And she says – well, it's crazy. She says that she's been visited a few times by a friend of mine. Who? I asked. It wasn't possible, because I never told anyone about Edda. And she takes out the newspaper and points to this picture.'

Judy reached for the page but he held it out of reach.

'No, I think I'll keep this one. It's interesting, actually. Tells us all about you and your husband, and of course your daughter: Francesca, is it? I don't know how I forgot that. And . . .' his face was animated ' . . . it gives the details of the next gala.'

Pulling out her phone, Judy made a show of touching the buttons. 'I'm calling Rory.'

He smiled, making a batting motion with his hand. 'Come on, put it away. We both know you're not going to do that.'

Butterflies fluttered in her stomach as he read the next sentence aloud. '*The dazzling yearly spectacle, which this year takes place in a château in Hérault, sees Society members from around the world come together in their finest jewels and glad rags. Last year's event saw Princess—*'

'Stop', Judy said, already knowing what was coming, reading it in the space between his words. 'No.'

'No what?'

'No, Jim.'

His face hardened. 'Judy. I'm not asking, but I'm also not asking for much. I'm just interested in a couple of details. Just as your husband, over there on Launceston Grove, might be interested in your visits to Edda, and of course our little sojourn to Somerset.'

'You can't prove anything. You've got nothing on me.'

'Oh, come on.' He laughed. 'You know I think highly of you, Jude. Too highly to imagine you would believe that. I tell you what I'm going to do . . . I'm going to take out this map—'

He reached for a piece of paper, printed from the internet, with the details of the venue – the château Rory had helped choose for its atmosphere of seclusion as well as its charm – followed by an aerial shot of the house and the surrounding gardens.

'I just need entrances and exits, that's all. And a copy of the guest list. Not asking much, am I?'

'I won't do it.'

'Yes, you will.' Jim's face hardened. 'Because you don't have a choice.'

Her heartbeat thumped as she made her way back to the house, rounding the corner before leaning back against the wall for support.

Shit.

Reaching into her pocket, she took out her phone and with trembling fingers she pressed Stop on the recording she had activated when she had pretended to call Rory.

Slipping the device back into her pocket, she made her way back to the house.

'What happened to the éclairs?' Rory asked when he saw her in the hall, empty-handed.

'I—' She paused and then walked towards the side table, glancing at the yellow vase as she reached into a drawer and pulled out a ten-pound note. Throwing her hands up to show how daft she was, she waved the money at her husband. 'My purse was empty.'

Kissing him hard on the lips, she smiled before heading back towards the door. 'Second time lucky.'

Judy

Hérault, July 2004

The drive from Montpellier airport to the house took just under two hours, along wide open roads lined with vineyards and deserted farms, long stretches of narrower paths shaded with trees, the sun twinkling through the leaves.

Sitting in silence in the back of the car, Judy kept her eyes on the immediate horizon as the featureless roads turned into smaller lanes, twisting and turning around the side of the mountain.

Francesca had finished her last exam the day before and Judy couldn't get her daughter out of her mind as they made their way towards the house. Part of her wondered whether she should have arranged something for Francesca as Marcia had for Laura, who was off to New York for a year, partly to do work experience on a magazine in a position earned entirely through nepotism. It wasn't as though Rory didn't have connections – he could have got Francesca an internship on the paper he wrote for, or with his publisher, who by this point had scooped up three more of his books.

Reaching a series of pretty crossroads and footbridges, she pictured Laura, off to the same city that she herself had arrived in, at more or less the same age, though in circumstances somewhat different.

When she did, Judy felt largely vindicated in her choice. Of course she knew Francesca was reeling at the idea of her best friend going to New York. And Judy felt for her – of course she did – but she didn't want to be the kind of mother who did things *for* her child. If Esther had taught her one thing, it was that it was no good relying on other people. Not even your own parents – *especially* not your own parents.

Which was precisely why she had also been so opposed to Rory giving Francesca an allowance on top of the rent for the flatshare near Hackney Downs – on the other side of London, as far away as she could get from the house in Kensington.

While Judy respected her daughter for choosing to move out and try on a different life for size, she knew it was a bad idea to keep giving her money; a disincentive to her truly finding her own path. But she hadn't wanted to make her give it up until she was at least settled in the flat.

The car closed in on the village where the main boulevard was drenched in light, and Judy sighed in relief at the familiarity of it all: the garage with stable doors next to the *tabac*, brimming with scooters; the group of men playing *pétanque* on a patch of dry grass.

She let herself imagine that everything was just as it always was.

The day of the gala, Judy spent the afternoon tending to the garden, sitting awhile in her favourite spot under the parasol once the sun beating on her back became too much.

A bead of sweat trickled along her hairline as she looked back at the house, admiring the pale sandstone.

The words of the article chimed through her mind. *The*

dazzling yearly spectacle, which this year takes place in a château in Hérault, sees Society members from around the world come together in their finest jewels and glad rags . . .

She strained to smile at Rory when he looked up from his seat in the kitchen, framed by the window, his hair neatly parted to one side. He waved lightly and then put down his paper and came out to join her, walking slowly along the path, his lightly tanned forearms visible as he rolled up the sleeves of his shirt.

'What are you doing?' she asked, looking up from the bag of compost she was slitting open with a scalpel.

'Helping you shovel some shit.'

Laughing, ruefully, she stood as he picked up a trowel. 'Well, in that case you're going to need a bigger shovel.'

'I'm sorry if I've been preoccupied,' Rory said a while later, re-emerging in the garden where she was admiring the space that she had cleared for the chicken coop they had been mooting as a possibility for somewhere down the line. 'But look, this has to end. Tonight.'

'Sorry?' Looking up at him, she felt the smile waver on her mouth. What did he know? Had Jim Doherty—

'I've been thinking,' he continued, taking a seat beside her and taking her hand, which was dirty with the remnants of the earth she had been digging, despite her gloves. 'Now that you don't have to be in London so much for Francesca, perhaps we could spend more time here.'

'Really?' Judy pushed a lock of hair under her sun hat, relief sparking down her spine. She would love that. Good God, she would love that. 'What's brought this on?'

He exhaled. 'I suppose I've got into bad habits. I mean, does the world really need another book on wine?'

She laughed at the weariness in his tone. 'I'm afraid I can't comment on that, but with all this digging we've definitely earned ourselves a bottle of the good stuff.'

His expression remained focused. 'I think I've been trying to make up for what I did to Caroline.'

With the heat sharpening against her skin, Judy waited. She could feel him treading carefully, as though what he was about to say required cautious navigation.

'I haven't been wholly honest with you. After what happened to my mother, when Caroline became ill I had a sort of breakdown. I struggled to cope—'

'Oh, Rory.' Sighing, she felt a rush of relief. Her heart could hardly keep up, as if her nerves were shot.

'No, please, just listen,' he went on. 'I wasn't there when she died. Or in the weeks beforehand. I went away, I left her and I—'

There was a gulping sound as he sobbed. It was the first time Judy had ever seen him cry, she realised.

'I am so ashamed of that. Caroline was a good woman, and she deserved . . . well, better than me. And she loved the Society, truly. So, after she died, I made a vow to continue her work there. But—' He turned to her. 'I think I went too full-throttle, at the expense of spending more time with you both. I know now that what I need to do is spend time with you. Francesca – I can't believe she's leaving us.' His voice cracked.

'Oh, Rory, she's not leaving us. She's leaving home. It's completely different.'

Even as she said it, Judy knew it was a lie. Their girl was turning into a woman, and it was wonderful and heartbreaking in equal measure.

'Do you think she'll be OK?'

Judy frowned. 'What do you mean?'

'I don't know. I guess as a father I don't have the same intuitive understanding—'

'Oh, bullshit,' Judy interrupted. 'Female intuition is a convenient way of absolving men of responsibility. If a woman understands her child better, my darling, then it's probably because she asks the uncomfortable questions and takes the time to listen to the answers. That's not intuition, that's invest-ment.' Softening, she reached for his hand, knowing too well the irony – or rather the hypocrisy – of her monologue. 'Intuition or not, you are a brilliant father. And I am a bril-liant mother. *Ergo*, our daughter is also brilliant.'

'Well, I can't argue with that. I wouldn't dare.'

Judy laughed, leaning into him. 'Seriously, though. I think everything's going to be fine.'

In that moment, she believed it might.

Judy

Hérault, July 2004

They took the new MG, top down, a gentle breeze blowing curls across Judy's face.

The château where the gala was being held was a twenty-minute drive. Judy wore a black satin dress with spaghetti straps and a short-sleeved mauve jacket, her lips blotted with red lipstick. For the occasion, she had traded in the usual horseshoe pendant for the diamond necklace Rory had bought her for her thirty-eighth birthday. Besides, she no longer needed that private reminder of her victory over Portia. Judy was happy. She knew who she was, and people like Portia Blythedon and Tamara de Burgh weren't going to ruin that. It was the party of the year; everyone understood this was an occasion to wear as many jewels as possible – and Judy didn't want to be the odd one out.

'A penny for them.' Rory looked over from the driver's seat and she met his gaze with a quizzical smile.

'Would you please stop ogling me and focus on the road?' Judy replied. 'I'm not quite ready to die.'

'You look beautiful, Judy.'

'I think I still have compost under my nails.' Placing her hand over his on the gearstick the way she used to, she looked back at the road, the evening sun casting a golden halo over the countryside, and imagined herself on a different highway, in another life.

The château was invisible from the road, until they dipped down into a valley and there it was, beyond high gates cutting across fields of grapes.

The dinner was held in the grand hall, which opened onto typically austere château gardens at the back.

Tamara and Edward de Burgh were the first people Judy saw as they walked in, Tamara dressed in a purple satin dress with an oversized pearl necklace, her diamond engagement ring glistening under a chandelier. At the sight of their arrival, Judy saw the other woman pause, her mouth twitching as her eyes moved from Rory to Judy and back again before they settled.

'Rory.' She spoke coolly, leaning in and air-kissing him on each cheek before pulling away and calling towards the waiter carrying oversized silver platters of Bouzigues oysters. 'I have to deal with something. We'll catch up later.' With a fleeting half-smile of acknowledgement, Tamara moved away from the couple, leaving a frosty air in her wake.

'What's wrong with her?' Judy asked under her breath as Rory turned to Edward, who was just finishing another conversation.

'It's been a while,' the older man said, turning to Rory.

'Too long,' Rory replied.

There was an air of tension between the men, changing shape as Edward moved his attention to Judy. 'You look radiant.'

Taking a glass of champagne from a passing waitress, she heard a clattering sound and turned instinctively towards it. A waiter was piling glasses onto a silver tray and Judy felt her heartbeat slow again as she looked past the guests in their shimmering dresses and dazzling diamonds and, despite herself, found herself picturing the wood at the back of the gardens.

Stay calm.

It had been years since they had been to this particular château and Judy had almost entirely forgotten it until Rory had mentioned it was to be the venue for tonight's special event. For so long, the annual gala had been held at the same house just outside Wellfleet, in the States. And then for a while in Cape Town, South Africa, before moving to Europe a few years ago – a move welcomed by the majority of its members, and by Judy herself. It was one of the châteaux to which they had taken Francesca as a child, pushing their young daughter around the formal gardens in a buggy, bringing a picnic to eat in the wooded area at the back of the estate, which provided shelter and plenty of space in which to get lost.

Dinner was served at 8.45 p.m., with Judy and Rory seated either side of an Australian couple – guests of honour of some sort who had flown in especially for the occasion. Judy seemed to have lost her appetite and she pushed forkfuls of beef medallion around her plate, fixing her face in an expression that she hoped represented vague interest. The man to her right – an investment banker who introduced himself simply as Mark – continued his diatribe on the new wave of natural wine importers who were gaining traction in the US. Her mind flashed to an image of Jim in his lock-up back in London, those long, fine fingers of his drumming the side of his legs as hers did now against the edge of the table.

'Of course, producers not too far from here, in the Loire Valley, have been practising biodynamic production since the 1950s. Despite its name, the process is a highly manipulated one—' Mark rattled on, not waiting for a response.

Nodding on cue, Judy glanced at the face of his Rolex watch and saw that it was 9.05 p.m. Excusing herself, she picked up her handbag and stood, heading across the dining room to the bathroom, catching Tamara's eye as she passed their table.

The bathroom was down a corridor, classical music playing discreetly through hidden speakers as Judy moved into the hall.

It was surely a bluff. Jim had been all talk; he was just ruffling her feathers. She hadn't heard a word from him since he'd accosted her outside her home last week. He had bottled it, or more likely he had never been planning to pull it off in the first place.

Either way, Jim Doherty was nothing to worry about. Feeling ridiculous for having been so panicked, she laughed as she pushed open the door to the bathroom.

And then she heard the scream.

Judy

At that first scream, the chamber orchestra fell silent. The door to the bathroom closed behind her, and then there was nothing, the air in the bathroom humming in the absence of any other sound.

Frozen to the spot, Judy stood, the world seeming to slow down around her. Keeping very still, she waited, straining to hear. But there was nothing. The only sound was the blood pumping in her ears. Had she imagined it?

Catching a glimpse of herself in the mirror, her eyes caught on the diamond necklace around her neck as a gunshot went off.

In the reflection of the glass, she watched herself lurch forward. Turning towards the bathroom door which led out into the hallway, she heard from somewhere beyond a commotion that became less distinct the more she strained to hear it.

Rory.

She couldn't be sure if she had spoken aloud as she stepped forward and pulled the door to the hall carefully open and stepped outside. Peering left, through to the dining room, she saw a section of tables and a guest's leg. Whoever it belonged to sat shaking on the floor.

'Put all your jewellery and watches on the table, and keep your eyes down!'

A silhouette marched past, a balaclava pulled down over the man's head. From his strained orders, he sounded young; in his twenties, perhaps. Sickness rose up in her throat. Jim had not mentioned guns – but then, what had she imagined would happen? Or what had she chosen not to imagine?

Rory.

Moving slowly back towards the dining room, she felt as though she were looking down from somewhere high above, watching herself, hunched over, as she peered around along the hall. And then, with a thump, she fell back into herself, the scene taking horrifying form around her. From her position, through the open doors to the dining room, she could just about make out the end of the table where she had been seated. Mark, the American she had been sitting beside, was crouched under the table reciting words that might have been a prayer as he worked to remove the Rolex from his wrist.

'Please!' a woman's voice cried out.

A sound like a gun being cocked was followed by a Mexican wave of whimpers spreading through the room.

'Shut up. Shut the fuck up! Put the jewellery and watches on the table then get the fuck down!'

Where was he?

Desperately, Judy searched for Rory as she strained to see his end of the table. But it was impossible without shifting herself closer to the door and risking being seen. Distracted by a sudden movement, she watched, as if in slow motion, as the American shuffled himself backwards from his position under the table.

No. He couldn't be . . .

Helpless, Judy watched as his hand reached towards the surface of the table.

Don't be a hero. Don't—

Blinking, she saw Jim's eyes glistening back at her from the driver's seat of his van on the road just around the corner from their family home, the place where Francesca had first toddled across the tiled floor; where she and her daughter called out to each other with offers of tea and reminders of the latest episode of their favourite sitcom about to start on the television.

Her stomach heaved again. The sensation was followed by the sound of a second bullet cracking through the air. It was an unmistakable sound, both strange and familiar at once.

A second bullet. Except, this time, something was different.

Stunned silence was followed, briefly, by a wave of panicked voices.

'They've stabbed him . . . Oh, my God, they've stabbed him!'

Running across the dining room towards the noise, her legs unstable, Judy called out her husband's name.

Mark's head was above the parapet by now, his hand curled around the base of a bottle he must have been intending to use as a weapon, his eyes wide in confusion.

Looking along the table, Judy searched for her husband.

The air in the dining hall was tinged with the acidity of wine and urine. Through tears, Judy made out the shape of two men just beyond the window, running away from the house towards the maze.

'Stay back, stay the fuck back!' one of the men called back towards the château, in English, a pistol held out in front of him.

And there was Rory, below his seat, his knees held up to his chest, his expression shell-shocked as she ran towards him.

'You're OK?' she sobbed as she reached him. Rory didn't respond and she threw her arms around him, holding him to her like a child clinging to a soft toy, as a frenzy of shouting rang out from gardens beyond the dining room that led down to the woods.

If you go down to the woods today . . .

Dry-heaving, Judy pictured Francesca in her buggy, laughing at the light dancing between the leaves as they sang.

Closing her eyes, she pushed the image away.

One, two, three.

When she opened them again, the scene around her played out as if in a dream sequence. Voices bled in from the terrace, followed by a burst of commotion as the scene sped up again.

When Judy stood, she saw the man splayed on the ground outside, past the glass doors. He was stomach-down on the terrace, his neck tilted unnaturally so that one side of his face was touching the earth, the other facing the sky. The balaclava obscured most of his face, but his left eye was visible, as was the kitchen knife sticking out of his back . . .

A young man. Early twenties, maybe. A man, hardly more than a child.

Francesca

London, July 2004

My parents left for France two days before Laura flew to New York to take up the internship a friend of Marcia's had arranged for her, unprompted, at a magazine called NYLON.

Marcia and Paul were due to fly out in a month's time, joining their daughter on the Lower East Side in an apartment owned by a family friend where Laura was staying for the duration of her stay. Given that Hugo was also abroad, working in Africa as part of his degree in international relations, and Johnny hadn't yet managed to get his driving licence, it was agreed that I should be the one to drive Laura to the airport.

I had hardly slept the night before. The sound of my flat-mate in the next room – an Austrian medical student who seemed to bring back a new partner every night – seeping in through the paper-thin walls at least provided some distraction from the circularity of my own thoughts.

With my exams now finished, the rest of my life stretched out in front of me, terrifying in its blankness. As I sat in the car outside the house in Primrose Hill, waiting for Laura to say her final goodbyes before heading to the airport, I leant forward to tune the radio, which was lurching between drum 'n' bass from a pirate station and the Scissor Sisters, and I felt a hand reach in through the open window and touch my arm.

'Fuck's sake!' I cried out, looking up and seeing Laura's boyfriend, Johnny, grinning back at me from the pavement.

'Shit, sorry, I thought you heard me coming.' He held out a placatory hand. 'Sorry.'

We had seen each other intermittently, at Laura and Hugo's, and at occasional house parties, over the past months. But Johnny looked different, having recently had his head shaved; his skin was a golden tan from days spent lying around on the Heath smoking weed.

'What you on?' he asked, his green eyes resting on mine.

Since the brief romance between Johnny and Laura at the New Year's Eve party a few years earlier, which had turned more serious in the past few months now that they were too old for Hugo to object to one of his friends dating his younger sister, I felt uncomfortable around Johnny in a way that I couldn't put a finger on.

'Aren't you saying goodbye to Laura?' I replied, glancing in the wing mirror, aware that she might come out at any moment. It was mid-July, and a line of perspiration was forming along the ridge of my upper lip.

'Yeah, I just did. With Hugo in Africa saving the world, it looks like it's just you and me.'

I laughed, uneasily.

'There's a party later,' Johnny said.

'Right.'

'You coming?'

Lighting a cigarette, I shook my head. 'I'm busy. I've just moved into a new flat in Hackney and I need to sort out some stuff.'

'There you go: the party is down the road. I'll be at the Cat and Mutton at the top of Broadway Market from about eight.'

'Good for you.'

He smiled, tapping the side of the door. 'See you later.'

Francesca

London, July 2004

The Cat and Mutton was already heaving by the time I arrived, some time after nine.

Even then I told myself I wasn't planning to go inside; that I was simply passing, on my evening stroll after the long drive to and from the airport. Giving myself time to decompress after the ordeal of saying goodbye to Laura and moving the first of my things out of the house and across London, alone, given that my parents were already in France.

I was dressed in cut-off denim shorts and an oversized vest top, my Reebok high-tops just like the ones my mum was wearing in a photo of her and my dad in Cape Cod the year they first met. It was a week since I had taken the room in a shared house near Hackney Downs, a part of London so geographically and sociologically removed from the well-heeled part of Kensington where I had grown up that it could almost be another country. Now, enveloped by the delicious chaos of east London – music blasting from car stereos; the smell of weed and barbecues drifting across from London Fields – I felt something shift and the possibility of a new life, a thousand different versions of myself, opening up in front of me.

'Oi oi.'

Johnny was part of a group strewn out across the tarmac, holding a pint in one hand, roll-up in the other. Since moving to England nearly four years earlier, his international school twang had been replaced by a faux-London patois. His preference for hip-hop music had broadened to include indie, drum 'n' bass and electronica. Any trace of his rich-kid Balearic upbringing was unconvincingly disguised with the help of scruffy drainpipe jeans, a white string vest and – tonight – a pair of braces that I worked hard not to comment on.

He didn't make any attempt to move at first; he just lay there beckoning to me, and I hesitated for a split second before walking over to him.

'Yes, Fran. I knew you'd come.'

Sitting up, he draped one arm over my shoulder and squeezed me into him like a long-lost friend, beaming as I sat on the pavement next to him. And I couldn't help but smile back.

Johnny rolled a joint, which we passed back and forth as we strolled arm-in-arm along Broadway Market, cutting onto the canal, feeling as though the city belonged to us.

'Where are we even going?' I asked as we headed north.

'King's Cross. You know that warehouse club that used to be Bagley's? Drum 'n' bass night. It's gonna be waaavey.'

Pulling a quarter-bottle of Glen's vodka from his back pocket, he took a swig and passed it to me. Feeling reckless, I finished it in three gulps, passing the empty bottle back to him; he tossed it to the ground, and both of us jumped back as the glass smashed into hundreds of pieces.

'Oh, my God, what are you doing? People cycle up and down here. And there are ducks—'

'Ducks?' Johnny bent over laughing. 'Oh, my days . . .'

His eyes lit up and he licked his lips, reaching into his pocket and pulling out a tiny plastic baggy filled with crystals. 'Give me your baby finger . . .'

Doing as I was told, I waited hesitantly as he licked the tip.

'There you go. Tonight, Francesca Harrington, is the beginning of the rest of your life. Whoever you were before, leave it here—'

'Shut up, Johnny.' I laughed, pushing him, gently.

'I mean it. All that? It's nothing. This – right now – is all there is.'

Puppeteering my finger into the bag and dabbing the powder, he indicated for me to suck the MDMA off the tip of my skin.

'Right? Now let's go!' he said, laughing as he ran ahead.

I understood exactly why they called it rushing.

As I stood on the cobbles in the queue outside the warehouse, next to a series of old railway arches, I held on to Johnny's arm as if to physically anchor myself to the ground as the MDMA took hold. It was as though my body was a fairground and a ride had taken off inside me without warning – all those pinging synapses, the screams of the thrill-seekers as they tumbled at speed, tilting one way and then the other.

When I tried to make sense of it all later, to piece together the details, I would have no idea how long I had stayed at the club, dancing under the giddying strobe. I would have no idea what time it was when I stumbled out into broad daylight, leaving Johnny there as I wandered back over Goods Way, towards the main road.

I would only remember that it was light, commuters weaving back and forth along the street outside King's Cross station;

streets which seemed to multiply as I crossed the three-lane intersection, registering cars honking somewhere in the distance.

Scrabbling in my pocket for a cigarette as I reached the other side of the road, I would only remember a single clear instant, through the haze. Leaning into the flame of the lighter and catching the headline on the billboard: LONDON MAN DEAD IN FRENCH CHÂTEAU ATTACK.

Judy

Judy took the first flight back to London the day after the gala dinner, telling Rory she wanted to get home to see Francesca.

It was true, in part.

Neither of them had spoken as they drove back to the old abbey, once the police had arrived at the scene and taken statements from the guests. Looking out at the dark roads that led away from the château, Judy had pictured the cordon being set up around the man in the balaclava, his dead eyes seeming to follow her as she accepted a blanket from one of the paramedics, who had noticed how hard she was shaking.

Tamara's face through the crowd, watching her.

Rory had hardly blinked when Judy leant in to kiss him goodbye the following morning.

Willing herself to stay calm as she waited for the plane to take off, she scanned the departures hall nonetheless, part of her expecting police to storm in at any moment and pull her away, kicking and screaming, to the station.

A man was dead. One of three armed robbers. Stabbed by the sous-chef with a kitchen knife seconds after the thief fired a warning shot.

Early twenties, the whispers of the policeman and paramedics had confirmed. He had been heard talking in English in the moments before he fired.

A man was dead, and there was only one person to blame.

Or, in fact, two people.

Francesca

London, July 2004

In a daze, I wandered towards the entrance of King's Cross station, the newspaper headline flashing in front of me as I went. The drugs in my system had drained away and I felt colder than I ever had in my life.

It must have been lunchtime, because a group of girls in school uniforms strutted past, eating chips from paper. The smell of vinegar hit my stomach. The sound of crackheads shouting at one another caused me to raise my hands to cover my ears.

In the shade of the train station, I crouched down against a wall, wrapping my arms around myself, shivering.

The headline, now visible from the front page of the paper stand by the entrance to the tube, goaded me as I forced myself to breathe in and out. Reaching into my pocket, I pulled out my phone, ignoring two missed calls from a number I didn't recognise, scanning through my contacts for the number of the house in France.

Scrolling down to MUM DAD FRANCE, I pressed call and waited while the phone rang. My father answered, his voice grave, and I felt myself cry out in relief.

'Dad! I thought you were dead!'

'Fran? You've heard?'

'It's in the newspaper. Your face was on the cover, in one of the pictures of the Society.' I couldn't be sure if I was making sense; I could hardly be sure of what I had seen, beyond a faded photograph of a table of men and women in evening dress, raising their glasses in a toast. I would only later learn that this photo was from a previous event, which the papers had got hold of and used to illustrate the piece.

'I thought you were dead,' I sobbed again, quietly, oblivious to the looks from strangers who passed.

'Oh, Fran, darling. I am absolutely fine. There was an attempted robbery at the dinner. A chef spotted one of the assailants and . . . he killed him.'

'It says the men had guns . . . That they were English?'

'I don't know.' There was a weariness to my father's voice. 'There were two other men. I believe they were startled, but yes, they were heard to be speaking English. I guess they're tracing this other man, the one who died. But we're OK, your mum and I. Where are you? It sounds—'

'Where's Mum?' There was a shift inside me as I asked, the nature of which I wasn't in the right frame of mind to engage with.

'She's on her way back to London. Fran?'

'Yes.'

'I love you.'

'I love you too, Dad.'

Holding the phone out in front of me after we rang off, I watched the screen go blank, and then the same unrecognised number from those previous missed calls flashed once more. When I answered, my voice sounded as though it belonged to someone else.

'Hello?'

255

'Where the fuck did you go?'

'Johnny?' There was a familiar hint of amusement in his tone that instantly comforted me.

'Fran, where are you? I'll come and find you.'

Judy

Jim was waiting on the towpath between King's Cross and Caledonian Road, his floppy hat and newspaper visible as Judy approached, a cyclist overtaking as she cut left towards the bench.

He was holding a bag in one hand with a sandwich inside, as if he was on a picnic.

Knocking away a piece of glass from a broken vodka bottle, Judy sat as far from him on the bench as she could manage.

Neither of them spoke. It was Jim who eventually broke the impasse.

'This has put me in a very difficult position.'

'What have you done?' Judy was breathless.

A man with a dog passed by along the canal, whistling as he went, and Judy looked away, her whole body bubbling with anger.

'We, Judy. I think you mean what have *we* done.'

'You're completely mad.'

He laughed, as if she had told a silly joke. 'Oh, come on, now, don't be coy. Take some credit.'

'A man *died*.' She looked at him then. 'He had a son, they're saying. A baby.'

'Indeed. And who do you think is facing hot water here? It's a fuck-up.'

He spoke about the young man's death as though he was referring to his luggage being lost in transit, or his car being towed. A nuisance, nothing more.

Trembling, Judy stood. Why had she even come here? Why hadn't she gone straight to the police?

She'd needed to be sure. As if it was ever in question.

'Come on,' Jim said, patting the bench as if she were a child sulking over the wrong flavour of ice cream. 'I didn't take you for a bleeding-heart liberal. The lad was a criminal. He knew what he was doing. He had a gun, for God's sake. But listen, don't be silly. Sit down.'

'I'm going to the police,' Judy said. 'You're not going to get away with this.'

'Oh!' He laughed. 'I see. And what are you going to tell them?'

'The truth.'

'The truth? Ah, yes. Great plan. I'll come with you. It will save them the hassle of arresting us separately. But listen, we do have a problem. Our robbery has ended up costing me very dear. The men, the flights, the weapons. And they didn't come back with anything, thanks to the fuck-up at your end.'

'My end?' She couldn't believe what she was hearing. They could have found out what they wanted to know without her – they hadn't needed Judy to make this happen. This was not her plan or her job. She had simply made it easier for them, pointing out a couple of entrances and exits. And she'd had to, hadn't she? It was that, or put her family in danger.

And yet how did she know that the boy who died hadn't been similarly duped? The thought had come to her in the small hours, as she lay wide awake.

She stood now.

'How's your daughter? Hope she's not too lonely in that flat of hers.'

Jim's words held her there.

'Judy.' He lowered his voice. 'Sit down.'

She waited a moment and he simply sighed.

'Come now,' he said again, and, once she had complied, he continued. 'Now, stop with the amateur dramatics, would you? I'm going to need some cash. It's not a question, and I know it's not a problem for you. I've seen how much your house is worth, you little gold-digger.' He said the words as if it were a private joke between them. 'Chip off the old block, eh?'

He shook his head, amusedly, and Judy imagined taking the plastic from his fingers and pulling it down over his head.

When he spoke again, his voice was still inflected with a hint of amusement. 'Do you want to hear a little story about your mother?' He leant in, enunciating his words. 'She was a whore, just like you.'

The air between them turned cold.

'I don't think I've told you this one before, have I? Some of us went and watched her dance a couple times in the clubs. "Dancing" is a bit of a stretch, if I'm honest. Oh, I'm sure she was good, back in the day, before the accident. Ballet, wasn't it? She used to talk about it a lot after a couple of drinks – which was most of the time, let's be honest. But by the time I knew her, the only thing she could point was her open hands towards the wallet of any man who would throw her a few quid, and then she'd do whatever it took to get it. She must have thought she'd struck gold when she found your father.'

Judy imagined doing it, then, the plastic between her long

fingers; picturing his piggy eyes bulge as she pulled the bag more tightly around his neck, watching the life drain from his body.

'I don't have any money.' Judy spoke clearly, not letting emotion creep into the cracks between the words.

'Well, you better find some. Rough neighbourhood, Hackney. I hope you look after that daughter of yours. It would be a terrible shame if something happened to her.'

'Don't you fucking—'

'Now, now.' Jim held up a placatory hand, making a soothing sound. 'If you don't have the money, I can give you another little job—'

But she was no longer listening. Her eyes were fixed on his hands as he held the plastic bag. Watching him, she felt her mind scanning back to the day they'd stood in his lock-up, just along the canal from where they now sat. Holding the memory in her mind, she scoured the image of the shelf, and there it was. And everything she thought she knew up until that point came tumbling down.

Judy

Her head swimming, Judy walked away from the canal, away from Jim Doherty, and towards the pieces of the jigsaw tumbling into place with the force of a tsunami.

A little way along the canal, the final stragglers were emptying out of the club that stood next to Jim's lock-up, and a stream of people in various states of inebriation spilled past as she made her way north. Somewhere near Camden Town, a tourist boat floated by, slowly cutting a path through the water, and Judy remembered taking Francesca on one similar when she was a little girl, watching her hold out a hand to touch the weeping willow which reached down over the water from the banks.

It was almost an hour later when, still shaking from the conversation with Jim, she stepped off the towpath at Camden Town and took the tube to Barnet, walking the short final distance to the care home.

A two-storey red-brick building, it stood at the end of a residential street framed by small suburban-style lawns, exactly as she had left it the last time she was here, although by now the whole world seemed to have tilted for reasons she momentarily put aside as she stepped into the reception area.

* * *

Her mother had only properly told her about her father once. It was the perfect story, and it made sense of everything. After that, Judy had never asked again, not wanting to think in too much depth about the questions that lay at the edge of what Esther had said: that he had been working in the Cabinet Office at the time they had met; that he was rich and handsome; that he was already married. They had met at the club on Maddox Street where her mother worked as a dancer.

Beyond that, Judy had drawn in the details herself: Piccadilly Circus a blaze of orange and red lights throbbing against a winter sky. The lights that circled the street advertising Cinzano and Coca-Cola.

Judy pictured her mother walking briskly, head held down against the rain, pushing her hands deeper inside the pockets of the red pea coat she had borrowed from the cupboard of her house-share off Fulham Palace Road.

The time, projected onto one of the buildings above a passing number three bus, would have read three minutes past seven as she passed a poster for *Doctor Zhivago*. A little way along, a young couple in white knee-high boots and brown corduroy flares, respectively, waited it out in a doorway until the weather eased. But Esther couldn't wait. She was late for work – Judy was sure she'd mentioned that. A few minutes later and he might have already spotted someone else who took his fancy. Funny how lives are made and lost in a split second.

Judy could almost hear the blaring of horns as she imagined her mother turning onto Maddox Street, a Bentley pulling up on the pavement a few moments later, the passenger winding down the window and noticing the young woman with the poise of a ballerina.

Pulling back a red velvet curtain the colour of blood, she saw Esther stepping onto the empty dance-floor, the Rolling

Stones' '(I Can't Get No) Satisfaction' throbbing through the low-lit room, empty tables discreetly placed around the edges.

As she'd grown older, Judy had found herself under no illusion as to what kind of club The Maddox had been, although she had never asked. She saw her mother undoing the buttons of her coat as she stepped inside, catching her own reflection in the panels of mirror that lined the wall behind the bar. Her image would have appeared slightly altered in each, her kohl eyeliner smudged at the edges.

After that, Judy tried not to imagine in too much detail. He was tall and handsome and rich, and Esther would have recognised him from the newspaper, though she wouldn't have said so. She was discreet, and she knew how to work people, a skill she had learnt on the market where she had run a stall for the past few years, following the car accident that had put paid to her career as a ballerina.

She had simply danced for him that night, and then – when he took a shine to the former ballerina with the soft Scottish lilt – she had done so most nights for the following months.

They had only slept together once – she had been clear on that detail – but once was all it took. When he'd arrived at his office in Westminster one morning and found Esther waiting for him, expectant in every sense, he'd nearly collapsed. He was a family man, Henry Porter had protested. Anything, he said . . . He would give her anything, but she had to leave him alone.

And so she did.

To his credit, Judy's father had kept to his side of the bargain, sending money for rent every month now that Esther could no longer work her two jobs as a nightclub dancer and a market trader. Even if she could have got a babysitter, she would have needed to sleep all day, given that her working hours were 8 p.m. to midday, which was hardly conducive to properly raising a child.

Two children, as it turned out. Twins. A boy with dark red hair, and a girl, with blonde curls and long pianist's fingers.

As she approached the care home, Jim Doherty's face lingering in Judy's memory, she felt a surge of anticipation.

It was late and visiting hours were nearly over, but the nurse on reception must have recognised her emotional state, for she didn't mention the time as she guided her through to the garden where Judy's mother sat, the roses in the garden scenting the air, sickly sweet.

She wore a pale yellow silk dressing gown over her pyjamas. Now in her late sixties, Esther was still too young for this place. And too beautiful.

When Esther looked up at her daughter, Judy imagined her as she had been as a young woman, practising her moves at the barre, her hair pulled back in a bun. When she tried to picture her after that, the vision slipped one way and another.

'Hi, Mum. Do you want to stay out here in the garden or shall we go inside?'

These days, it was impossible to know what state she might be in. Judy remembered the doctor's analogy about the effect of dementia on a person's brain, when Judy had first brought Esther here: how the brain stored memories on a series of shelves; that dementia caused those shelves to rattle so that anything which had been on there before the illness started would be at the back and tend to stay fixed, while everything else was progressively shaken away.

It had always been amazing to Judy what her mother did and did not remember, and she had found this visual explanation helpful, picturing the shelves in the flat in Marylebone, the photograph of Keir at the centre, on a family holiday aged five, holding a rainbow trout at the edge of a loch, grinning ear-to-ear.

Either side of the picture, the old pointe ballet shoes, and an abstract bronze given to Esther by Judy and Keir's father, she'd told them. The one that had formed part of a pair. One for her, the other for him.

'I want to go home. They won't let me go home.' Esther reached for Judy's hand, her expression imploring.

'OK, Mum. Listen to me. We need to talk about my father.'

Francesca

'Oi, you missed the last tunes . . . That was banging.' Johnny sat down beside me on the pavement outside King's Cross station, studying my face. 'You OK?'

Taking the spliff from his hand, I shook my head. His green eyes were clouded with red, his pupils no larger than pinpricks. Despite his distorted appearance, it was a face I knew, one I associated with Laura. When I thought of my friend, I felt a stab of rejection. Why did Laura always get everything, so easily; even things she didn't really want?

Where would she be by now? Already in New York? God it was so cold. Exhaling the smoke in a long line, I struggled to work out how long it had been since I had dropped her at the airport.

'I don't even know what time it is,' I said, leaning into him.

'Time we had another dab,' Johnny said, reaching into his pocket for the last of the drugs.

'You can't do that here!'

Laughing, he licked his finger and dipped it into the bag. 'I'm Johnny B, I can do what the fuck I like.'

Francesca

'As I said, we'll be taking no questions,' Hugo says, slipping effortlessly into professional mode as he follows me back into the house, turning to shield the front door from the group of reporters calling out their requests before closing it firmly behind us.

Walking back upstairs in a daze, I pass Lily's room; the room that was once mine; where my mother read to me as a child, just as she did later to Lily; where I had sat, puzzled after overhearing my father's hushed phone call with Tamara the night we learnt about the burglary at the de Burghs' home in Somerset, in the days after that summer in Mallorca; where I had grinned with pride the night of Laura's parents' New Year's Eve party, more than twenty years ago, so overjoyed that our parents were becoming friends.

Squeezing my eyes shut, I push these thoughts away. I don't want to think about what came later. I don't want to think about any of it, though I know I can only hold the memories at bay for so long.

When I blink, I picture Johnny, his body pressed against mine, my hands pulling at his hair, willing him closer.

Judy

London, July 2004

It was still light when Judy got home, opening a bottle of wine and drinking most of it alone in the garden, seated at the circular wrought-iron table she had bought in Bermondsey market not long after they had moved back to London.

Letting her mind briefly slide back to those days, the scent of the roses carrying on the air, for a moment she felt it was possible to believe everything was still as it had been.

But it wasn't. Everything was fucked, and yet it could be right again. All Judy had to do was tell Rory the truth – or at least part of it.

She would tell him about Esther, and about Keir, the dead brother she could never allow herself to name. About Jim. All of it. Just as he had confided in her about Caroline. They both had their secrets, after all.

If there was one thing she had learnt in those moments in the château when she'd believed Rory's life was in danger, it was that she didn't need a nest egg. She didn't need a Plan B. Plan A was as good as it could get. She had everything she needed: a man she adored and a daughter she loved more than she could ever hope to express. She had everything. And now, with Francesca no longer in school, Judy and Rory were free to go together on the kinds of adventures she had dreamed of in bed when she was a girl; the kinds she'd told the others about in the dorm room at night.

Isla Mujeres would be theirs: the island of women, with the addition of the only man she had ever really wanted. And then from there, who knew? The world was their oyster.

There was nothing to be scared of, except her own lies. She had the power to make it right. It wouldn't be easy, but nothing worth having in life ever was.

She would do it the moment he came home.

It was dark by the time she made her decision, a wave of serene relief flooding over her as she walked back inside, the clock in the kitchen reading nine o'clock.

Picturing her mother asleep in the care home, Rory in bed at the house in France, Judy walked through the hallway.

Looking around, she felt her thoughts move back through shelves of memory.

The sound of Genesis playing in the street outside Aunt Susan's brownstone in South Brooklyn.

Marnie crouched down outside the vineyard in Wellfleet, hammer in hand, her eyes smiling as she looked up at Judy for the first time.

Rory's gaze meeting hers at the party on the Cape.

Finally, Judy's thoughts settled again on the bronze statue in her mother's flat. The one she had been given by Judy's father. The only thing he had ever given her, Esther had told her one night, tears forming in her eyes, breaking down and crying, but saying she didn't know what the girl was talking about, the next time Judy brought it up.

Draining the dregs from her glass as she locked the French doors, Judy made her way upstairs, pouring the rest of the bottle as she went.

In the hall, she paused by the phone and tried Francesca's number, finding herself relieved when the phone went to voicemail. Of all the lies she had ever told, lying to her daughter had always been the hardest.

After leaving a brief message on her voicemail, she considered calling Rory but told herself she didn't because it was too late, and he might already be asleep.

Leaving the empty bottle and glass on the side table next to the phone, Judy headed up.

Despite the tsunami of thoughts, sleep came after a while, and when she awoke it was to a vague awareness of a noise coming from downstairs.

Francesca

It was dark again by the time we got back to his flat, laughing as he scrambled for the keys.

'I swear to God, Fran, it's true, they're actually lizards. Picture Prince Charles's face and tell me I'm not right,' Johnny said as he placed the key in the lock.

Outside, Shoreditch buzzed with life that felt at once reassuring in its immediacy, and distant, as though the people milling around at the junction behind them, and the music spilling from the open windows of cars, were taking place in another world.

When I looked back later, I would tell myself I had only gone back to Johnny's flat to have a line of the coke he had scored in one of the pubs on Caledonian Road before we were thrown out for racking up in the toilets. I had missed a whole night's sleep and was delirious with exhaustion and the chemical rewiring that enabled me somehow to stay upright as I followed him in through the door. I would tell myself I was too high to be alone, that I wasn't thinking straight.

But, whatever the truth was, on the ethics of whether he should have done it or not given my obvious state, the fact was that when he leant in and pulled off my top I didn't even think about trying to stop him. Did Laura's face flash in front of me as I clawed at the boy she had always assumed, like everything else, would naturally be hers?

It was only after the fact, as I lay shaking beside him on the mattress on the floor, that I felt the sly retreat of whatever it was that had emboldened me just minutes earlier.

Pulling myself up to sitting, I didn't look at him as I reached for my clothes, my denim shorts and vest top feeling insubstantial as I pulled them on.

Johnny was leaning over to reach for a Rizla and called after me, just once, as I walked away from him through the bedroom door, picking up a black hoodie and some rolled-up bank notes from the table and stepping out into the night.

Fucking hell, what had I done?

Reaching into my pocket, I stepped out of Johnny's flat onto Shoreditch High Street, pulling out my phone to check the time, my fingers brushing against the bunch of keys.

It was 1.42 a.m. and the voicemail symbol flashed in the corner of the screen. Pausing, I pressed listen, pulling up the hood of Johnny's sweatshirt. The message was from a couple of hours earlier.

Francesca, it's Mum. I'm back in London and I just wondered how you are. Call me when you can, or pop over. I'm going to be on my own here tonight, so . . . There was a pause. *I'm sure you're too busy but I just thought I'd call and say hello. Love you.*

The sound of my mother's voice was a punch to the gut and the tears that had been building fell now, coursing down my cheeks as I walked towards the minicab sign flashing on the other side of the road.

Finally, the thoughts I had held at bay since I'd first seen the headline this afternoon ambushed me. Was it possible that Judy had something to do with the robbery? I didn't want to

believe it – a man was dead – but could it really be uncon-
nected? My mother was the best person I knew – could it
really be that she was also a thief and a liar? Two opposing
facts, both possibly true.

Everywhere she went, trouble followed.

That was what Tamara and my father had been talking
about that afternoon not long before the New Year's Eve party
at Laura's. I had gone to the loo and they hadn't known I was
listening, as Tamara raged at Rory, swearing blind that it was
his wife who was behind the robbery at their home in Somerset.
Tamara accusing my father of marrying a liar and a phoney.
Telling him that he'd jumped in with any old whore because
he was so guilty about not being there for Caroline when she
was sick, for leaving her to die alone.

I pulled the hoodie tightly around me, a car honking its
horn as it screeched past. I thought I might be sick.

It made no sense that I should travel across London instead
of heading to my place on Hackney Downs, just a few
minutes down the road, except that I couldn't live like this
any longer.

I was an adult now. I had my own flat, my own life. I
needed to know the truth, and I knew that Judy would tell
me if I asked. Just as she had baited me to ask that time in
France as we sat across from one another in the garden, using
Lady Audley's Secret as a false pretext as we spoke in riddles.

Besides, I wanted my mother. Any animosity I harboured
towards her paled into insignificance compared to the need
to be home; to be safe.

Emboldened by the thought of us having it out, clearing
the fog that had taken hold between us, there was no hesita-
tion as I walked into the cabin and asked the man behind
the glass window if I could have a car to take me south.

I still had my old house keys; I could slip into my old bed and have a few hours' sleep before my mother even woke up.

'What's your name? I'll call you when . . . Actually there he is, pulling up on the other side of the road. The silver Vauxhall.'

I nodded in thanks.

Yes, in the morning we would talk. Finally I would find the words to ask the questions I had been pushing away for so long.

For now, I just needed to get the taxi to take me as close to my parents' home as it could with the twenty-five pounds I had taken from Johnny's table. And then I could rest.

The rolled-up notes only got me as far as Hyde Park.

The air was fresh against my cheeks as I got out of the car and made the final leg of the journey on foot, my exhaustion turning to relief as I spotted my parents' house still in darkness. I reached into my pocket for the keys, opening the front gate. And it was then that I heard the shouting.

Judy

There was the sound again as Judy moved out of the bedroom and into the hallway. The house was plunged in the kind of darkness that was rare to witness in summer.

With her biological clock speeding towards the menopause, she often found herself waking in the night, unable to draw herself out of her own thoughts. But generally that happened just before four o'clock when, at this time of year, the birds would be starting their dawn chorus.

Judy hadn't checked the clock before moving out of the bedroom, but all around her the house was silent, and as she reached the top of the stairs she realised the noise was coming from her husband's study.

Rory, she knew, was still in France. It was highly unlikely that Francesca – the only other person with a key – would be letting herself in at this hour. Even if she had decided to come back to her parents' house after a night out on the other side of town from her flatshare, there was no way she would be rooting around in her father's study.

Thinking of Jim and his final words to her before she left him on the towpath the previous day, Judy reached the bottom of the stairs and moved carefully towards the side table where the empty wine bottle from that evening still stood. Circling her fingers around its neck, she moved towards the study door, pausing only for a second before she opened it, the familiar face turning to her so that she froze.

'What are you doing here?'

Rory's demeanour was almost unrecognisable, hunched over the chair in front of his desk. The drawer was open, and papers spilled out over the green leather surface.

'What are you doing here? You didn't tell me you were coming back so soon?' Judy asked again but still her presence didn't seem to register. The room was partially lit by the lamp beside the door, casting Rory half in shadow.

'You bought me this desk, didn't you?' he said, without looking up. From his slurring it was clear he had been drinking.

'You scared me to death . . . What are you—'

'I don't know why I bother keeping it locked; it's not like there's anything worth stealing in here,' he said, thoughtfully, and then laughed in a way that caused Judy's fingers to tense around the neck of the bottle in her hand. 'Not that it matters. You have a spare key, I imagine.'

'Rory, what's going on?'

Grimacing, he stood, using a hand to steady himself. 'You know, the French police came back after you left. They seem to think this "botched robbery" as people are calling it was planned with the help of someone on the inside.' He paused, looking up at her finally, and she saw that his eyes were rimmed with red. 'Someone who knew the area and could give a tip-off on how to arrive and escape unnoticed.'

'Well, that's—'

'Tamara thinks it's you.' Taking a step from behind the desk, he chuckled. 'She was quite jubilant, actually. You know, she rather has it in for you. She thinks it was you who was behind the theft at her place in Somerset.'

'Rory, you're clearly drunk . . .' Shaking, Judy reached for something decisive to say, to defend herself against these accusations, but the ground seemed to move beneath her.

It was all happening too fast. This was nothing like how her confession was supposed to go. She had no control, no time to work out the infinite iterations of how this could possibly play out.

'What's that got to do with anything?' His tone shifted. 'Other stuff, too. She says you stole her scarf.' There was a brief pause as he waited for his wife to respond and then he hooted with laughter. 'You know, that red and green thing you always wear? Always fucking going on about it, she was. She thinks you stole it at that party where we met.'

'Tamara de Burgh is completely fucking mad.' Judy's voice, when she finally found it, was level.

His eyes turned cold then. 'You know, I don't think you ever told me who invited you.'

'What?' Her voice was a whisper and she made no attempt to wipe away the tears that were now rolling down her cheeks.

'The party in Wellfleet, where we first met . . . Who was it? We had a blazing row about it, actually, Tamara and me. You remember, before the party we were supposed to go to at their house on New Year's Eve that time? It's weird – you never even asked why it was cancelled so last-minute. Or why, after that, we hardly saw them again other than at the occasional Society event.'

'They were hardly our close friends. I could barely stand the woman—'

'It was *me* who cancelled, since you still haven't asked. After defending you against Tamara's—'

'Please, Rory. Why are you doing this?'

'What were you even doing on the Cape that summer, Just Judy? You said your father had an interest in wine and then you said you were visiting your aunt. But I don't know who your father was, and I don't know who your aunt was. It turns out I don't know anything about you at all.'

'Stop it.' Judy's voice was little more than a husk. The air felt thick, as though a wall had grown up between them, and she struggled to breathe, unable to reach out to the man she loved.

'What was it like, then, watching your mother die of bone cancer?' he continued, finding his footing. His voice was measured, as though he was thriving on the air she now lacked. 'Which type was it, specifically, by the way? I don't think you ever said. Such a coincidence, that both our mothers should—'

'My father was a con-man! All right?' She shouted the words, almost with relief.

She thought of the previous evening, her mother's fearful face staring back at her in the garden of the care home. *I don't want to talk about your father. I want to go home.* Esther's voice had echoed in her mind as she'd walked away from the garden, back towards the red-brick building, moving through reception with its single vase of plastic flowers and up the mint-green linoleum stairs, turning the key in the lock of her mother's room, that sad little space so devoid of life.

Taking it in, Judy had noted the old wool blanket tucked at the end of the mechanically operated single bed. The shelves, laid out almost exactly as they had been at the flat for all of Judy's childhood: the truth about her own life hiding in plain sight. The framed photo of Keir, the pointe ballet shoes, the postcard of Skye. Amidst it all: the statue, one of two identical bronzes.

Matching the one that she had seen on the shelf in Jim Doherty's lock-up.

'You want to know who my father really was?' Judy cried to Rory, delirious from having finally learnt the truth. The seal was well and truly broken. 'My father was a charlatan. My whole life I thought my father was a politician, but it turns out I had no idea—'

'Well, welcome to the club, Judy, except I still don't know who my *wife* is!' Rory gave a hoot of laughter. 'How's that for top trumps?'

'Stop it. Stop saying that, Rory. You know who I am. I'm Judy. I'm—'

'You're a *liar!*'

Before she could stop herself, Judy threw the bottle. She didn't know if she was aiming at him, or if she just wanted to stop what was happening. But the moment it landed and she heard the smash, everything shifted.

Francesca

'Have you rung Lily?' It's exactly the sort of practical question at which Hugo excels.

'Not yet,' I say, trying not to think of our daughter on the other side of the world. Our daughter – and yes, I will always consider her *ours* – who walks around with her face almost permanently attached to a screen. It won't be long before she sees the news reports and my statement.

Taking a step towards the bay, I look down from our bedroom window at the grey London street, which is finally devoid of journalists. With a sigh of tainted relief, I imagine them already back in their cars or on their phones as they march towards Gloucester Road tube station, pulling together their stories for that evening's deadline.

Turning to Hugo, I hold my arms crossed over my chest. 'Do you think I did the right thing?'

He considers the question a moment before continuing in such a way that I wonder which unanswered questions he is also addressing.

'I think you did the only thing you could. If that's what you really think. That Judy didn't do it,' Hugo responds, in a measured voice.

'She didn't do it.' I turn so that he won't see my lie. 'I don't know what to think.'

'Francesca—'

There are any number of questions he might be preparing to ask me, but I can't face any of them. He understands. Hugo has always known what I need, and been prepared to give it to me, without asking for anything in return.

'Hugo, I can't do this now . . . Please?'

He stays where he is, giving me the space I need, and I picture him the day Laura came home from New York, my excitement at seeing my best friend again spliced with the fact of all that had happened since she had been away.

My mother had given me a lift to the house in Primrose Hill, three-month-old Lily snoozing in the car seat. It was one of the first times I had been out of the house since the funeral, other than our daily walks through Hyde Park after Lily was born. As I'd stood on Laura's doorstep, watching Judy drive away, having promised to come and pick us up again as soon as I was ready, I had felt my heartbeat speed up. There were so many reasons to feel nervous, but the moment the front door opened, and I found Hugo smiling back at me, his skin deeply tanned from his time in Africa as part of his degree in international relations, I had felt calm and child-like again.

'What's her name?' Hugo had asked, taking the car seat from me. Before I could answer, Laura had come running into the hall, screeching with excitement and then hushing herself when she remembered the three-month-old stirring under the constraint of the seatbelt.

That night, Marcia and Paul had hosted a reunion party and, after a glass of Dutch courage, Hugo had confessed then and there that he had always been in love with me. When I saw the way he looked at Lily, I knew that he was the right one.

Not long afterwards, Johnny went into rehab, and, when he came out, he and Laura got together.

Given all that had happened, it was the perfect ending, almost.

'Fran?'

In the present, Hugo's voice draws me out of the memory and I flicker with unease when I see his expression.

Following his gaze to the street through the glass, I place a hand on the window to steady myself as I hear the sound of the gate opening and closing and then I inhale, my breath catching in my lungs as the figure on the path looks up and it all comes flooding back.

Judy

The bottle hit the lamp and smashed, the house descending once more into darkness.

Turning, instinctively, Judy ran out into the hall, fear chasing her along with the sound of Rory's footsteps.

Her husband would never lay a finger on her – she could trust that, couldn't she?

And yet what did she really know any more? She was under threat. Everywhere she looked, the world she had so carefully created was closing in on her.

'You're not leaving. Talk to me! I deserve to know, Judy—' Rory followed her into the hall, grabbing Judy's arm so that they were suddenly facing each other.

'Get off me!' she shouted, not seeing the figure silhouetted in the doorway behind the spot where Rory stood.

Not noticing the open door, or their daughter stepping inside, picking up the vase from the side table.

Keir's vase. The one he had been carrying home from the market – a birthday present for their mother – the day he died.

Not noticing anything until it was too late. Until she heard the crack, and watched her husband drop to the floor, his head ricocheting off the edge of the stairs.

By the time she turned on the light, Francesca was already shaking, kneeling beside her father, her eyes wide with fear. *Oh, my God.* Judy's daughter repeated the words, trance-like, as the realisation of what she had done coursed visibly through her.

Putting her hand on her daughter's shoulder's to steady herself, Judy leant down as if peering at a stranger. Beneath them, Rory's neck was twisted, a small pool of blood appearing from under the side of his head nearest the stairs. There was not even a mark on the left-hand side where the vase had struck. Francesca had barely touched him.

And yet.

'Rory?'

She heard her own voice as if it belonged to someone else as she called his name. Her husband's name. A name she had said so many times, in so many ways. But never like this.

Nothing about this lifeless figure was Rory, her Rory.

Kneeling in front of him, Judy watched her own hand as if it belonged to someone else, trembling as she held it in front of her husband's mouth and felt for his breath on her palm.

Why did she not touch him?

She couldn't. This wasn't Rory. Something very strange had happened. Whoever this person was, she didn't want to touch him. It was horrible, this man in her hallway—

'Mum?'

Francesca's voice sliced through the ringing silence.

The hallway started to spin, the black and white tiles distorted. Sitting back from the body, Judy thought she would vomit.

'Oh, God.'

'Mum.' Her daughter's voice brought her to, again. 'I didn't know Dad was here. I thought . . . No one else was supposed to be here. In your message, you said . . .'

Francesca was shaking, her voice like Judy had never heard it before. She thought of all the times she had comforted her daughter. After the falls from her bike; the time her pet hamster had died; disappointing test results. She thought of all the ways she had heard that voice grow and shift, subtly and entirely, from one thing to something else. From an infant cry to the voice of a young woman. Changing so that it would be unrecognisable except to the person who had known and loved her all her life.

But never before had Judy heard this voice.

'I didn't—'

Judy felt herself regain control. Watching her daughter spiral, she pulled the other way. She had to get herself together. She had to think.

When she looked down, she saw Rory with a sudden clarity. This was Rory, her husband, and he was dead. She heard the noise again: the sound of his head as it hit the corner of the stairs, and then the tiles.

'He was supposed to be in France,' Francesca sobbed.

Christ – Judy's mind skipped back to the message she had left on her daughter's voicemail not long before she went to bed.

Looking at Francesca more closely, Judy saw instantly how high she was.

Her husband was dead and her daughter had killed him. No. Her daughter had hit him because she thought he was an intruder. And he fell, and he hit his head, and he died.

'It's not your fault. Call an ambulance,' Judy said, her practical mind taking over.

But as Francesca stood, she felt her arm move out to grab her. When she spoke again, she was calm and efficient, the initial fight or flight mode settling into something else, something more cautious. More measured. 'Wait. It's too late. Don't—'

'But—'

Forcing herself to sit forward and feel for her husband's pulse, Judy said it again.

'Don't call anyone. Just wait, please . . .'

Thinking ahead as if it were a chess game, Judy tried to imagine what would happen next, picturing the police arriving at the scene; her daughter, high on drugs, her fingerprints all over the vase that had struck her father. The vase that had been bought by her brother. The only other person Judy had ever loved as much as she had Rory and Francesca. Her brother who was dead. Her husband who was dead. She would not lose her daughter. She would not.

They would simply explain that it was an accident, she silently reasoned. A horrific accident. They could say he tripped. Except for the shouting – how could they explain that? And the nature of the fall? Any pathologist would work out that he had been struck first. Even if the blow from the vase hadn't killed him, it had led to his death.

The police would accept that it was self-defence, wouldn't they? Or perceived self-defence by a young woman high on drugs. Francesca would be charged with manslaughter at worst. And yet, still, Francesca was not even quite eighteen – she couldn't manage a stint in jail, no matter how lenient. She was high as a kite. If she got the wrong judge and was made an example of—

The solution was obvious. Judy would take the blame. Of course she would. Any mother would. And yet, could Francesca really survive without either of her parents; one of them dead, the other in jail? It was unthinkable. But what was the alternative?

There would be countless traces of DNA, of course. Judy had seen a programme on it recently, a documentary on how fifty-year-old traces had provided a break in the case of a serial killer from the 1960s. A tiny amount was all that was needed. In this case, a cushion found at one of the crime scenes had provided a close Y-chromosome DNA match to a family member of the suspected killer. It was estimated that the half-life of DNA is just over five hundred years, so in ideal conditions it would last almost seven million years. That fact had blown her mind. Not least because of the questions she still had over her own paternity.

The problem with DNA matching was making a call when genes were too close to match. Like with Keir and herself, she had thought at the time. Except that in their case they were male and female, and DNA mapping would show that.

Two members of the same immediate family: two sisters, or two brothers, would be too close to call. Likewise, a mother and daughter.

Or a father and son.

Judy stood up now, the thought already formed in her mind. As if it had been there waiting for her, all along.

'Francesca, you need to listen to me. You can't be here. The state of you . . . If the police come here now and see you . . .'

'No . . .' Francesca shook her head but Judy took a step towards her and cupped her face in her hands.

'Darling, listen to me. Does anyone know that you came here?'

She shook her head. Her teeth were chattering.

'Right. I need you to go, right now. You need to keep your hood up and walk as far as you can away from the flat without being seen, and then you need to flag down a taxi and take it close to your flat but not right outside.' Judy paused. 'Do you have money?'

As she shook her head again, Francesca's face shone pale in the moonlight that sliced through the glass in the doorway. Judy watched her daughter's chocolate-brown eyes widen with fear.

'Here.' Reaching into the drawer under the phone where she kept the emergency stash, Judy handed her daughter three twenty-pound notes. 'You need to get back home, without seeing or talking to anyone. I will call you in the morning, and you will not have been here tonight. Do you understand me?'

Judy

The painting was only twenty-one by twenty-one inches. It had been an engagement present from Rory's father to his mother, an original Picasso sketch. Not exactly priceless, but more than enough, for now.

As she removed it from its place on the wall, Judy pictured the day she and Rory had hung it there, not long after they moved into the house.

Forcing herself to focus, Judy placed the picture in one of the tote bags hanging on the pegs by the door and attended to what needed to be done next.

The vase – a rich yellow colour, hand-painted with red roses – had somehow remained intact, despite the blow. It was the force of the fall, rather than the strike itself, it would be confirmed later, that had killed him.

Picking it up, Judy thought of Rory, working hard to clear her mind of the image of her daughter clinging to the vase, her eyes dropping tears on to her father's lifeless body. Judy moved through the kitchen and into the garden, to do what needed to be done. That was the trick to being a good gambler, after all. You couldn't control the hand you were dealt, and you couldn't always walk away. Sometimes, even when the odds seemed too close to call, you had to take a leap of faith. It was all about weighing up how much you had to lose, and there was no way Judy was going to lose her daughter as well as her husband.

Besides, she had a contingency plan.

It was half an hour later when she opened the door at the back of the garden, avoiding the cameras she knew covered the front of several houses on the street, wearing a navy scarf pulled around her head, hiding her blonde hair. She kept her head down and disappeared into the alley behind the house, weaving through dark residential streets before emerging again at Hyde Park.

Hailing a cab outside the Royal Albert Hall, she sat directly behind the driver so as to best obscure her own face, focusing her eyes towards the window as the car moved north through London, pushing against the image of Rory, alone, on the cold tiled floor.

In the small hours of the morning, the air outside Bagley's warehouse shook with music, and Judy paid the taxi driver before weaving through the crowd, across the cobbles and down into the arches. The familiar smell of damp made her gag, her whole body trembling with the reverberations of the bass from the street above as she walked through to the end of the passageway, leaving the artwork, wrapped in a suitably innocuous plastic bag, outside Jim's lock-up.

The four-word note inside: *Now we're even. J.*

It was less than twenty minutes before she was in another taxi, making her way back west up the Euston Road, getting out at the far end of Gloucester Road and walking the rest of the way home via the quietest streets.

By the time she picked up the receiver in the hallway of the house and dialled 999 it was 3.30 a.m.

'I need an ambulance,' Judy said. 'It's my husband.'

Judy

London, August 2004

The clouds above Brompton Road Cemetery hung like sodden cotton balls as they moved inside the chapel, both dressed in black, their fingers barely touching.

The weight of the organ was softened by a single violin, the familiar bars of Elgar's 'Nimrod' both reassuring and painful as mother and daughter placed one foot in front of the other.

The title was a play on words, Judy remembered with a sad smile, 'Nimrod' referring to the descendant of Ham depicted in Genesis as a mighty hunter.

Moving beneath vast Corinthian columns that supported a circular lead-covered dome, Judy thought of the words she had scanned in the information leaflet as she booked the service for Rory's cremation. *Marigolds were used to symbolise sadness by Victorians who used flowers to convey hidden messages: red roses for I love you; the hyacinth begging for forgiveness.*

Closing her eyes briefly, she pictured her husband at the table in the kitchen in France the day she'd discovered she was pregnant, the crossword laid out on the table in front of him. Judy's surprise at the joy she felt vibrating through her as she stood in the doorway, watching this man she hardly knew reading the clues aloud to himself, moving his glasses down his nose as he scoured the page.

'Nimrod, four letters.'

'Dolt,' she had said as she moved behind him, laughing when he started.

'You almost gave me a heart attack.'

'Well,' she replied, taking her place in front of him. 'I'm afraid you can't die yet. We're going to have a baby to look after.'

Blindsided by a sudden rush of emotion as the music reached its crescendo, Judy walked through the centre aisle, rows of seats laid out on either side. Squeezing her daughter's hand more tightly, she inhaled deeply.

'I don't know if I can do this,' Francesca whispered as they reached the front of the church, her complexion pale from the morning sickness that had begun to take hold.

'Yes, you can.' Judy kept her face fixed forward as she spoke, the organ music coming to a close. 'We have to. Trust me, darling. I will always look after you. No matter what.'

Francesca

From the bedroom window, I watch Detective Joy Brown, accompanied by a second officer, walking up the steps towards our front door.

'I'll get it,' Hugo says.

'It's fine. I'll go.' Inhaling, I steady myself, aware of my palms pressed against the window pane, leaving a print as I pull away and move out into the hall and towards the stairs.

'Have you found her?' Opening the front door, I look from one officer to the other in an effort to understand.

'Francesca, can we come in?'

When Hugo joins me in the doorway, I reach out to him for stability.

'What's going on? Tell me, please.' My voice is almost a whisper.

Detective Brown inhales, the male officer next to her taking off his hat as Hugo leads them through to the sitting room.

'Take a seat,' the detective says, as if this is her home not mine.

The last time we were face to face like this was the time, years ago, when I was interviewed as a 'significant witness' in my father's murder investigation. A younger version of this same woman explained that my interview would be recorded and used as the basis for a witness statement; that, as and when any court case took place, I could be summoned for questioning by the prosecution based on any statement I gave at this point. Though, of course, no court case had ever happened.

'I'm fine as I am,' I say, my eyes not leaving hers; as if with one false move everything will come clattering down. As if it hasn't already.

'Francesca,' the detective continues, 'your mother has gone.'

'She can't be gone,' I repeat, with a laugh as though what she is suggesting is plainly absurd. 'It's ridiculous. She's nearly sixty years old. She's hardly going to be able to outrun a police officer—'

'She had a gun and she—'

'A gun?' I stop them. 'No. That not possible.'

'When the *gendarme* arrived, she shot him and drove off.' The detective exchanges a look with Hugo. 'Perhaps your husband could get us some water?'

'Water?' I repeat.

'Of course.' Hugo squeezes my arm reassuringly before walking into the kitchen and I bristle, the second officer following behind.

Waiting a moment, the detective continues. 'Francesca, there's something else you need to know. The evening before your father died, your mother was involved in the death of another man.'

'What?'

'We have evidence.' Reaching down into her bag, the detective pulls out a file. My eyes remain fixed on her as Hugo walks back into the living room carrying a glass of water in each hand. He hands one to me and the other to her.

She looks tired, I notice, a weariness evident in the hollows of her eyes. I watch her fish her hand into her pocket and pull out a packet of pills, slitting the silver film of the packet with her thumbnail and slipping a couple into her mouth.

The house is so quiet now, it's hard to believe that just hours ago the front porch was buzzing with reporters.

It's hard to believe a lot of things.

'Of course you are well aware that after your father was killed, the finger of suspicion started to fall on your mother,' the detective begins. 'There was never any evidence, so the case remained unsolved. Your mother always insisted it was a bungled robbery – that Rory, having just arrived back from France in the middle of the night, must have caught someone trying to rob the place and they scarpered, grabbing the nearest thing they could, which just happened to be a Picasso.'

There is an air of sarcasm in the detective's voice at that, but she clears it away as she continues, taking a sip of water as the second officer returns.

'We had no way of proving otherwise,' Joy Brown says. 'But of course, there were things that pointed towards an altercation. The smashed wine bottle in the study with your mother's fingerprints on it; the argument the neighbours over-heard taking place in the minutes before the—' Appearing to rearrange her thoughts, she continues, 'Beforehand.'

Taking another drink, Detective Brown gathers herself.

'Then, about a month ago, I received a call from an attorney in the US. He had been working for a client there, he said, who had been funding an ongoing private investigation into a spate of thefts that had taken place in the USA and France over the past twenty or so years. These crimes were connected to members of the International Wine Society, which the investigator – or rather, his client, dated back to the 1980s.'

'What?'

I look at Hugo as he speaks, resenting him for the interruption, and then turn my attention back to the detective.

Putting down her glass, she continues. 'The person his client was gathering evidence against was your mother. The original investigation started years ago, in 2004, not long after your father died, in fact. The person who was payrolling it gave up. She got ill and was distracted, or rather, reading between the lines, her husband made her give it up. Then, a year ago, it was started again.'

'Why so many years later?' Hugo asks, and the detective shrugs.

'The woman died. It was her final wish, according to her husband, for the case to be reopened.'

'Tamara de Burgh,' I say, walking to the bookshelf, taking a packet of cigarettes that Hugo uses the tobacco from to roll his joints, and lighting one without meeting his eye. 'She died from complications relating to her diabetes.'

'This time, the husband brought in someone new, an investigator here in the UK, to squeeze some different angles. And this investigator tracked down a new witness,' the detective continues.

'Let me see that.' Hugo steps forward and takes the bundle from the detective's hands. 'Tamara de Burgh.' Looking at me, he asks, 'As in Tamara and Edward?'

'She was convinced Judy was responsible for the death of your father – I've got it all here,' Detective Brown intervenes, clearly satisfied to finally have both my and Hugo's full attention. 'The investigator was incredibly vigilant, tracing your mother's life all the way back to the moment she arrived in America – New York City, to be precise – in 1983. He spoke to her aunt there who confirmed she had run away in 1985, ending up shortly after, from what this PI put together, in Massachusetts, where she met your father.'

I smoke in silence as the detective continues.

'The transcripts are all there. Interviews with a past employer from a vineyard in Cape Cod who confirms that there were reports of stealing at the establishment while Judy was working there as a receptionist in the summer of 1985, using the name of Porter. Though she never came under suspicion at the time. Too well liked, it seems.'

In the unfurling silence, I move slowly across the room to join Hugo as he continues to scan through the papers.

'There is nothing concrete here. This is all completely circumstantial,' he concludes after a moment, reading snippets aloud from the cover letter.

'*I have evidence implicating Judy Harrington in the death of her husband who, it is my belief, had discovered she was a fraud who had sought to ingratiate herself into high society . . .*

'*A barman in Wellfleet, Cape Cod, attested to the fact that in 1985 Judy came into Mac's Bar on Main Street and asked if she could dispose of a bin bag in the private rubbish stores at the back of his bar. When he looked inside, he saw newspaper cuttings and papers relating to Rory Harrington, whom it is my belief Judy Harrington – née McVee – targeted after reading about the death of his wife, Caroline, and more recently his father . . .*

'*A chancer who acquired a fake persona in order to—*'

Stopping suddenly, Hugo scoffs. 'I'm sorry, but this is ridiculous. It would never stand up in court, even if the CPS—'

'No.' Detective Brown's tone is sharper now. 'This wouldn't, not on its own. Not without some sort of evidence – camera footage, for example, or ideally DNA. That's why we haven't been able to push the case forward sooner.'

I know how badly Joy Brown had wanted to solve this case. If it had been me, I would have felt the same. It was almost too perfect: the smashed bottle with Judy's fingerprints all over the neck – explicable, though, given that my father and my mother had been the ones drinking from it together earlier that evening, by Judy's testimony. And who could argue with that? There had also been the shouting, loud enough that it was later commented on by neighbours when they were asked if they had heard or seen anything suspicious in the run-up to the moment when Rory died. That, too, had been explained away; the raised voices had been part of the tussle with the intruder. No neighbour had directly claimed to have heard a second male voice, but they couldn't swear there wasn't one.

The missing Picasso substantiated my mother's story that she had come down and found her husband like that, her hypothesis being that he must have disturbed a burglar.

And there had never been a murder weapon found. There was nothing, demonstrably, that could link anyone to the crime. Until now.

'There's something else.' Detective Brown pulls out another file. 'Recently, Edward de Burgh got in touch with the family of a British man who was killed at a Wine Society gala in France. He was part of a robbery that went wrong. The widow – who had refused to speak to the PI the first time around – had died by then, and one of the children told the new investigator that after his father was killed a woman had sent them money.

'The child, who recently turned twenty-one, has just inherited his share. He said it was weird. All the accompanying legal notice said was that the anonymous woman who had given him the money was a friend of their dad's and was somehow involved in the robbery in which he had died.'

The end of my cigarette burns dangerously close to my skin, and I turn and drop the butt into the fireplace. I stay there, with my back to the room.

What the hell is happening?

Exhaling, the detective continues in her measured tones. 'The thing is, it's doubly strange because we received this bundle of evidence, and then a few days later we had a tip-off on the location of the Picasso that was taken the night your father was killed. When we visited the person who owned it, we were able to trace it back to a man called Jim Doherty. The same man who was the mutual friend of the robber who died.'

Jim Doherty? I stare, at the unfamiliar name.

The detective puts down her cup. 'And there's a letter for you, Francesca. It's from Judy. It should explain a few things. But you might want to sit down.'

Judy

London, 2014

The morning of Lily's ninth birthday, Judy woke early and took the tube to Covent Garden.

It was a perfectly mild Saturday in April, and she ordered a coffee at one of the outside tables at Ladurée, watching the early morning crowd milling in the piazza. At her feet, in a tall cardboard box tied with ribbon, sat the *macarons* she had picked out in soft pinks and yellows and greens.

Francesca had arranged to take Lily and a few friends to the open-air cinema the following day, but today – her actual birthday – was for Lily's family. This included Hugo's sister Laura and her husband Johnny, as well as Hugo's parents, Marcia and Paul. Given how much time Francesca and Laura had spent together over the years, Judy knew them all well, and had even grown fond of them as the years crept by. But on occasions like this she felt distinctly outnumbered. Marcia's overbearing presence and Paul's sense of his own importance accentuated the absence of her confidant, the person with whom she could privately have rolled her eyes and laughed.

It had been little surprise when, despite Hugo's assurances that they had everything under control, Marcia had insisted on bringing her signature lamb dish, as well as the birthday cake.

Not one for competitive grandparenting, Judy had nominated herself for adult dessert and wine duty. Not least because if she was going to get through this afternoon she would need ample amounts of the latter, ordering a crate of champagne and another of red from Rory's favourite supplier.

She tried not to let herself think of what their lives might look like if Rory had still been alive, but it was hard.

Ten years. Christ.

Immediately, she pushed the thought aside – she was not going to risk blubbing in public. Neither Francesca nor Judy had acknowledged the coming anniversary to one another, but still it was hard not to remember; not to wonder about all that might have been different if Rory was still here.

One thing was for certain: Judy would not still be living in the same house as her daughter and her daughter's boyfriend. Not that she would have changed the arrangement as it had unfolded. Never for a moment had she resented Hugo's gradual insinuation into their lives. Judy adored the man and he, in turn, adored Francesca and Lily, and with Hugo around, the dynamic in the house had improved immeasurably.

Without him there as their daily audience, who knew what might have slipped out. Hugo's presence was a distraction from the memories the house contained.

The waiter passed and Judy signalled for the bill.

'Just the coffee?' he asked.

Smiling in confirmation, she thought how well the arrangement had worked over the years. Hugo was on hand to help lug things around the garden when his mother-not-in-law came home with new chimneystacks and bags of turf. In turn, she was there to act as babysitter or to read bedtime stories to Lily while Francesca and Hugo worked late; Hugo at his Chambers, her daughter at the little firm on Parkway where, to Judy's bafflement, having taken up her legal studies later than originally planned – in London rather than in Bristol – she seemed perfectly content working to help resolve other people's familial spats.

Baffling, but fine by Judy. As long as her daughter was making her own living, without relying financially on someone else, Judy was happy with however Francesca chose to do it.

Her daughter, also now a mother.

Francesca's pregnancy had come as a shock, of course. She was only eighteen years old, with no boyfriend, no job. But somehow it hadn't felt entirely surprising. Given everything else that had just happened, the news when it came had felt like another turn in an uncontrollable series of events. Of course Francesca might have decided to have an abortion and head straight to university, having got the grades she needed – straight As, no less – but she had chosen not to. It had been a relief for them both in a way, once the police had cleared out, to have something to focus on; a way to atone, to pour goodness into the dark chasm that had opened up in the middle of their lives.

And Lily wasn't just good, she was perfect. Unlike Francesca, Judy's granddaughter was fair with curly hair, just like Judy and just like Esther, the great-grandmother the girl would never know.

Francesca had taken most of her looks from her father, but Lily seemed to be almost wholly McVee.

Almost, but not quite.

A one-night stand after a party. That was what Francesca said when Judy had asked who the father was, and she hadn't pressed further. Lily didn't need a father; she had a mother and a grandmother, and no child would ever be more loved.

And then, one day, she had a father, too. Hugo. The dynamics between them all worked well, for a while. Maybe they would have continued to work. But, as Lily grew older, something shifted. Slight enough as to almost be imperceptible, but still Judy felt it at times, like when she came home and found the three of them splayed out in front of a film: Francesca and Hugo on the sofa; Lily curled up on Rory's armchair. Seeing Judy walk in, they would each grin and budge up, making room. But there was never quite enough space. It wasn't resentment that Judy felt, so much as relief. She was no longer needed – though if she ever was, she would always be there.

Enjoying the moment of contentment, reflecting on all she had, enlivened by what she still had to come, Judy smiled as the waiter placed the bill on the table. Taking four pounds in cash from her purse, she left the money on the plate, along with change for a tip.

Picking up the box of *macarons*, she made her way across the piazza towards the tube. The sopranos who had once cried their heartache to one another across the cobbles had been replaced by an electric guitarist singing along to a pre-recorded song by Simply Red. Christ, weren't they all suffering enough already? London had lost something – or perhaps it was she who had changed – though she doubted that. Homes left empty as tax benefits. Chain cafés owned by millionaires. The big guys taking things at every turn. Where was the room for the individual?

Judy resented it, the officiousness and lack of freedom in the city, more and more, the older she got.

Taking a step into the station, she heard a voice behind her. '*Madame!*'

Turning, Judy saw that the voice belonged to the waiter from the café, who was out of breath from running.

Tipping her head enquiringly, she smiled back at him. 'Yes?'

'My colleague just told me – you forgot to pay for the *macarons*.'

Following the direction of his stare, Judy looked at the box in her hand and started. 'Did I? Christ, I'm sorry. I thought I'd – goodness, how embarrassing, I must be losing it.'

The first guests arrived just after two.

'I'll get it,' Judy said when the door knocker sounded, eager for the excuse to leave the kitchen where Francesca, more stressed than the occasion necessitated, was tearing candles out from their packet.

'Laura!' It was hard not to beam at the sight of her daughter's oldest friend in the doorway, her face swollen with the telltale signs of pregnancy. 'Come in, come in! You look magnificent.'

'I look like a frog.' Laura smiled, weakly, kissing Judy on both cheeks and stepping past so that she was faced with Johnny, dressed in tight jeans and Converse, smiling in the sort of over-compensatory manner that suggested he and Laura had been interrupted mid-argument. Even Judy had to admit that the boy had been a knockout in his youth, though time had made him worn at the edges.

His hands were clammy as they shook and Judy nodded politely, not quite feeling the smile she wore as she let him inside.

'Mum, did you get any alcohol-free drinks?' Francesca called out from the kitchen, her wine glass already empty. What was that, her third? It was unusual to see her daughter drink more than a glass, particularly in the daytime, and Judy replied with a pointed calmness serving to accentuate the frenzy in Francesca's tone.

'There's squash.'

'Laura's an adult, she doesn't want Ribena. I told you she was preg—'

'It's fine, I'll have water! Actually, I'm going to make a cup of tea. Does anyone else want one?'

'I'll have one of those,' Johnny said, moving to the fridge and reaching for the bottle of champagne as Francesca reached up and took the tea bags from the cupboard and with the other hand smoothed down her hair.

'Hey!' When Hugo walked in, he was trailed by Lily, beaming in the new birthday dress he had chosen for her at a boutique on the King's Road. The child had her grandmother's colouring, the same loose blonde curls, but there was something distinct about her appearance, too. It was the line of her nose, almost aquiline above bee-stung lips.

Looking between the eyes in the room, Judy paused on Johnny, the unusual green of his, punctuated by pupils like pinpricks. And the same long nose and full mouth.

Taking a large gulp of her drink, Judy felt something like a pinch in her stomach.

When had she realised, for sure, who her granddaughter's biological father was? It was hard to identify the exact moment. The realisation had unfolded in waves.

She had never liked Laura's husband, that much she knew for sure. What was there to like?

Was she shocked? Hardly. Judy hadn't been shocked, or even unimpressed. She just wished Francesca could have talked to her. But everything from around that time was knotted together. To try to pick apart any single strand might lead to their unravelling. They both understood that much.

'Is that the door?' It was Laura who heard the knocking.

'You stay here. I'll get it,' Judy said, taking the moment she needed to gather herself, and moving towards the hall.

'Judy!' Marcia wore a blue kaftan printed with oversized parakeets in bright yellow and green. She held a large box wrapped with a ribbon and a gold birthday bag hung from her tanned wrists, which were stacked with bangles.

As the women kissed each other on the cheek, Judy was engulfed by a mist of heavy perfume, Marcia calling out Lily's name as she made her way inside the house.

'Paul, you look extraordinary.'

Judy smiled to herself as she ushered Laura's father inside. He seemed to become more of a parody with every year that passed, and now wore a white turtleneck with circular tortoiseshell glasses and lace-up suede shoes.

'Everything OK?' he asked, and Judy touched her cheek.

'Hmm? Oh, yes.' Signalling to the casserole dish he was holding, she indicated towards the kitchen. 'Bring that through. We're all in there.'

Marcia was holding court in the centre of the room, cooing as her adopted granddaughter opened the box she had lifted from the gold gift bag.

'I love it,' Lily said, pulling out the Build-a-Bear and hugging it tightly. 'It's the best. And so is this,' she added quickly, spotting Judy in the doorway. 'Grandma Judy gave it to me.'

Her granddaughter held up the necklace she was wearing: a green emerald shining in its new setting alongside a silver horseshoe.

Judy no longer needed the memento. A 'legacy piece', Marcia or Tamara might have called it. Perhaps it was Judy's way of throwing her past into the light and challenging someone to call her on it. Or maybe it was one of her little jokes to herself. Either way, she felt a bit bad now, watching Marcia lean forward and study the necklace, her expression darkening. Not that regret ever got anyone anywhere.

'Gosh. That's – it's beautiful. Funnily enough, I had a stone just like this one. Years ago. In a different setting. It was stole—'

'Now listen,' Judy said, 'I wanted to make a quick toast to say a very, very happy birthday to our beloved Lily. To thank

Francesca and Hugo for being the very best parents a girl could wish to have. And also to make an announcement. I've decided that, at the end of summer, I'm going to move to France, permanently.'

'Mum?' There was a collective murmur and she held up her hand, silencing them all, avoiding her daughter's enquiring gaze. She couldn't let herself be persuaded out of doing the right thing.

'Excuse me, but this is reason to celebrate, not to be sad. I had to wait, to be sure that Hugo was sufficiently brilliant to take up the mantle – after all, I know I've set the bar very high.' Judy's eyes scanned the room then, meeting each face in turn, looking away when her eyes reached Johnny. Her expression softened. 'Seriously – and you know I don't like being too serious – Hugo, I am so grateful for everything you have done for Lily, and for Francesca.' Batting away the ensuing chorus of *ahh*s, she continued. 'And Francesca, you should be congratulated for being the very best mother. You don't need any of us, but we are here nonetheless. And Lily, we love you.'

She was no longer needed – but if the time ever came, Judy would always be there.

When she looked at her daughter, she saw tears streaming down her face. Judy gave her a wink in reassurance. 'To the next chapter.'

After all, there was always room for one more. Surely?

Francesca

London, 17 September 2024, 2.45 p.m.

'I don't understand. None of this makes sense.'

For once today, I'm telling the truth. I have no idea what's happening.

Detective Brown waits a moment before reaching again for the file, this time taking out a couple of photocopies of pages in handwriting I recognise instantly. 'It looks as if she'd been working on it for a while. She must have left it out after you called her and she realised her time was up.'

I picture myself, a few hours ago, dialling the number to the house in France, as she had instructed me to.

'The French police still have the original – they sent a photocopy of what she wrote.'

Queasy, my fingers trembling, I take the printout from the detective's outstretched hand.

Dear Francesca,
Above all else, I want to say that I'm sorry.
While I accept that you will probably hate me for all that I have done – how could you not? – I don't want you to remember me and feel sorry for me. Your anger I can accept, but your pity I cannot.

While I can't expect you to forgive me, I hope in some way you will understand.

I mean it when I say I had a wonderful life – and you were the best thing about it. There are things I regret. Of course there are. But you are not one of them.

It's true when I say that the robbery at the château wasn't my fault. I was blackmailed into being part of it. But a man died, and I accept my role in that. I accept that what follows now is part of a delayed punishment.

Hugo takes a step forward but I hold out an arm to keep him at bay. Tears welling, I struggle to refocus on the page, trying to make sense of what I'm reading.

I'm sorry I couldn't be honest with you about the person I was before I met your father, or how I came to know of him. But things spiralled. Not that I would change it for the world.

I was just nineteen when Rory and I met. I had read about him, you see, in a newspaper clipping: the ultimate bachelor; the single son of the late Montgomery Basil Harrington.

Montgomery Basil Harrington. What a name!

The moment I saw the article about the handsome bereaved orphan son of a millionaire wine mogul, I knew I had my new chapter, my shiny new beginning.

What I hadn't anticipated was that I would fall in love. And I fell hard – of course I did. Your father was the love-liest, kindest man I ever met, and he adored me, which helped. And he was rich! Together we had the kind of life I could only have dreamed of. Except that I didn't want to be solely reliant on someone else – I couldn't be. I know that can be hard for people to understand but I had my mother to look after, and the only piece of advice she ever gave me was to make sure I was never indebted to a man. She had made that mistake and I had seen, first-hand, what it was like. I didn't want to put myself – or you – at risk in that way. I'm not saying I didn't trust your father, but you can never be sure. Especially given where I came from. Besides, I had lied to him from the start. By the time I realised my feelings for him, it was too late. If he'd divorced me, I would have had nothing. I couldn't risk that. I had to plan ahead. I had to safeguard our future, no matter the outcome.

But really, the truth is, I <u>chose</u> the life I led. And I'm sorry if it hurts you to hear this, but it was fun! Most of the time. At least it was, until it wasn't any more.

I don't blame Jim Doherty for what happened to your father, not wholly. Jim was the one who struck the blow, but if I hadn't done business with him in the first place your father would still be alive now.

I look up at the detective, the room seeming to sway around me so that I feel I might be sick.

None of this makes sense. This was not the plan we had made.

She was going to run. She was going to—

A *gun?*

Holding on to the arm of the sofa for stability, I ignore the sound of Hugo calling out to me, again returning my attention to the note.

Jim Doherty is poison. I realise that now. If only I'd seen it then. I blame myself for all of it – I need you to know that.

We first met when I was pregnant with you. He'd worked on the antique markets in Portobello and Bermondsey – for forever, it seemed – and was an old friend of my mother's. He recognised me as Esther's daughter, and the next time I went we had a cup of tea together, which became a regular thing. I liked him and I trusted him. It turned out he was even more of a crook than I was.

We started working together – him organising the bigger jobs and taking a cut of the profit, including the robbery at Tamara's house in Somerset.

The whole nightmare at the château in France, though, was never part of the plan. By then, I was all out. I wanted a normal life, with you and your father. But Jim blackmailed me into being part of it. When it went wrong, he blamed me. That was what really happened the night your father was killed.

Rory had just got back from France. We had been drinking a bottle of wine in the study and he went upstairs to use the loo when there was a knock at the front door. I had left a voicemail on your phone earlier in the evening so I thought it might be you, having heard what had happened at the château and coming to see if we were OK – it had been all over the English news by then.

But, when I answered, it was him. Jim Doherty.

I tried to usher him away before Rory came to see who it was, but Jim pushed himself into the house, saying I owed him money for the job. I told him I didn't have any. I tried to get him out, telling him this was nothing to do with us. He lunged at me and I threw a bottle of wine at him but it hit the lamp instead.

Your father must have heard us arguing because he came downstairs. That's when Jim started laughing, telling me I needed to tell Rory the truth. The whole thing is a blur. One minute we were all shouting at each other, your father not knowing who this man was and grappling to get him out of the house; Jim telling Rory that I was behind the robbery, that I was a fraud. But your father wouldn't believe him. He said he was going to call the police. He went for the phone, and that's when I turned and saw Jim hit him over the head with the vase.

Closing my eyes, I inhale before reading on.

Once it was clear your father was gone, Jim made me help cover it up, threatening to hurt you if I didn't. He took the Picasso sketch in the hall to make it look like a robbery gone wrong, and then he sold the picture, claiming the money would go towards my debt to him for the failed robbery at the château.

These days, with this knowledge, the police should find it easy enough to trace the Picasso.

Somehow this is the hardest thing to write, but it is also the most important: the vase is still buried in the garden at the house on Launceston Grove, under the roses. Jim was wearing gloves the night of the attack so I can't be wholly sure what trace of him will have survived, but I'm hopeful – confident, even – that when it's dug up, they will find Jim Doherty's DNA, along with mine.

There is also enclosed, along with this letter, a USB stick containing a digital recording I made years earlier on my phone, of the conversation in which he attempts to blackmail me to be part of the château robbery in which Peter Ellis died. So you see, I am to blame, in part, along with Jim Doherty, for the death of two men.

I wish I could have told you this face to face. I wish I could have lived to look you in the eye. But I'm a coward.

There is a lot I could put up with in life, but I cannot abide the possibility of being trapped. In your mind, picture me at peace, at last; the wind in my hair, the sun kissing my cheeks.

Picture the blue sky and the golden sand, and me like a butterfly floating free in the wind.

Mum

'What is this?' My tone is one of baffled outrage, but of course I know what this is.

A suicide note. How could I not have seen this coming?

'At this stage, we don't know. If she intended to run off, then can you think of anywhere your mother might have gone?'

Detective Brown's voice breaks through my thoughts and I exhale, genuinely dumbfounded. The shock has numbed me so that I cannot be sure whether the tears on my cheeks are fresh.

A butterfly? Is she fucking *mad*? What did she think this was: a game? A fairytale? Immediately, I know this is the answer. She has cast herself as the anti-hero in the story of her own life, while spinning me a different yarn.

'And they're saying she shot someone?' I manage.

How can this be? And yet, what had I expected? It is almost laughable that I had trusted her. That I had allowed myself to believe that she could cause enough of a distraction that she could somehow escape and then reappear again once the coast was clear.

How could I have let myself think that this might have some sort of happy ending?

Because I wanted to believe – and because Judy is good at this. It is what she does, and I have fallen for it, just as she knew I would.

'A policeman – he died on the scene.'

I heave, and Hugo runs to put an arm round me.

For once, I had believed her; I had trusted that my mother was being honest with me, that I had understood the plan, that I was part of it. Now it turns out I understood nothing. My mother has *killed*—

'We haven't been to the house in France for a while. A long while, actually,' Hugo says. 'I don't understand where she would get a gun. It doesn't make sense—'

'According to French police, the gun was similar to those used by local pig farmers who hunt nearby. It's possible that she sourced one through them.'

Picturing the man in high-vis, the stone shed behind him with the rifles inside, I almost laugh, despite myself. But no laughter comes. Instead my voice is distant.

'A policeman?' I say. Everything is landing in parts, my brain struggling to process all that is happening. My mother is not a killer, that much I know. Don't I?

Hugo takes my hand.

'I'm so sorry. I know this is hard, but I need you to think,' the detective says. 'Is there anyone your mother could have turned to for help?'

Judy

Hérault, August 2024

She was sitting in her favourite spot on the front terrace of the old abbey when the phone rang.

Judy's legs no longer moved as quickly as they used to, and she sighed as she made her way through the hall, the tattered cover of the book she was reading still pressed between her fingers.

There had been the odd cold call of late, which, here on the perimeter of the village that Judy cherished for its sense of seclusion, somehow felt like even more of an intrusion than it had in London, almost like an unbidden arm reaching in from the outside world.

For a moment she hoped it might be Lily but remembering her granddaughter was in Thailand, Judy felt a pang of disappointment, followed by a thrill at the thought of the girl out there having new adventures.

'Hello?'

At first, she didn't even recognise the voice. How long had it been since she had last heard it – forty years? And then the penny dropped.

New York City.

The flutter of snow outside the Rockefeller Center.

Genesis booming from a car stereo on a sunny day.

When she thought of herself then, it was hard to reconcile that figure with the person she had since become.

But people never changed, not really.

'Aunt Susan, is that you?'

'Judy.' Her aunt's voice on the other end of the line was chiselled with age, softer and harder all at once.

It was possible for two seemingly incompatible things to be true, after all. Without paradox, there wouldn't be progress. This was another thing she found herself wanting to shout from the rooftops: did no one remember a time when two people might simply agree to disagree? That someone might be right and wrong; something might be black *and* white and an infinite variety of shades in between?

Thirty-one years older than Judy, her mother's sister sounded old, though Susan's Scottish accent remained as strong as ever, despite the decades spent in the United States.

Of course she was old – they both were, relatively. And Judy was happy with that. Wasn't it Maurice Chevalier who'd said that growing old was a gift when you considered the alternative?

Maurice Chevalier. Christ, she hadn't thought about that man in years.

'Judy, are you there?'

'Sorry, yes. It's good to hear you.' As she said it, she felt herself brace. Why would Aunt Susan be calling Judy at home in France, decades later – to reprimand her for taking off with a few dollar bills from her purse back in 1985? To scold her niece for not calling in the intervening years?

Of course she knew that her mother would have told her only sister that Judy was all right, but that wasn't really the point; she had never felt good about having run off like that. Not that she had dwelt on it much, either.

'Judy, the police have been here. They've been asking questions. Questions about you.'

And then she understood.

She had never believed in fate, not the kind that a person didn't make for themselves, though in a way she wished she did. It would make it all so much easier to accept, to wash one's hands of one's mistakes, if we could simply tell ourselves that our lives weren't all cause and effect. That we weren't somehow in control of – or responsible for – our own destinies.

We all made the choices that we made, and we lived with the consequences. It would be easier for Judy to accept what had happened if she could tell herself a sob story; if what she had had before all this was tragic and dire.

But that wouldn't be true.

It was just that she had wanted something else – something more – and nobody was going to give it to her. It was as Mrs Briscoe had said: if she wanted another life, she had to take it. And that was what she did.

Judy processed Aunt Susan's words, waiting for her to speak again, and then she exhaled, understanding that this was it. The moment she had been half-expecting for more than forty years.

There was nothing left but to decide whether to run or to hold.

It was not long after Judy's seventeenth birthday and she was in her mother's living room, home for the final summer holidays before her last year at school, the day the man she had always believed to be her father had dropped dead.

They were sitting opposite one another at the table, Judy reading her favourite novel while her mother scanned the pages of the newspaper. The moment Judy looked up and saw her mother's face, she knew something was wrong.

'What's happened?' she asked, watching her mother put down her paper and walk into the kitchen, the sound of the freezer door opening followed by the clinking of ice.

When Esther said nothing in reply, Judy stood and, going over to where her mother had been sitting, she picked up the obituary that lay open on the sofa cushion. Quietly pulling out the story about the dead politician, she let the rest of the newspaper fall to the floor, instinctively understanding that this was something she needed to keep.

When Esther walked in again a moment later, she set down her glass on the side counter, picked up the remains of the paper and tossed it into the fire.

'It's your father. He's dead,' she said simply, lighting a match and dropping it into the grate, watching the paper burn.

Stunned, Judy had said nothing in reply, folding the obituary into the size of a bookmark and placing the only remaining evidence of the father she had never met into the pages of *Lady Audley's Secret*.

Weeks later, when it became clear that there would be no more money for school or for rent, that her education had been paid up to the end of the term but then she would have to go and live with her aunt for a while in New York, she felt a sense of liberation.

There was nothing her mother could do to support them; as far as Judy was aware, Esther hadn't even left the flat in over a year. The truth was, Judy had known for a long time that Esther couldn't bear to have her remaining child around even for as long as the summer holidays. Judy's presence brought back such painful memories of Keir that, faced with the prospect of the girl living with her full time, Esther had panicked. And Aunt Susan was the only person who would have her, even if merely out of a sense of duty.

Maybe she should have felt sad, or rejected. But she didn't. Judy felt emboldened, determined to make a life for herself that was better than the one she was leaving behind. Esther didn't have what it took to be a mother. Whatever cards she had been dealt had been torn away again the day her son died in front of her.

But Judy was born to be lucky, she could feel it. She just hadn't had her chance yet; the opportunity hadn't presented itself. Until it did – and then it was up to Judy to play her hand well; to make a life for herself and for her mother.

And if you were going to make a life, Judy reasoned, you might as well make it one worth living.

Judy

At this time of year, the medicinal gardens were empty apart from the odd worker who appeared in flashes through the miniature box-hedge maze, paying little attention to the older woman whiling away an afternoon amidst the blooms.

Hidden off the beaten track, the grounds were divided into specific sections that stood incongruously side by side: statues evoking the Italian Renaissance next to an English cottage at the edge of a wood, giving the impression of being somewhere impossibly beautiful, and nowhere at all.

It was an oasis, even at the height of the school holidays when families descended on the area in droves, flocking to the riverbanks and the châteaux that littered the tourist maps sold in the *tabacs* in town. Judy had only stumbled upon this particular garden the summer she'd first returned to France after Rory died. It had taken almost a year to work up the – what was it? Not courage, as such – to come back to the village that had been so perfectly theirs.

Back then, the garden, discovered quite by chance on one of those directionless drives Judy so loved, had become a sanctuary; a place to sit and reflect, away from the ghosts that still chased her through the house.

As she passed a patio area tiled in Moroccan reds and blues, her mind shunted back to another, more formal garden in the grounds of a château. They said, didn't they, that when the end was hurtling towards us, our life would flash before our eyes. But Judy felt no sudden lurching; she felt things still and crystallise, her thoughts resting on a single day in September, decades ago.

September was her favourite month. One she still thought of as a time for new pencil cases and new beginnings. A time when she would head back to school in Sussex for the start of term – passing the train journey reading library copies of the *Famous Five*, *Treasure Island* and *Robin Hood* as the carriage trundled through the English countryside; practising the coin-vanishing magic trick her mother had taught her, Esther's words echoing in her mind. *It's like a mystery story. The secret is to distract your audience so that they are looking in the wrong direction when the trick takes place.*

It was the same with crosswords, Esther had explained, that autumn day, just before she went back to school. Except with crosswords there were codes, too. There was a logic and a method to how clues were crafted; the secret was to recognise what you were looking for; to balance knowledge with instinct. Once you had sought out the hidden words, and anagrams, it was legitimate to use your gut, to not be frightened to go with what felt right.

Of course, you had to accept that sometimes what felt right would be wrong.

The afternoon had taken on some cloud, which was a relief, as Judy strolled through the gardens, her thoughts returning to the present. Her hands held behind her back, she passed the poplar trees and spotted him on the bench, as arranged: Patrice, seated by a section of echinacea. She came towards him on the path, passing a stone pond with a cherub throwing out a gentle trickle of water from its mouth.

Judy's face broke into an instinctive smile at the sight of her old friend, muscle memory kicking in before the reality of what was about to unfold pulled her back by the throat.

'*Bonjour,*' Judy said as she leant down and kissed him on either cheek. In the mid-afternoon light, his pale skin was tinted with the telltale pallor of a man who was reaching the end of his days. '*Ça va, Patrice?*'

Batting away her look of genuine concern, he replied with a light shrug. '*Comme ci, comme ça.* Shall we walk?'

Standing with a groan, he took her arm and led his old friend along the path with a forced vitality.

'I'm dying, of course.'

'We are all dying, it's the only thing we all have in common,' Judy replied, plainly, and Patrice patted her arm.

'It's true. Life's only certainty, and the greatest unknown. But I—' He made a gesture. 'Well. We've both been shown how life can be snatched away at any time. We use what we have.'

'Yes.'

The last time she had seen Patrice had been the twenty-fifth anniversary memorial of the death of his late wife, which had taken place on the hottest day of 2022, delayed for two years by the global pandemic. Judy had only met Cristal a few times, but Rory and Judy had both been to the original cremation, along with half the village. Patrice was well liked, and so was Cristal.

Her and Patrice's sense of kinship had been heightened by their respective losses. They could count each other as friends, and there weren't too many people Judy could say that of.

That same year, the mercury had hit forty in parts of northern England that you would think from the news reports had never previously seen sunlight. Here in France, fires had raged through the countryside. 'If we don't reduce our use of greenhouse gas by forty-five per cent by 2030 then the world is literally going to go up in flames,' Lily had asserted, seriously, that summer. She was sitting splay-legged on the sofa in the drawing room of the old abbey, her phone resting in its usual spot in the crook of her hand as she spoke, addressing her grandmother as Judy circled the room looking for her handbag. 'Net zero by 2050,' Lily continued. 'That's literally massive.'

'Literally?' Judy repeated, suppressing a smile. Aged seventeen, her granddaughter had mastered that particular tone of lethargy and despair that belonged to a certain breed of London private schoolgirl. With various lockdowns and Francesca's increasingly hectic work schedule, this was the first time Francesca and Lily had visited in two years – Judy's longest time away from the girls since she had moved back, permanently, to Hérault. Judy was struck both by how perfectly teenage Lily had become, and how wholly unchanged.

'It's true. That's only twenty-eight years away—'

'I don't doubt it.' Retrieving her bag from beneath a cushion, Judy pulled out a cigarette from the tin she decanted them into and placed it between her lips.

When she drew it away again, she noticed the smudge of red on the filter and her mind flipped back briefly to another evening, a lifetime ago, the cheap taste of the Max Factor lipstick she had purloined from the department store on Fifth Avenue fresh on her lips.

'You shouldn't smoke,' Lily said. 'Do you have any idea what the tobacco industry is responsible for?'

'I had heard something,' Judy replied, drily, casting about for a lighter. 'If we're all going to be dead soon, we might as well go up in a blaze of glory,' she added, pulling out a matchbook and lighting up before turning to face Lily, her expression becoming more serious. 'I understand what you're saying, and it's admirable to care. But you can't carry the weight of the world on your shoulders. You know? You can only do what you can to be a good "global citizen" or whatever they're calling it these days. It's important that you enjoy your life, too. All this introspection—'

Lily groaned. 'I know, I know. My generation are all narcissists and we're—'

'I've never said that.'

'Yes, you have. Constantly.'

'Well, maybe I have and maybe I had a point. Anyway, you clearly misunderstood what I was actually saying. I'm not averse to selfishness – quite the opposite. It's the *performance* of it all that's so—' Judy sighed in demonstration. 'Exhausting. When did people stop living like no one was watching? Because let me tell you, no one is. Everyone is too busy thinking about themselves. And if they're not – they should be.'

'Hot take, Grandma. You should start your own range of demotivational T-shirts. You'd make a killing.'

In the garden, Patrice stared back at her with milky eyes. 'You look troubled, Judy.'

Smiling sadly, she nodded. 'You could say that. I'm getting wistful in my old age, it's a terrible habit.'

'Can I help?'

And then her expression changed. 'I hope so.'

Francesca

London, August 2024

Kyle, my paralegal, leant up against the doorway of my office, the young man's eyes red-rimmed from lack of sleep, his right leg crossed in front of his left.

Holding the legal bundle in one hand, he scratched his shaven head with the other. Poor boy. The more he tried to look casual, the more I could tell how hard he was trying not to be sick.

There had been a post-work party after yesterday's win that I hadn't been in the mood for, and I could still practically smell the vodka on his breath as I watched him, backing out of the office under the scrutiny of my gaze.

Honestly, I didn't care whether Kyle was hung-over or not, but I did care if he was incapable of working at full pelt. If Kyle was going to be good enough – or, more to the point, any good to me – he was going to have to either clean up his act or get better at dealing with the consequences. When I was his age, I was a college student pulling all-nighters so I could keep up with my coursework, a pre-schooler asleep in the next room.

Intently setting down my pen – the silver Parker Hugo had given me the day I had taken this job – I sat back in my chair to consider Kyle with my full attention. What must he think of me: his boss with the expensive-looking long bob, oversized collar and thin cashmere sweater worn tucked into a pencil skirt? Middle-aged and too loaded to be doing this job, I imagined. Beyond that, he probably thought about me very little at all.

I was preparing to give him the gentle bollocking he deserved when my computer beeped. Spotting Lily's name at the top of my inbox, I felt my spirits lift, and dismissed Kyle with a wave. 'Leave the papers there and go and have a coffee. And brush your teeth. We'll catch up tomorrow.'

Wheeling my chair closer to my desk, my heart beating a little faster, I pictured Lily, her face furrowed with concentration, typing at a pay-per-minute internet café on the Khao San Road.

Was there even still such thing as an internet café in 2024? Admittedly my experience of Bangkok was limited to a few chapters of *The Beach*, which I had read when my daughter was tiny, in lieu of the kind of gap year my more self-entitled peers saw as a rite of passage – and then snippets of the copy of the *Lonely Planet* I had bought the day she announced her trip to southeast Asia, starting in Thailand; the two of us reading up on the places she planned to visit.

Hi! The first hostel on Khao San Road was grossss (actual cockroaches – did you know if you squash them you spread their babies everywhere, wtf?). Found a new one in Chinatown overlooking the water, and we're heading to one of the islands tomorrow. I'll write when I get there. Give Hugo a hug from me . . . Love you. Lx

It was hardly the weekly low-down Lily had promised, but at least it was something. And honestly, what did I expect? Lily was nineteen. She was travelling the world with friends.

Sending her mother a detailed summary of the experience was hardly likely to be top of her list of priorities.

Still, I was thrilled she was getting to do this trip at all. The kind of thing I never had the chance to do. Not that I would have changed that for the world. There were plenty of aspects of my life that I would alter in a heartbeat, but Lily was not one of them.

Re-reading the message, trying to picture the places my daughter mentioned, I was interrupted by a French number I didn't recognise flashing up on my phone.

I answered with a tentative slant to my voice. 'Hello?'

'Fran—'

'Mum, where are you, what's this number?'

'It's a payphone. I need you to meet me.'

My mother's tone made me pause.

'Where?'

'Toulouse. I'll give you an address. Do you have a pen? Don't tell anyone.'

It is impossible, weeks later – knowing what I know now – to say for definite whether I would have said yes, had I fully understood the course of events I would be triggering.

But I didn't.

Francesca

It was a half-hour cycle from Camden Town to the house. There were so many more security cameras in London than there had been when I was growing up. I felt as though I was being followed as I pedalled, faster than usual, along the canal, my feet pushing hard against the treads as I emerged on Lisson Grove, my mind already working through the scant details Judy had provided.

A gust of wind caught me off-guard as I made my way west through the tourists gathered in Hyde Park, and for a fraction of a second I imagined the wheels slipping out from under me, the slightest turn enough to tip me in front of the cars that hurtled past.

Ten minutes later, letting myself in through the front door, I found the house empty as I had expected. Hugo was preparing for a case and would still be at Chambers for hours yet.

Now that Lily was old enough to be spreading her wings, maybe Hugo and I could call time on the farce of our loveless – or at least sexless – marriage. Or maybe we'd bumble along as we always had since the infatuation of our youth had worn off.

For now, in any case, I had more important things on my mind.

Dumping my coat and bag on the kitchen island, I clutched my laptop as I moved towards the fridge and took out a bottle of wine, pouring myself a large glass before turning the radio on low. Slipping off the mid-heeled boots I had settled on as a suitable compromise between stylish and comfortable (soon discovering they were neither) in those first baffling days as a solicitor after years at home looking after Lily, I finally allowed myself to consider, properly, what lay ahead: my past and present hanging precariously in the balance.

Opening my laptop, I typed in the password and waited for the whirring sound to pass before entering the words *train London Toulouse* into the search engine.

From the radio, Rosemary Joshua and Sarah Connolly's rendering of Handel's '*Io t'abbraccio*' drifted through the speakers, and the sound transported me back to the cobbled streets of the Covent Garden piazza; the scent of my mother's perfume as we crossed towards the doll's house boutique on that shopping expedition before my first ever trip to Deià. The summer it all began.

My screensaver was an image taken at that same house, Casa Salas. A photo of me and Hugo with baby Lily in the mid-2000s. We were nineteen and twenty, respectively – both still practically babies ourselves: sun-kissed and relatively care-free.

I focus on the image as I wait for details of the train times to load. Hugo's arms wrapped around my waist, one of his blue eyes appearing half-closed; my own dark, heavy-lashed eyes laughing as I supported the baby in one arm and held the camera aloft with the other hand, turning it around to try to capture all our faces.

Perhaps we really had been in love then. Perhaps we still were, in our own way. Love, like people, changed with time.

As the train times appeared, I bolstered myself, following Judy's instructions, booking a ticket to Toulouse for the next morning.

Judy

Toulouse, August 2024

Judy drove a Ford these days, nothing fancy but something reliable enough to get her from A to B. It took a little over three hours, taking the scenic route so as best to enjoy the Canal du Midi.

As she drove, her mind drifted back through the shelves of memory, resting on an image of Portia Blythedon the day she finally got her revenge.

It had been so easy, sneaking into Harriet's jewellery box and pulling out two necklaces: one encrusted with rubies, which Judy placed under Portia's pillow; the other a tiny horseshoe pendant which she slipped inside the lining of her shoe.

It had been simply to teach her a lesson, really; taking from one mean, spoilt bully and framing another in the process. Weeding out the root, so that all the other flowers could flourish, just as Mrs Briscoe had taught her. And it had felt good. The power Judy had experienced as she watched her nemesis's tear-streaked face looking back at her from the back window of the car as her parents drove her away . . . Judy had felt it again, afresh, every time she sat in the dorm room in the months to come; the other girls gathering round as she told them stories of the multiple versions of the life she had built for herself, uninterrupted by Portia's withering laughter.

Revenge had tasted sweet. Most people were good and bad. But some just needed to be eliminated altogether.

At that thought, Jim Doherty's face appeared in Judy's mind's eye. Touching the horseshoe necklace, she pressed her foot more firmly on the accelerator, the plan already taking form.

Francesca was there waiting when Judy approached the café, moving carefully through the town square towards the parasol under which her daughter sat, half of her face concealed behind sunglasses.

When she looked up, Judy smiled. 'Hello, darling. Should we walk?'

Francesca

Toulouse, August 2024

'How was the journey?' Judy asked.

'Mum, what is this about?' I replied, confused and annoyed by her obliqueness.

'Where did you tell Hugo you were going?'

'Can we stop with the small talk, please?' I reached for one of my mother's cigarettes as we moved across cobbled streets.

'Francesca. What I am about to ask isn't just a matter of protecting you – it's about protecting Lily.'

'Mum—'

'OK, OK. I got a call from my aunt in New York. The police are going to reopen the case against me.'

'What?' Aunt Susan? What the hell did she have to do with this? 'But you were exonerated,' I said, reaching for one of the many questions that fought for precedence.

'No, they couldn't find any evidence. It's different.'

'That's because there wasn't any. Because you didn't—'

'Francesca.' Stopping, she turned to face me, her expression imploring. 'Listen to me. If they keep on looking into this, if they keep digging – what are they going to find?'

We both stopped, the bells of the church above us striking two.

'OK. So what do we do?' I said, lowering my voice to match hers.

'We take control.'

Standing straight, I took the lighter from Judy's extended hand and lit my cigarette. The first drag gave me a head rush.

'They already think I did it. If I can convince them that they're right and get away for a while—' my mother continued.

'Get away where?' I asked, so ready – so desperate – to believe that she had the answer. 'What are you talking about—'

'Look, I have a plan. But you have to trust me.'

And so I did.

Francesca

London, 17 September 2024, 6.45 a.m.

It was almost light when I stepped out of bed, slipping on the grey leggings and running jacket I had laid out the day before.

Hugo didn't stir, gently breathing beside the empty space where I had hardly slept. Air brushed my face as I opened the front door and stepped outside, giving a final glance back at the house.

The streets of Kensington were still largely quiet at this time of morning, and I listened to one of my usual playlists as I ran down Launceston Grove, weaving through residential streets and over a leafy square before emerging onto Kensington High Street.

It was one of the few phone boxes I was able to find within an appropriate distance and out of direct view of a street camera, and the irony that I could see the offices of the *Daily Mail* as I dialled the number of its reception was not lost on me.

'News desk,' the voice at the other end of the line said, defensively. It would be someone at the tail end of the night shift, when the likelihood of someone answering the phone was much higher than in the middle of a busy working day. Just as Judy predicted.

'Hi. I have tip-off for a story.'

'Oh, yeah?' The man at the end of the line sounded ready to hang up, but knew he had to hear me out first, even if, at this time of day, he expected a nutter or someone having a laugh.

'The police are looking into the death of Rory Harrington again, the socialite wine writer. The case was closed after they couldn't find enough evidence, back in 2004. But there's fresh evidence, and his wife Judy Harrington is the prime suspect.'

'That's interesting.' He sounded surprised, and I felt sick at the excitement in his voice. 'Can I ask a couple of questions—'

Before he could say anything further, I hung up, my eyes brimming with tears as I turned and ran towards Hyde Park, pounding the pavement past the Royal Albert Hall, my thoughts tumbling over one another.

It was done. Judy was right, of course. If the police continued to investigate my mother's past, what else would they find? What truths would they uncover? This way, by controlling the flow of information, we could stop them in their tracks.

She had been willing to take the fall, to say that it was her, not me, who accidentally killed my father. I could have told the truth and accepted the consequences, but Judy was convinced she could make this work, and Judy was nothing if not persuasive. If there was one thing she could do, she said, it was to spin a yarn. She could disappear. If Lord Lucan could do it, why couldn't she?

I had to trust her. What choice did I have? It was that or be prepared to spend the rest of my life behind bars.

And I chose to believe – or maybe I just chose to save myself.

* * *

It was just past eight by the time I got back to the house, noting the smell of coffee drifting through the hallway the moment I let myself in.

'Good run?'

Pulling off my trainers, I left them beside the gold-buckled loafers I put there the night before. 'Yeah, good. Just my usual route. I'm going to have a quick shower. What time are you heading in?'

'I haven't got court until this afternoon, so I was going to work here for a while first.'

I smiled back at him as I headed towards the stairs. 'Great.'

'Why did you never tell me Johnny was Lily's father?' Judy had asked, her final question before we parted ways in Toulouse.

I thought for a moment before answering. It had never occurred to me that my mother might have guessed – that she hadn't believed my assertion that the baby was the product of a one-night stand with a stranger. Looking back, how could I expect anything else? She knew me better than I knew myself.

'I didn't want to think about it.'

'Does Hugo know?'

I nodded.

'Laura?'

'God no,' I replied quickly, shuddering at the thought.

'Sometimes we end up carrying secrets just because we've got so used to keeping them,' she said, unusually pensive. 'If I'd been more honest with your father—'

'Mum, stop.'

She did. But she was right. I didn't understand why she had kept so much of her life from us, but I saw, too, that sometimes the things we weren't prepared to share with others said more about us and our insecurities, about our need for control, than it did about the relationships themselves.

Half an hour after I got back from my run, I was doing up the buttons of my cream shirt, the steam from the shower obliterating the view in the mirror, when I heard the doorbell ring, followed shortly by Hugo calling up the stairs.

'Francesca, there's a journalist at the door. I think you should come down.'

The plan was simple, really. To take as much of the truth as we could offer and parcel it into the version of history we wanted to present – and then let the police believe they had pieced together the clues for themselves.

Once Aunt Susan got in touch, Judy had explained, it was clear the police were going to reopen the case – or were likely to. In order to ensure I was never exposed, she was going to put herself in the frame and then run.

It was better, she said, that I knew none of the details. When the time was right, she would get in touch.

The press had to be brought in from the beginning, of course. How else could we trigger the first event that would enable everything else to play out? Once the media knew that the case was being looked at again, their first reaction would be to come to the house and alert me. Then, I would be free to go to the police and demand to be brought in on what they knew. I would make myself an ally, offering up details that would lead them to a conclusion they would believe they'd arrived at themselves.

Telling the press also had the advantage of creating a degree of external pressure for the police to solve the case as quickly as possible, without exploring too many alternatives.

But everything about the plan had been wrong from the moment I had made the call to the old abbey. She was never supposed to answer the phone. By that point, she was supposed to be already on her way to wherever it was she was hiding out. I was supposed to go straight to the police station once her phone went unanswered.

When she picked up, I knew something wasn't right. Immediately, I understood that I was being bent to her will, being made a participant in a game where I had no idea of the rules.

It was only once I saw what she was really doing that I realised why she had kept me out of the loop. She needed my reaction to be genuine. She needed the world to see me give my speech to the press, genuinely baffled. People believed what they saw with their own eyes. And I was never the sort of actor she was.

If she was going to take her own life, then my reaction had to be one of real horror.

The plan had been that she would cause a distraction and run away. But Patrice? The thought of my mother killing anyone, let alone her friend . . .

Bringing in the media was her warped idea of fun; that much I could understand; that aspect of the whole thing was pure Judy. I think that she liked the spectacle of it, that she revelled in the idea of this being her final showpiece: taking centre stage and feeling the eyes of the world looking in the wrong direction as she clicked her fingers and turned her own star to dust.

She would never go to prison. She could never disappear quietly, either.

She loved a good story too much to go out without a bang.

Francesca

London, January 2025

Lily is downstairs in the kitchen, humming along to Cyndi Lauper on the speakers, when I come down to breakfast. Looking up from the counter, she smiles with that same rallying spirit that I know and adore her for.

'Toast?'

'Not yet,' I say, filling the kettle and placing it on its cradle.

'You need to eat, Mum. At your age if you get too skinny you start to look like Skeletor. You have to choose: face or arse, and I say face all the way.' My daughter continues humming music between mouthfuls. 'Post's over there, by the way.'

It is the first postal delivery of the new year. As expected, Christmas has been a strangely quiet affair this year, and I skim through the envelopes as I wait for the kettle to boil, noting Hugo has already left.

Beyond a circular there are two letters of note. The first is neatly typed. One of the generic kinds that one expects after the death of a parent – though given how few friends Judy kept, and the assumptions made by those who knew her, these have been markedly few.

Dear Francesca,
I was so sorry to hear about the death of your mother.
No doubt she will be watching you from wherever she is now.
All my love,

<u>*Julie Masser*</u>

Glancing at the envelope, I note a postmark I don't recognise, the sender either a friend from the village whom I have never met, or someone I have simply forgotten.

So much has shifted, and it's hard to keep track of where my real memories end and the stories my mother told begin.

The second has a north London postal stamp. Inside is a handwritten letter on a thin piece of white paper. As I read on, my stomach tightens.

The care home is further north than Primrose Hill, in a part of London I don't know at all, London proper giving way to suburbs as I follow the directions on the satnav.

Of all the things Judy failed to tell me, this hurts the most. And yet I hadn't mentioned it to Lily, had I? This is something I have to do alone. What use would it do at this stage other than to further sully my daughter's opinion of the grandmother she still hero-worships, in spite of everything?

We all have our justifications for the choices we make. We all think we know how best to protect the ones we love.

From the tone of the letter, I am not sure how long this woman has left, or how many visitors she can tolerate.

'I'm here to see Esther McVee,' I tell the receptionist.

'Lovely, and your name is?'

'Francesca.' Pausing, the words surreal on my lips, I continue. 'I'm her granddaughter.'

* * *

Upstairs in the bedroom, a care worker who introduces herself as Irene keeps vigil at the side of the bed.

'It was me who sent the letter. It's so good to meet you,' she says, with genuine warmth. 'I'm sorry it has to be in such circumstances. She hasn't got long now.'

'No.' My voice is raspy with emotion. Hovering in the doorway, I don't know where to put myself. And then I see her, a carbon copy of Judy, accelerated almost three decades. The same soft blonde curls and full lips that skipped a generation with me and passed straight down to Lily.

Gripping the handle of the door, part of me wants to turn and run.

'Sit with her a moment. She would like that. Can I get you a tea? It tastes like shite but it's better than the coffee.'

Irene's voice is soft and soothing, and I feel my heartbeat steady. 'I'd love one,' I nod as she passes, touching my arm affectionately as she does.

Turning to the bed where the old woman lies, propped up on a pile of cushions, a wool blanket pulled up around her, I see that her eyes are closed.

Inwardly, I run through all the things I want to say. Instead, I simply take her hand.

'Hello, Grandma.'

'Thank you for coming,' Irene says, hugging me as we stand in the reception area, once our time is up.

'Thank you for letting me know about Esther.'

'When I read about your mother in the paper, and you were mentioned . . .' She sighs. 'I know it's a useless thing to hear, but I'm very sorry. I wasn't sure, to be honest, if I should get in touch. But she is your grandmother, and she's dying. You have a right to know. Esther has a right . . . It wasn't

343

hard to find the address.' Irene hesitates. 'They've arrested a man in relation to your father's murder, haven't they?'

'Jim Doherty.' My chest tightens. 'I believe he knew my grandmother, once upon a time.'

'Yes,' Irene replies, glancing away.

'Irene, how long have you known Esther?'

'For many, many years.' Irene smiles, warmly, scratching her cheekbone. 'We were neighbours. After Esther became unwell, I worked as her carer, coming into the flat in Marylebone a couple of times a week, and then more regularly. I knew your mother, too. She was a good daughter. She was desperate for Esther to be able to stay at home but in time it wasn't possible; it was getting dangerous. She kept forgetting things – leaving pans on the hob, candles lit overnight . . . Bringing her here was the right thing to do. Even if it wasn't easy. That's why it's so hard to believe what was written about her. Judy was always different – a free spirit, I suppose you'd call it – but I never—'

'Irene,' I interrupt, before I lose my nerve. 'Is there somewhere we can talk properly?'

We sit on a bench in the garden and I light a cigarette, offering one to Irene and laying the box on the seat between us when she declines.

'I'm just going to ask you this directly because I'm not sure if there's any other way. Do you know, is Jim Doherty my grandfather?'

The silence that ensues confirms what I already suspected.

It had been troubling me, though I'd tried to ignore it, the question of how Jim Doherty's DNA had come to be on the vase my mother had buried in the garden the night Rory died. A vase that had sat in the same spot, never leaving the house, ever since I could remember. The only possible explanation was impossible – unless it wasn't.

Recalling a case Hugo had worked on where it hadn't been clear whether the DNA had belonged to the father or the son, I had remembered how, in the end, it had been too close a match to call. Yet, even as the pieces of the puzzle came together, something hadn't fitted. I had dealt with enough paternity enquiries in my time in family law to know that DNA would also show if a sample was male or female. So, even if Jim was Judy's real father, their DNA would not match that closely.

'Irene, I don't suppose you know whether my mother had a brother?'

The older woman's eyes narrow. 'Why do you ask?'

Holding myself perfectly still, I improvise. 'She mentioned him once, but I was too young and selfish to really pay attention to what she was saying.'

Irene smiles, sadly. 'Keir. He was a sweet kid. Always laughing. He was silly, you know? Thoughtful, too. After he died, your grandmother was never the same. I mean, who would blame her? She saw it happen. She was looking out at the street, watching her boy return home from the market with the yellow vase he had picked out for her birthday. It was hand-painted with red roses. Her favourite. He was always so thoughtful.' Irene closes her eyes before pressing on. 'She saw the whole thing. The truck reversing, without warning. Keir looking up at her as he stepped backwards off the pavement. It must have been awful for Judy, too. She was there as well, when it happened.'

When Irene stops, she reaches for the packet of cigarettes. 'I will have one those, if you don't mind.'

'Of course.' Pushing the packet towards her, I hold my

breath as I listen to Irene light up and inhale before continuing, my heart splintering with the thought that my mother had never confided in me, nor presumably in my father, about the brother she had lost.

'By the time Judy ran into the sitting room, to see what had happened, Esther was out on the street with Keir, but the child . . . He was still holding the vase he had bought her.'

Something clicks, and I shift forward on my seat.

Suppressing a sudden bout of tears, Irene shakes her head. 'After Keir died, Esther retreated into herself. She couldn't cope. It was me who suggested sending Judy away to boarding school. What with the money Henry Porter still sent every month, there was enough to cover the fees. I regret it now, of course. It just seemed like the right thing to do. Esther wasn't really there – she was a shell. And your mother, she was . . . well, she was only eleven. It was extremely hard for her. It was a tragedy.'

Irene looks again at her watch.

'Look, I'm so sorry but I have to get going. Will you come again, or . . .'

We both understand that Esther is not long for this world, and I nod. 'I'll come back as soon as I can.'

Smiling, Irene squeezes my hand. 'OK . . .'

As I stand and begin to walk away, Irene's voice calls me back. 'Francesca?'

'Yes?'

Pausing, she breathes in as though still unsure whether she should continue. 'Your mother was here, asking the same question. The same day your father was killed. I don't know if that's – I just thought you should know.'

'What's that?'

'I'd just arrived on shift and heard a commotion in the garden. When I got there, your grandmother was very upset. She said your mother had been asking her about that man. About Jim Doherty.'

'Did Judy ever mention him to you?'

'Once. A little while later. She asked – just like you – if I knew of him.'

'And what did you say?'

'I told her the truth, but it felt like a betrayal. Esther used to confide in me. I hate to say it, but I think I was her only friend.' Irene pauses. 'But there's no point hiding it from you either. Jim Doherty raped your grandmother. They worked together on the same market. He was kind to her for a while, gave her a present even – this weird bronze statue thing, which you might have seen up there on the shelf. And then, one night, he came to the club where she worked as a dancer and he . . .'

In the silence, tears roll down my face.

'I'm so sorry to tell you that. And about Keir. It's a lot. I just – I thought you should know. He wasn't – isn't – a good man.'

'Why did she keep it? The statue. I don't understand. Why would she want—'

Irene shakes her head. 'I don't know. Maybe, in a way, she loved him. Maybe she couldn't bring herself to . . . I'm sorry.'

She stubs out her cigarette and stands. My head swims with all I have learnt.

'One last thing. Your mother – she gave me some money. The last time she was in London. She insisted on it. She said she wanted to express her gratitude for all that I had done for Esther over the years. She wanted me to go travelling – she was always on about that. Seeing the world. Southeast Asia,

Mexico . . . Anyway, I thought you should know, in case you need the money. I don't want to take—'

I smile. 'No, you keep it. I'm pleased she did that. She's right, you should take a holiday. Life is short, right?'

Francesca

London, February 2025

Rain beats against the car window. Ahead of us, the gates to
the cemetery await.

Cutting the engine, Lily and I sit for a moment in silence
before my daughter speaks. 'Are you OK?'

Taking her hand, I swallow and smile. 'I'm OK. Are you?'

'I think so.'

'You know your grandmother loved you very much, don't
you?'

Lily's young face is focused downwards, any bravado falling
away as she fiddles with the yin-yang ring she brought back
from Thailand, cutting her trip short without a second thought
after she heard Judy was gone.

She had been doing so well up until now but, despite her
brave face, she is still only nineteen.

I haven't had the heart to tell her about Esther, the
great-grandmother she never knew. Irene called a few days
ago to say that Esther had passed away. In a way, it was a
relief. At this point, Lily and I need to move on.

For a while, I let myself believe that my mother is still alive,
that she was being honest with me when she said she would
simply be going away. But of course I know now that this is

simply what she had to say in order for me to go along with her plan.

The plan to frame the man who raped her mother for the death of her husband. You couldn't make it up – unless, of course, you were Judy.

And I had believed the version of events she gave me, in spite of everything. I had believed that she would slip away quietly once I had given her the signal. That she would escape across the border on a fake passport she had procured, in the way that only Judy could, with the help of a friend. I had believed that one day, when the time was right, my mother would make herself known, and Lily and I would see her again.

I had believed, I suppose, because I wanted to. Because it allowed me to feel better about her taking the fall for what I did. And why not? She had got away with so much, for so long. Why not this, too?

She had killed a man. Her own neighbour. That, I really couldn't understand.

'How do they know she is dead if they haven't found . . . her.'

Struggling for breath, I steady myself with one hand against the car door. 'Lily, I know it's hard. It's really fucking hard—'

'But why aren't they out there looking for her? They only found her car – that doesn't mean anything—'

'It wasn't just her car. It was where they found it. The direction of the river would have—' I look away, trying not to picture my mother's lifeless body floating out to sea.

'They dredged the river. She wasn't there,' Lily says, animatedly.

'But they found her shoe,' I reply.

'So? None of it makes sense. If she had a gun, why would she not just have shot herself there and then?'

'Lily—'

'The police seem to have given up! Why aren't they—'

'That's not true.'

Although it is, in a way. It is over. How can I tell my daughter that she should be relieved? That, in framing Jim and forfeiting herself, Judy has saved us both?

It is over – isn't it?

Without a body, there will merely be a memorial service. It is only right that we hold it here, in the same place where my father is buried. But now that the time has come, I'm not sure I have the strength to leave the car.

The only person I want right now – to hold me, to scream at, to beg for answers to all the unanswered questions she has left me with – is gone.

My thoughts are interrupted by a knock on the car window. When I look up, Hugo and Laura stand under an umbrella, side by side, Laura's eldest daughter between them.

Immediately, I remember the card Johnny sent. On the front was a bunch of lilies and the words *I'm sorry for your loss.*

'Are you coming?' Laura beckons and Lily gets out of the car ahead of me, walking over and taking Eva's hand.

Wiping away a tear before it fully forms, I smile as I watch Hugo, Lily and Eva walk together in the rain towards the cemetery and the chapel beyond.

Finally opening the driver's door, I step out, and Laura holds out an umbrella. As I lean into my friend, the weight of years of secrets falls away.

'I have something I need to tell you—' I say before I can stop myself.

Laura keeps her eyes on our girls, almost fifteen years apart in age. 'Fran, this isn't the time.'

'Please. Laura, it's import—'

'I said *no*, Fran.' Laura keeps her voice level but, when she turns to face me, the look in her eyes tells me this level of self-control is taking everything that she has. 'I already know,' she adds, and I freeze, unsure whether I have heard her right.

'How long have you—' My voice is small.

'Let's not do this now.' Laura squeezes my hand. 'Please.'

'But why didn't you say anything?'

'Why?' Biting her lip, Laura searches my face, both our eyes brimming with tears. 'Don't make me do this, Fran. You're my best friend. I've already lost my husband. Some things are better off left in the past.'

Laura's expression is imploring, and I tilt my head in acquiescence as she continues.

'You know, Fran, sometimes our punishment is to live with our secrets. To keep them to ourselves, to feel the weight of them. However big or small.' She keeps her eyes steady on mine, her voice softening. 'You have a daughter who needs you. She needs you *here*. Do you understand what I'm saying?'

A question forming on my lips, I simply nod, wondering what else she has surmised.

'Mum?' Lily's voice calls to me from the entrance to the church.

'Come on,' Laura says. 'Our family needs us.'

'Yes.' I smile. 'Let's go.'

Stepping forward, I think of Judy and try to picture her the way she would want to be remembered. Almost as though she is calling out to me from wherever she is now.

Pushing the thought aside, I concentrate on the living. Laura and Lily flank me on either side as I move through a sea of people I don't recognise. My port in a storm. My very own island of women.

The thought catches me off guard. And then I remember, with a sudden clarity that stops me in my tracks. An image of my mother in France, the summer after my GCSEs. Judy returning after our argument over dinner, holding a bowl of figs, her face bright, as if nothing had happened.

Under her arm, the crossword she had printed from the *Times* website earlier that day. The bowl of figs untouched as I watched her scan through the questions, automatically underlining those that could be solved by anagrams.

'I wonder how Laura and her family are getting on in Mexico?' she had asked, without looking up. 'We should go there one day. The Yucatán Peninsula – I've always wanted to visit. Apparently there's a road along one stretch where at a certain time of year you hardly see the sky for yellow butterflies. Isn't that gorgeous? And there's an island.' She paused, looking up as if reaching for the name. 'Isla Mujeres. The island of women. Doesn't that sound fabulous? One day, I'll take you there. That's a promise.'

As Laura, Lily and I walk forward towards the chapel, I picture again the condolence note and the signature, 'Julie Masser', and I can't help but let out a laugh.

EPILOGUE

Judy had never intended the shot to hit Patrice. Her plan had only ever been for him to arrive at the house, at the arranged time, and for her to take out the gun and aim it at him – for the benefit of anyone who might have been passing along the road that led past the village and unwittingly witnessed the old Englishwoman's escape, once they learnt, later, that this was what it had been.

But once she'd raised the idea in its basic form, Patrice had pleaded with her.

She had begged him not to ask her to do it. Even if the bullet striking him would make it more convincing to the police that she had, in a panic, killed the policeman and run a little way to the deepest, wildest part of the river, where, struck by the enormity of what she had done – she had taken her own life.

Even then – Judy was not a killer.

Please, he had said. He was dying. He was in pain. He wanted it to be over.

And she understood that. This way, they could go out together in a blaze of glory.

They were Thelma and Louis, he'd joked, and she had laughed at that. They had laughed and laughed and then

Patrice had taken her hand, looking her plain in the eye in the midst of the medicinal garden that was no longer any use to him. He was her friend, and he was dying. And he was willing to help her to protect her daughter, wasn't he? His price was the highest either of them could consider. But in the end, she felt she had no choice.

It was the least she could do.

'Mum, what are you doing?'

Lily stands ahead of me in the line for Departures.

'Just doing a final check,' I reply, running my hands through the contents of my carry-on.

'The fifth final check?'

'All right, madam, just because you're a seasoned traveller . . . This is a big thing for me!'

'I know.' Lily loops her arm through mine as we head towards passport control.

'Francesca Harrington-Talbot and Lily Harrington-Talbot. Going anywhere nice?' the man behind the desk asks, looking from my passport to my daughter's and back again.

'My daughter's going off to travel the world before starting university – I'm joining her for the first leg of the trip.' I smile. 'Mexico.'

'How long are you staying?'

I have no idea, I think.

Smiling, I reply. 'Two weeks.'

I keep my eyes fixed on the landscape outside the window of the coach as we make our way from Cancún airport to where we will catch the boat to the island.

'Finished,' Lily says, as we approach our stop. When I turn, I see the copy of *Lady Audley's Secret* I had lent her for the trip. The article, which had been tucked into the front page, is now open on my daughter's knee.

'What's this? It's, like, forty years old,' Lily says, scanning through the profile of the deceased Cabinet minister.

With a pang of regret, I shrug. 'I guess your grandmother used it as a bookmark and forgot to take it out. That was her favourite novel.'

'Yeah.' Lily smiles, sadly.

'And what's your assessment, then, future English scholar? Was Lady Audley mad?'

'I mean, yeah.' My daughter laughs, pushing a blonde curl away from her face. 'She was batshit. But I also think she was doing what she felt she had to, and what she wanted. That's kind of cool. She was smart and unpredictable.'

'Yes.' I nod. 'She was.'

We take the boat from Cancún to Isla Mujeres. It's evening by the time we reach the island, the sun setting behind the palms that line the shore.

Watching Lily move ahead towards one of the hammocks propped between the trees, I think of the note. The letters of the name, 'Julie Masser', rearranging themselves in my mind.

'I'll have a piña colada,' Lily calls out as I reach the beach bar, the sand soft beneath my feet.

'Welcome to Isla Mujeres,' the barman says.

Smiling, I turn back towards the beach and my daughter. When I turn again, I spot a figure in a straw hat just visible in the periphery of my vision.

Above, the sky is blue.

Ahead, a butterfly floating free in the wind.

Acknowledgements

This book was (largely) a joy to write, and was pounded into shape by a number of people, to whom I am very grateful.

Above all, my thanks to my brilliant friend and first reader, Victoria Hollingsworth, for your insight, rallying and direction, when I felt lost. You are clever and generous and, of course, you were right.

Without the professional eye of my much relied-upon second reader, former policeman Richard Hart, I might have found myself somewhat red-faced. Thank you for your diligence, and for always making yourself available for my often basic questions.

To Dennis L. Everson, my man-on-the-ground in Wellfleet: I owe you a plate of oysters, or at least a coffee at the Isokon when you're next in town.

To my agents, Veronique Baxter and Emily Hayward Whitlock, you have my unwavering gratitude; and to Christie Hickman, Stephanie Glencross, Suzie Dooré, Sophia Schoepfer, Sian Richefond and Linda McQueen – thank you for helping make this book better than it would otherwise have been.

A huge thank you, as always, to my husband, Barney and our children, for making life off the page one I'd never want to rewrite.

As a legal disclaimer, let it be known that neither my mum,

Jo, nor my late grandmother, Joan, are/were, to my knowledge, jewel thieves, but the best bits of Judy's spirit are based on them.

Finally, to my much-loved team at Borough Press, in particular Ann Bissell and Fliss Denham – what fun it has been.